A S

"Kindly release my arm, which you are bruising," Anne demanded.

"You are lying," Lord Leatham replied. "I am not hurting your arm in the least. Admit it."

"No, you are not hurting me," Anne had to admit. "But I am opposed to the use of physical force in any and all situations."

His answer to that took her aback. His free hand cupped her cheek, and he leaned toward her. Anne sighed softly just before their lips met.

"You should not have done that," Anne murmured. But try as she might, she could not bring herself to move away from him. For that force that held her now did not come from him alone. . . .

CHARLOTTE DOLAN attended Eastern Illinois University and earned a master's degree in German from Middlebury College. She has lived throughout the United States and in Montreal, Taiwan, Germany, and the Soviet Union. She is the mother of three children and currently makes her home in Idaho Falls, Idaho, with her husband and daughter.

THREE LORDS
FOR
LADY ANNE

by

Charlotte Louise Dolan

A SIGNET BOOK

SIGNET
Published by the Penguin Group
Penguin Books USA Inc., 375 Hudson Street,
New York, New York, 10014, U.S.A.
Penguin Books Ltd, 27 Wrights Lane, London W8 5TZ, England
Penguin Books Australia Ltd, Ringwood, Victoria, Australia
Penguin Books Canada Ltd, 10 Alcorn Ave. Suite 300,
Toronto, Ontario, Canada M4V 3B2
Penguin Books (N.Z.) Ltd, 182-190 Wairau Road,
Auckland 10, New Zealand

Penguin Books Ltd, Registered Offices:
Harmondsworth, Middlesex, England

First published by Signet, an imprint of New American Library,
a division of Penguin Books USA Inc.

First Printing, October, 1991

10 9 8 7 6 5 4 3 2 1

*Dedicated
to
my mother-in-law,
Virginia Bess Fisher Dolan,
for twenty-five years
of
love, affection, and friendship.*

I wish to thank Dee Hendrickson and Mary Jo Putney for their advice and encouragement, and I wish to thank Vickey Duffey, formerly of Devonshire, England, and now of Idaho Falls. I also wish to thank Russ Burnham, my favorite Mohawk, for letting me borrow his great-grandfather's name.

Prologue

August 1794

THERE WAS NOTHING about the elegant traveling coach to cause comment. Axelford Cross was not so far off the beaten path that the villagers were inclined to give the gold and red equipage pulled by four beautifully matched blacks more than a passing glance.

Eyebrows were raised, however, when the coachman, rather than continuing at a brisk pace on down the road toward Leeds, pulled his team to a halt in front of the small house rented for the last several years by Mrs. Carlisle. She was, as the black-smith's wife was quick to point out to the landlady at the Brimming Goblet, only an insignificant widow from somewhere in the south of England—respectable, but not one to push herself forward unbecomingly.

On the other hand, as the postmaster pointed out to the new schoolmaster, the widow did receive an inordinate number of letters, many of them franked by assorted peers of the realm.

Perhaps, remarked the vicar's wife to the squire's wife, with the widow's obvious connections, might not dear Mrs. Carlisle be a welcome addition to the Altar Guild? With a murmur of assent, the squire's wife decided on the basis of one imposing coachman, two liveried grooms, and four armed outriders, that the time had come to give the widow a copy of her closely guarded and much sought-after receipt for pickled beets. There was no need, of course, to mention such beneficence to her companion. Good friend though she was, the vicar's wife never received visits from ladies whose raiment had the unmistakable touch of an expensive London modiste.

As for the elegant lady who descended from the carriage, Lady Letitia was well aware of the watchful eyes and wagging tongues, and in a back part of her mind she automatically

9

considered whether there might not be some way to use them to advantage. Following the housekeeper into a sitting room decorated more for comfort than for elegance, she contemplated the possibility of prying her friend out of the country and back to London where she belonged.

"Letty! My dear, whatever brings you to such an out-of-the-way spot as this?" With great alacrity and a look of guilt, the widow rose from the settee and, hands held out in welcome, hurried to embrace her visitor.

Lady Letitia Amerdythe returned the embrace, then stepped back to survey her friend through a critical eye. A novel fallen to the floor and a half-empty box of bonbons told their own story. "Well, Amelia, I did not undertake this journey for my health, of that you may be certain. The roads were abominable, and I feel as though several of my back teeth have been jolted quite out of their sockets. It is your health, or rather the reports I have received from all three of your daughters of your lack of health, that has persuaded me to undertake such an arduous journey. Why you have chosen to immure yourself in the wilds of Yorkshire instead of establishing yourself in Bath or maintaining possession of your London residence, I am sure I cannot fathom. You had as well taken yourself off to a nunnery."

Without waiting for her friend to remember her manners, Lady Letitia seated herself on a chair conveniently placed next to the settee, but the widow remained standing, looking like nothing so much as a schoolchild called upon to recite an ill-prepared lesson.

"Oh, my dear, I am so sorry you have made this journey for naught. I never thought—that is, it never occurred to me . . ."

"Indeed, and well you should blush. Here you are in the pink of health, looking positively half your age, when I expected to find you prostrate on your deathbed, for so your daughters have led me to believe."

"Well, there you have it." Amelia seated herself again on the settee, then as unobtrusively as possible she slipped the box of sweets out of sight behind a pillow. "Why you should have believed a word I wrote them, I am sure I cannot comprehend. And you know perfectly well that I have *immured* myself here precisely because of those same daughters. It was the only way I could discourage them from constantly descending upon me, or what is worse, foisting their repellent offspring onto dear Grandmama. Well this grandmama has no interest in the wretched brats. That is what nannies and governesses are for.''

"You did, however, cancel your annual round of visits to them this year claiming ill health, did you not?"

"Well, yes, but that was merely a ruse. Really, you cannot have any idea how much I dread visiting them each autumn. Lizzie is increasing again, which will make nine—*nine*—and every one of the poor things the spitting image of Sandervale— not a chin among the lot of them. And Harriet has seven, and Ermelda six, with no end in sight. Well, I will tell you right out, they did not get such bourgeois ideas from me.''

The widow stopped abruptly, then all the stiffness went out of her, and she relaxed back on her pillows. "Oh, Letty, you are too wicked. You were never for a moment worried about my health, were you? You might as well confess. I have never been able to fool you with my little fabrications before, and I cannot believe you would be taken in by any gossip passed on by my daughters, who you know perfectly well take after their father and have more hair than wit.''

"No, my dear Amelia, I did not honestly believe you were about to expire. I am on my way to join a very special friend in Edinburgh and decided a short detour was in order to visit you and discover the real reason you have decided to stay in the north this year."

The widow gave a positively girlish giggle. "Oh, my dear, I simply could not tear myself away from the farce that has been unfolding in the village. I declare, it would be a *succès fou* on the stage in London. Were I a playwright, I would title it, 'The Encroaching Mushroom.' But come, I shall have the house-keeper show you to my guest room and give you an opportunity to rid yourself of your travel stains, and then we shall meet for tea and I shall tell you all about the folly and pretensions that make life in a little country village so fascinating."

Mrs. Pierce-Smythe was not her usual calm self when she entered the drawing room to join her husband for tea. She was, in fact, so excited by the news she had just received, she had an impulse to do something wildly indecorous, such as bestow a kiss on Mr. Pierce-Smythe.

"You are late, my dear. The tea will be cold by this time."

A slight frown crossed Mrs. Pierce-Smythe's face, not at her husband's admonition, but at the sight of the two girls seated side by side on the settee. She had forgotten it was Wednesday, the governess's half day off, and the schoolroom party was therefore taking tea with the adults.

Scarcely able to control her impatience to tell her husband the wonderful news, she nevertheless seated herself beside him and calmly laid a hand on the teapot. It had indeed grown tepid. "Lady Gloriana, take this back to the kitchen and fetch a fresh pot."

She waited only until the door had closed behind her young relative, then turned back to her husband. "My dear, I have received the most shocking information. Lady Letitia Amerdythe is here—*here* in this very village—and she is visiting Mrs. Carlisle."

"I am sure that is all very interesting, my dear, but I deplore unpunctuality, as I believe I have mentioned to you before."

"Mr. Pierce-Smythe—" his wife drew herself up and affixed him with her most imperious look, "there is nothing and nobody more important in the *ton* than Lady Letitia. No door is shut to her, and she has arranged more marriages—*advantageous* marriages—than, than, oh, than anyone. And she is having tea with that little nobody. I would give my eyeteeth if only we could invite her here for dinner."

"And whyever can we not? I fancy I am somebody in this district, and I am more accustomed to people angling for invitations than declining them out of hand."

"Because I have never acknowledged that wretched widow, that is why. Indeed, you told me yourself she was not worth cultivating. But on the other hand . . ." She thought for a moment, then began to smile. "If Lady Letitia is taking tea at that house . . . Yes, she may well be so desperate for some decent cooking that she will overlook the lack of acquaintance-ship. It is worth risking a refusal. And indeed, now that I think on it, all we need do is address the invitation to Mrs. Carlisle and her guest, and I am sure they will neither of them hesitate to accept."

"But, Mama," her daughter Rosabelle said with a pretty pout on her face, "are you forgetting about Lady Gloriana? Surely all our prospects will be lost if Lady Letitia once catches sight of that great gawk."

Just at that moment the door opened to admit Lady Gloriana with the fresh pot of tea. The eyes of the three other people in the room followed the young girl, and none of them were pleased with what they saw. Not even her rounded shoulders could disguise the fact that she was a veritable giantess. Why she towered a good nine or ten inches over Mr. Pierce-Smythe, and although she had stopped growing a year ago, shortly after she had passed her fourteenth birthday, it was too late; the damage was done.

Mrs. Pierce-Smythe quickly reviewed the dilemma that had stumped her for the past year—what to do about an impoverished young relative who has become inconvenient, yet who, as the daughter of an earl, cannot simply be turned out into the world. And since everyone of consequence in the district knew of her presence in the Pierce-Smythe household, tongues would wag if she were simply shut up out of sight and out of mind in her room.

On the other hand, Mrs. Pierce-Smythe realized full well, nothing could be more fatal to her own dainty daughter's chances of contracting a brilliant marriage than to continue letting Lady Gloriana appear in public. Because what man of sense would wish to ally himself with a family known to have produced such a freak?

Deciding finally that the potential benefits of cultivating an acquaintance with Lady Letitia, whose friendship would guarantee herself and her daughter entrée into the highest levels of London society, more than outweighed the penalties liable to be inflicted in Yorkshire for offending the sensibilities of local society, Mrs. Pierce-Smythe resolutely made her decision. "Lady Gloriana, we are expecting company this evening. You will dine on a tray in your room."

"Amelia, I do not consider myself to be difficult to please, but I must point out to you that these scones are hard as rocks, the macaroons are burned on the bottom, and the junket is sagging ominously at the knees. I fear, in fact, that the only firm thing about it is its intention to slither off the plate and make the acquaintance of the tablecloth. Might I suggest that with the ample funds your husband left at your disposal you consider hiring a reasonably competent cook?''

"Oh, but Mrs. Skinner is a pearl beyond price; I could never let her go. Although I will admit she has never quite learned the knack of dressing a joint properly, she has a veritable genius for ferreting out gossip. Nothing that goes on in the village escapes her.''

"Then speaking of gossip, since I am not to be allowed to assuage my physical hunger properly, perhaps you might fill me in on the rest of the story of the local mushroom.''

"Try the bread and butter. It is quite safe; I buy it in the village. As to the mushroom, he goes by the name of Mr. Pierce-Smythe, although I have it from a reliable source—''

"Your cook?''

"Exactly. That his grandfather was a plain Mr. Smith, who started life as a higgler, peddling his wares from door to door. Now I have not heard it said that he was actually dishonest, but it would seem that his trading practices were sharp enough that by the time he died he was a successful shop owner in Manchester. His son, who changed his name to Smythe, claimed to be a respectable banker, but he was really nothing more than a demmed cent-per-cent. Which brings us to the present generation.

"He styles himself a gentleman, but there has always been something a little off about him. He is more or less our generation, and he married Miss Rosemary Pierce. Perhaps you remember her mother Rosamund? A Calkins, she was, the granddaughter of some wretched little Irish viscount, always hanging around the fringes of society. No taint of the shop, mind you, and she was acknowledged by the family, albeit grudgingly. Married the fourth son of a seventh son or something like that— the Lincolnshire Pierces, but sadly fallen away." Amelia paused to butter another slice of bread for herself.

"I recall the family. Rather a nondescript lot, even the best of them."

"Exactly. Miss Rosemary had pretensions of beauty but lacked a dowry, and with nothing else to recommend her, she was assumed to be on the shelf until her father struck a bargain with our Mr. Smythe. I would hate to have to judge which of the two got the best of that bargain. The higgler's grandson has plenty of money, I will grant you that, but he is at least twenty years her senior and she was no spring chicken. They have only the one child—a daughter named Rosabelle. So many roses, it is enough to make a body feel nauseated."

"It is probably only the strawberry preserves. I noticed a spot of mold on them."

"More than likely. Now where was I?"

"The daughter, Rosabelle."

"No, no, the daughter has nothing to do with the story. She is only nine or ten or some such age. It is the cousin who is of interest—the Countess of Faussley, widow of the fifth earl, also supposedly from Lincolnshire, although I have never heard of the family."

"I have."

"You have? Oh, my dear Letty, let me ring for some fresh tea and then you must tell me all you know. And do start at the beginning. You know how I abhor the custom of coming into the opera in the middle of the first act."

"Well, the title is not a very old one, less than seventy years, I believe, and already extinct, so it is small wonder you have never heard of it. The first earl was a minor baron who saved the life of the king, or so the entitlement reads."

"How is it I have never heard of such a deed of daring?"

"It is not the kind of tale that normally appears in the history books, my dear, for whatever the baron may have claimed, the story that circulated quite freely among the servants is that his aid to the king consisted of marrying a certain Anne Newbold, a young woman of good family who aspired to enter the ranks of royalty through the bedroom door. She had, most unfortunately for the king, not only a glorious face and a stunning figure, but also an irate father, several hulking brothers, and numerous uncles who had their fingers in all the political pies of the era.''

"Such a delightful story, it is too bad it is only servant's gossip.''

"Well, as to that, I have seen a portrait of the second earl, and he bore a striking resemblance to the royal family and none at all to his younger brother and sister, so it is quite possible the first earl did save the king's life in a manner of speaking.''

"Do you mean to tell me that the earls of Faussley had royal blood in their veins?''

"Only the second earl. He was still a bachelor when he managed to eat his way into an early grave, so the title devolved on his next younger brother, whom I had the misfortune to accompany once to a concert in London. A more boring escort I have never endured—puritanical in his morality, coupled with a most limited understanding. That was before he succeeded to his brother's honors. After he became the third earl, he quitted London and devoted his life to piously mismanaging his affairs. He married one of Leighton's daughters, I forget which one. Had two sons, the elder every bit as pious a nonentity as his father.''

"That would be the fourth earl?''

"Yes, he died of the measles about a year after his father's death. Had no gumption at all.''

"I must say, Letty, that except for the first earl's wife, you are describing a very boring set of people. I expected a more entertaining story from you.''

"Ah, but we are now come to Reginald, the younger brother of the fourth earl of Faussley. He was the most engaging black sheep you would ever want to meet. A trial to his parents from the day of his birth. I have heard he came backward into the world and continued from that day forth to behave in a way that was invariably the exact opposite of what his parents wished. Ran rampant through the flocks of nubile young maidens in Lincolnshire and was not averse to sampling the attractions of bored young matrons, either. On only one occasion did his parents succeed in bringing him to obey their dictates, and that was in the matter of the spinster daughter of the vicar of Droneyfelds.''

''That would be the countess who came here purporting to be the cousin of Mrs. Pierce-Smythe?''

''The relationship is indeed there—third cousin twice removed or second cousin thrice removed, it matters not. What matters is that Reginald seduced her while promising her marriage, a regrettable habit of his. Unfortunately for him, on this one occasion he made the mistake of setting pen to paper, and the vicar threatened to bring suit. This was while the third earl was still alive, and he sided with the vicar. Even so, I believe it required the assistance of three sturdy plowmen to bring his son to the altar, and I suppose in due course the babe was born.''

''Indeed, she is Lady Gloriana Marybell Dorinda Elizabeth Hemsworth, presently aged fifteen years, and quite the central figure in my farce. I shall tell you all about her as soon as you have finished your part of the story.''

''There is little more to tell. Marriage and fatherhood did not have the hoped-for steadying effect on Reginald, and as soon as he inherited the title, he departed for London. After three years of flitting from bedroom to bedroom, he was finally killed in a duel by a cuckolded husband. Which concludes my knowledge of the family, since until this day, I had no idea what became of the vicar's daughter and her offspring.''

''Well, according to Mrs. Skinner, who had it from the Pierce-Smythe coachman, the bailiffs were already pounding on the door of Faussley Hall, attempting to evict the countess, when Mrs. Pierce-Smythe arrived and invited her cousin for a visit.''

''Aaah, and the welcome was extended for as long as the countess was willing to acknowledge the relationship?''

''Oh, Letty, you are always so cynical. But in this case you are correct. I will not say the countess ever fawned over them, but she did refer to them more frequently than necessary as Dear Cousin Willard and Dear Cousin Rosemary.''

''And such is the way of the world, that doors hitherto closed to the higgler's grandson were now magically opened.''

''Of course. Can you doubt it? Unfortunately, the countess had a deplorable habit of quacking herself. I believe it was 'Dr. Blackwell's Golden Elixir,' guaranteed to restore the youthful bloom to her cheeks, which finally secured her a permanent spot in the churchyard.''

"Rather a setback for the Pierce-Smythes, it would seem.''

"Oh, they made a beautiful recovery. Simply substituted the daughter for the mother, as it were. Only ten years of age at the time, but admirably trained to recite 'Dear Uncle Willard' and 'Dear Aunt Rosemary' on cue. The great disaster began the year Lady Gloriana turned thirteen and began to grow.''

"She became fat?''

"No, although I will allow she would be more pleasing if she lost a stone or two. The problem is she has grown so tall. I myself have remarked her standing next to the blacksmith, who is known to be six feet three, and I would estimate she is no more than an inch shorter than he is. Such a catastrophe for the Pierce-Smythes, who would have done better not to inflict the presence of schoolgirls upon their adult company, for you must know, I do not at all approve of such modern practices. But having once introduced her to society at such a tender age, how can they now shut her up in the attic, so to speak?

"As sorry as I feel for the gel, I must admit I have enjoyed watching the Pierce-Smythes try to come about. When Lady Gloriana reached five feet nine or so, they sent a letter off posthaste to the vicar, her grandfather, requesting he come and remove her, but he had already gone to claim his heavenly reward.''

There was a light rap at the door, then the housekeeper entered bearing not only the fresh tea, but also a letter from Mrs. Pierce-Smythe.

Perusing the missive, Amelia gasped. "The gall of that woman. She has the nerve to invite me and my houseguest to dine with her *en famille* this evening. You may count on it, Letty, she has ferreted out your identity, even though she pretends not to know your name. Have I not told you she was encroaching? Of course I shall decline.''

"Do not be so hasty. I am not at all sure my stomach is up to another of the burnt offerings from your kitchen. I assume Mrs. Pierce-Smythe has chosen her cook for her culinary abilities rather than for her propensity to gossip?''

"Actually, she has a French chef, and her idea of potluck will probably be a dozen courses of four removes each. But my dear Letty, do please consider that if I should accept her hospitality, which I have not the slightest intention of doing, I would then be forced to acknowledge her, and though I am not so high in the instep that I am unwilling to give the squire's wife a nod on Sunday, one must draw the line somewhere."

"But my dear, surely you do not wish me to miss such an opportunity to observe this farce first hand?"

"Do not try to turn me up sweet, Letty. I know perfectly well what your intentions are. You plan to—to interfere. That has always been the chief difference between us. Where I am content to observe, you delight in playing the role of *deus ex machina.*"

"My dear departed second husband, Mr. Edward Newbold, was wont to call it meddling, but even he agreed I am a dab hand at arranging other people's lives."

"Newbold! I knew that name sounded familiar. Was he perhaps . . ."

"Related to the enterprising Miss Newbold? Her nephew, in fact, which is how I was so fortunate as to hear the whole story. Quite the most lusty of my husbands, so if his aunt was anything like him, it is understandable that the king should have been led to stray from the strait and narrow path. I feel compelled, therefore, to do my puny best to aid my husband's unfortunate young cousin. But you need not accompany me. I am quite capable of depressing the pretensions of mushrooms."

"Well, if you refuse to listen to reason, I might as well make a start on packing. Once you mention how I am your very dear friend, and somehow I feel sure you will find the opportunity to do so, that wretched woman will give me no peace. She will be ringing my doorbell at all hours and lying in wait for me every time I set foot outside my garden. I declare, you have made it necessary for me to endure three months of visiting my daughters after I have been so successful in wriggling out of that obligation this year. I only hope that I will be gone long enough for Mrs. Pierce-Smythe to lose interest in me."

"You might, if you prefer, accompany me to Edinburgh."

"And why, pray, should I do that?"

"Well, to begin with, you could stand up with me."

"Letty, you are not planning to walk down the aisle a fourth time!"

"But what is a woman without a man beside her? I confess, dear George caught me in a moment of weakness, and I accepted his offer. We are to be wed in the Cathedral in Edinburgh. That seems suitably far removed from London so that we can avoid attracting undue attention, especially from my sons and daughters-in-law."

"Attention? Can it be— Is George perhaps Mr.— No, he cannot be."

"Mr. George Morrough? But of course. What other George do I number in my acquaintance?"'

"But Letty, he is a good five years younger than you and a veritable nabob!"

"Are you accusing me of being a cradle robber or a fortune hunter? I assure you, I am neither. It is his other attributes that have persuaded me to agree to the match."

"Letty!"

"I was referring, of course, to his educated mind and his amusing wit. Pray, what did you think I meant?"

Amelia Carlisle blushed, but did not answer the question.

Feeling as if she had wandered by mistake into a gross parody of a rose garden which did not belong in her worst nightmare, Lady Letitia seated herself on the only gilt chair in the Pierce-Smythes' drawing room that was not ornamented with yellow roses done in needlepoint. To compound the horror of her surroundings, giant pink tea roses adorned the wallpaper and were repeated in the carpet. Tucked into the corners of the settees were plump pillows embroidered with improbable orange roses, which clashed dreadfully with the lavender roses in the upholstery. Nor had Mrs. Pierce-Smythe neglected the real roses, which were arranged flamboyantly in large vases scattered here and there around the room.

After closing her eyes for a moment to gather her strength, and realizing nothing could shut out the overpowering perfume of the flowers, Lady Letitia managed to smile sweetly at her hostess. "It was really fortuitous of you to issue your kind invitation to dine with you this evening. I can only regret that Mrs. Carlisle, who is, as I am sure you know, my very *dearest* friend, was unable to accompany me this evening. I had meant to call upon you on the morrow, but this will give me a better chance to become acquainted with my late husband's young cousin."

"Cousin?"

Three blank stares met Lady Letitia's imperturbable gaze. "But of course, dear Lady Gloriana. How does she get on? She will be joining us for dinner, will she not?"

"Oh, of course," Mrs. Pierce-Smythe said faintly. "I had better . . . if you will excuse me, I shall see what is delaying her."

With an expression on her face that more nearly resembled a grimace than a smile, she hurriedly left the room.

Her husband harrumphed and cleared his throat, but made no other attempt to entertain his guest. The joys of dining *en famille* were vastly overrated in Lady Letitia's considered opinion. On the other hand, with a few embellishments, the account of this evening should make a vastly amusing story for dear George.

"I am ten years old now," Rosabelle said, apparently feeling called upon to take up the conversational slack left by her mother's sudden departure. Her legs crossed daintily at the ankle, her rose-colored skirts arrayed neatly around her, and her hands folded primly in her lap, she sat beside her remaining parent, who bestowed a doting look on her. "My father bought me a little gray pony for my birthday. She is the most *beautiful* pony in the whole world, and I love her dearly. And I have the most cunning saddle that is all my very own. My riding habit is pink. That is my favorite color."

"And very pretty you look in it, too, my sweet." Her father beamed down at her and patted her hand.

Nauseating child, Lady Letitia thought. Someone should tell her that she would be vastly more attractive if she were not so smugly conscious of her own looks. And someone should tell her parents that ten-year-old children are better kept in the schoolroom, no matter how precocious their parents think them.

"Ah, here we are are now." Mrs. Pierce-Smythe sailed into the room, trailed by . . .

Gracious me, Lady Letitia thought, what have I gotten myself mixed up in? Any ideas she might have had about taking the chit along with her to Edinburgh died aborning.

Lady Gloriana's height was the least of her problems. Her posture was deplorable in the extreme, her complexion was spotty, her lank brown hair did not deserve mention, and in the appalling frock Mrs. Pierce-Smythe had forced her into, she had no more shape than a bag of flour tied around the middle. Without looking up, the girl mumbled her greetings.

"Now that we are all here, let us go in to dinner. My dear Mr. Pierce-Smythe, if you will escort our guest, the girls and I shall be pleased to follow."

What to do, what to do? Lady Letitia's situation, instead of improving, became steadily worse. As the evening progressed it became clear to her that Mr. Pierce-Smythe considered the intellect of females only slightly greater than that of cabbages, and the education Lady Gloriana had apparently so far received fitted her for nothing other than staring blankly into space and eating chocolates, her present occupation.

It was only during the fourth course, when her host was expounding on the deleterious effects for females of the slightest physical exertion, that an image arose in Lady Letitia's mind— the image of the woman whose idea of a little walk to settle one's meal was a brisk fifteen-mile hike done in double-time.

She paused to consider. Lady Sidonia was dear Edward's first cousin, which would make her Lady Gloriana's great-aunt. Perfect. A bit eccentric, Sidie was exactly what the poor overgrown girl needed to recover from the harm caused her by ten years of being exposed to the Pierce-Smythes.

There would, of course, be no problem with persuading the Pierce-Smythes that Lady Sidonia had more need of her grand-niece's company than they did.

But how to convince Sidie to bother herself with the chit when she had no experience with raising children of her own? Nor any interest in the younger generation. In fact, Sidie had once expressed a strong aversion to having anything to do with anyone under the age of twenty, and even that she allowed was frequently still a bit too young.

All in all, if 'twere done, 'twere best done without warning, Lady Letitia decided. I shall simply write a letter and send it along with the child. Martinet though she can be, dear Sidie will surely not be so hard-hearted as to send back her own flesh and blood. Especially not when I describe to her Mr. Pierce-Smythe's views on the type of education suitable for females.

> . . . and my dear, then he said that reading history was known to cause softening of the brain in females, and it were best if such complicated subjects were left strictly to men, who are better able to understand the politics involved.

Lady Sidonia skimmed the rest of the letter, then glanced up at the girl standing forlornly in front of her.

Well, the bones were good, or would be if they were not buried under a layer of puppy fat. Whether the mind was still functional after years of disuse was another question. Looking down at the letter again, she re-read the last sentence. "If you can take care of her until she is eighteen, then I will see to finding her a husband."

A husband, bah! Husbands were totally unnecessary encumbrances. "Preposterous," she muttered out loud.

" 'Tis not my fault." The girl in front of her wiped her eyes with a sleeve that had apparently served her quite some time as a handkerchief. "It truly is not."

Lady Sidonia rose to her feet. "Stand up straight, gel, shoulders back. Let us have a look at you."

Her eyes still downcast, the girl made a half-hearted attempt to square her shoulders, then slowly her gaze traveled from Lady Sidonia's stout boots up past her black split riding skirt, up, up, until she was eyeball to eyeball with the older woman.

"But . . . but you are as tall as I am!" she cried with the first show of spirit Lady Sidonia had yet seen in her.

"Of course I am. We get it from my mother, your

great-grandmother. Anne Newbold she was. Almost caught herself a king, she did, although I never could see why she should have wanted a dunderhead like him. Aye, you have got her height, but we have yet to see if you have also inherited any of her wit or gumption.''

Chapter One

May 1806

"I BELIEVE there has been some mistake. I do not accept temporary positions." Miss Anne Hemsworth, a most highly recommended governess, rose majestically to her feet and looked down at her would-be employer.

He was a short man, though he did his best to disguise the fact by wearing shoes with extremely high heels. Dressed as he was in a deep plum jacket, which was padded at the shoulders and nipped in at the waist, and biscuit-colored ummentionables, his lilac waistcoat would have been unexceptional were it not for mother-of-pearl buttons of extraordinary size. They and his collar, which was too high to permit the turning of his head, proclaimed him a dandy.

His unlined face gave the impression of youth, and on first making his acquaintance, Anne had thought him to be only slightly older than her own seven and twenty years. But upon closer inspection, a certain sagging about the jowls led her to believe he was already on the shady side of forty.

Now, however, frown lines wrinkled his forehead. "But— but, do please reconsider. It is an excellent offer I am making you."

He reached for her arm to detain her, but she avoided his hand and turned to leave. The little man scurried after her, reminding her of a toy poodle being dragged along on a leash. Not that she had anything against poodles, except, of course, those of the breed that had a tendency to yap constantly.

Her tolerance for lapdogs did not extend, however, to short men who seemed unable to raise their eyes above the level of her bosom.

"But you would be passing up the opportunity to work in the household of a marquess. Only do think how it would raise your consequence to have a reference from an actual marquess.''

Added to his propensity to rub his hands surreptitiously on his unmentionables every time he looked at her, this was the last straw. Having spent the first fifteen years of her life trading on the fact that she was Lady Gloriana Marybell Dorinda Elizabeth Hemsworth, the daughter of the earl of Faussley, and having spent the last twelve learning to stand on her own two feet, Anne was not at all in doubt as to which was more rewarding. She knew better than most people how little real value a title carried.

Pausing at the door of the hotel parlor where the interview was being conducted, she turned to face Mr. Trussell. ''I have no need of references from a ten-year-old marquess. My reputation is already such that I am able to pick and choose where I will.'' Surveying him impassively from top to bottom, she concluded, ''And I do not choose to be in your employ.''

Deliberately throwing back her shoulders, which only made his eyes goggle all the more, she turned and sailed majestically through the doorway.

Mrs. Dorothy Wiggins, for the last twenty-one years part owner and sole manager of one of London's most elite employment agencies, sat at her wide oak desk and listened to Anne describe the abortive interview she had just terminated.

Really, Lady Letitia had been mistaken in her belief that it would be an easy matter to maneuver Anne into taking the position in Devon. But as difficult as it might be, Dorothy was in full agreement with her friend and partner that allowing Anne to waste her life as a governess, to live and die a spinster, was a crime against nature. It was therefore up to Dorothy to convince Anne to accept this temporary position in Devon, even though Lady Letitia was keeping her own counsel as to who the prospective bridegroom was.

''It is all very well and good to know one's worth, but before one can pick and choose, one must have more than one job to pick and choose among,'' Mrs. Wiggins pointed out. ''And in the autumn, of course, there will undoubtedly be an abundance of positions open. But with summer upon us, it is not the best time of the year to be between positions.'' If one discounted, of course, the two ladies who had specifically requested that they be notified the moment Anne became free to accept a new position.

"Be that as it may, I am not the slightest bit inclined to be in the employ of that little worm of a man."

"My dear, Mr. Creighton Trussell is most highly esteemed and a perfect gentleman. I should not describe him in such slighting terms if I were you."

"If he had slavered over your hand and drooled every time he gawked at your bosom, you would think it a mild enough description."

"Surely by this time you have accustomed yourself to attracting attention. You cannot blame the poor man for taking one look at you and becoming completely besotted."

"Besotted? Is that what you call it when a man is so lost to propriety as to stare rudely at a woman's chest?"

"Of course. This may come as a shock to you, my dear Anne, but your singular height is not the only reason men's heads turn when you walk down the street. Indeed, I would say it is not even one of the principle reasons. Even dressed as a governess, you are quite beautiful, and you need not point out that you are not at all in the mode. This Season's ideal of beauty may be a little china doll dressed in ribbons and flounces, but that will not stop men from appreciating your flawless skin—"

"Which only makes me look healthy, rather than interesting—"

"And your thick, glossy hair—"

"With its unruly curls. Really, Mrs. Wiggins, you are making me sound like a horse you are trying to fob off on some unsuspecting gapeseed. Next you will be trying to convince me that I am virtually a pocket Venus, when you know very well I am everywhere oversized."

"Not really oversized, my dear. I have seldom seen anyone with a more perfectly proportioned figure."

"If one is interested in the overlarge, the overabundent, the over—"

Mrs. Wiggins held up one hand. "Enough! I shall refrain from trying to cure you of your blindness where your own looks are concerned. But I am not ready to let you throw aside a perfectly good position because you have taken a dislike to your prospective employer. To begin with, may I point out that you would not actually be working for Mr. Trussell, but rather for Lord Leatham, the twins' legal guardian?''

"Who is safely out of reach in Turkey or Afghanistan or some such heathen place, which leaves the day-to-day management of Wylington Manor in the hands of that incompetent, sniveling little—''

"Exactly! The situation positively cries out for the attention of a sensible woman such as yourself.''

Anne burst out laughing. "What you mean to say is that I am that worst of all creatures, a managing female. And having never been to Wylington Manor, how would you know how well or how poorly it is run?''

"Well, to begin with, I have sent six—no seven—governesses all the way down there to Devon in the last four months. The most capable lasted a bare fortnight, and their comments when they bolted back to London ranged from 'heathen savages' to . . . let me see.'' She flipped through several papers on her desk. "To 'hell-born brats' and 'spawns of the Devil.' And their descriptions of the living conditions were every bit as bad. You see, it is a situation positively demanding your abilities.''

"The one flaw being that in September the twins will be packed off to Harrow.''

"Would you not enjoy a summer by the sea?'' Mrs. Wiggins did her best to make her voice sound beguiling.

"Wylington Manor lies in the middle of Dartmoor, some fifteen miles from the coast,'' Anne corrected her friend. "I had rather spend the summer visiting my great-aunt, who is getting on in years, and who writes that she misses me.''

"Lady Sidonia is healthy as a horse and will likely see us all in our graves, so do not try to gull me. And you know perfectly well that after three days in one another's company you are both at daggers drawn.''

"Nonsense, we could not be more alike in our way of thinking.''

"Exactly. I have never yet known a household with room for two managing females.''

"Touché.''

"Besides, Mr. Trussell has offered you a full year's salary for only three months' work."

"I am not that hard up for money."

Anne was now smiling at her, which Dorothy hoped was a sign the younger woman was weakening.

"You might also consider this. Although Miss Alice Feathertoner, who was married off last week to young Mr. Claymore, was in all ways a shining example of your ability as a governess, you must admit that she was not the least bit of a challenge. Virtually any of the governesses who are handled by this agency could have turned her out in a creditable manner, so sweet and compliant as she is. On the other hand, if you take this job in Devon, you will be taking on a considerable challenge. Moreover, it is a challenge others have tried and failed to meet—*and*," she added, without giving Anne a chance for a rebuttal, "I seem to recall that you have a partiality for clotted cream. Need I remind you that strawberries are just coming into season?"

"Unfair tactics, Mrs. Wiggins." Anne could no longer hold back her laughter. "Very well, I shall let you pack me off to Devon, but if I come back at the end of the summer as fat as a Christmas goose, it will all be on your shoulders."

She stood up, but did not immediately leave. "Tell me, my dear Mrs. Wiggins, now that you have persuaded me to go against my better judgment, do you know if any of the other governesses are in London at the moment? The ones who did not find clotted cream adequate compensation for living at Wylington Manor?"

"Why, yes. Miss Jennings has accepted a position as companion to Lady d'Auberville, and I believe they have not yet departed for Bath. But why do you ask?"

"As my great-aunt Sidonia used to say, 'A general is only as good as his spies.' I intend to know as many details about those two boys and their tricks as possible before I match wits with them."

Watching her depart, Mrs. Wiggins speculated on the man Lady Letitia had picked to win the hand of Lady Anne. That it could not be Mr. Trussell was obvious. On the other hand, as Anne had mentioned in passing, Lord Leatham was never in England long enough to pursue even a lightning courtship. The only other eligible bachelor in the vicinity of Wylington Manor was Lord Thorverton, and he was already engaged to be married.

More than likely this temporary position was in the nature of a stop-gap. Lady Letitia was undoubtedly planning something for the little Season in the fall and was now merely guaranteeing that Lady Anne would be unemployed and available then, while at the same time solving what had become a thorny problem for the agency.

"It is really a shame dear Mr. Trussell was not left in charge of the twins. He is their uncle, you know—their mother's brother, and such a sweet man. So courteous in every respect, but with no real authority to take charge of their lives. He confided in me what a terrible blow it was when he discovered the twins' guardianship had been left to Lord Leatham. Perhaps you have heard of him? He is not even their uncle, although the boys are accustomed to referring to him as such. He is merely their father's second cousin and quite a barbarous man. Only imagine, months go by without a word from him and then he simply descends upon the household with no warning, encourages the boys in their wildness, and then departs, leaving poor Mr. Trussell to try to undo the harm. Such a dear man, and he does his best, but it is an impossible situation. More tea?"

"No, thank you. I really must be going. I do appreciate your helpfulness." Anne rose to her feet and pulled on her gloves.

Miss Jennings escorted her to the door. "Really, I do not think Lord Wylington and Lord Anthony are beyond salvaging. They have such angelic smiles, I am sure they must also have good hearts. If only they could be completely removed from the influence of the baron, then perhaps they might be more willing to follow the model of their dear uncle, who is in every way the perfect gentleman."

The woman was a complete ninny, Anne decided while walking at a brisk pace back to her lodgings. A useful source of information, to be sure, but Miss Jennings's ability to evaluate other people's character was woefully deficient.

Which was adequate reason for Anne to resolve then and there to be especially wary when confronted by two "angelic smiles."

"The expenditures are a bit high, but well within normal bounds. I cannot see any discrepancies in the accounts that would tend to support your suspicions that Mr. Trussell is playing ducks and drakes with your wards' money. If you perhaps had some evidence?"

Bronson Roebuck, Lord Leatham, regarded his solicitor, Mr. Johnston, through half-closed eyes. Evidence? Did the man take Creighton Trussell for such a fool that he would leave signed documents lying around stating that he was embezzling money from the Wylington estate? Indeed, it was a lucky thing George Morrough, one of his late father's old cronies, had felt it his responsibility to drop a word in Bronson's ear about Trussell's activities.

"My wards' uncle has been spending money on his wardrobe and his mistress at a rate that patently exceeds his funds."

"But my dear Lord Leatham, surely you know there are any number of ways a gentleman can augment his income. Mr. Trussell may have won large sums at cards, for example, or speculated successfully on 'Change, or even borrowed from a cent-per-cent, which while certainly unwise, is not at all illegal. And I must point out, the estate books are fully in order."

"To be sure, such things are possible." Except of course, for the fact that the Bow Street runner Morrough had recommended had easily discovered that Creighton, rather than winning the required sums, had been steadily losing money on the horses and at cards—a great deal of money, in fact.

Would the solicitor evince more interest if he learned that the runner had not been able to locate any money-lender who had had dealings with Trussell? Would the solicitor merely find more excuses if he were told the extreme lengths Trussell had gone to hide the fact that he was the owner of the lease on that little house in Mayfair presently occupied by the latest redhead beauty to grace the ranks of opera dancers at Covent Gardens?

More than likely, Mr. Johnston would interpret Trussell's furtive actions as being merely the discretion of a prudent man.

Solicitors, it would seem, were not trained to operate on suspicions. They required positive evidence.

It was little consolation for Bronson to consider that he himself would have been dead on more than a dozen occasions in foreign lands if he had not taken action quickly and efficiently, when the said action was supported by nothing more than the flimsiest of suspicions.

But if evidence was required in Merrie Olde England, then evidence would be found. Bronson rose to his feet.

The solicitor hurried around his desk to open the door for him. "And you will, of course, leave a copy of your itinerary with my clerk? So we will know where to forward such papers as require your signature?"

"My departure plans are as yet uncertain. It may be necessary to postpone my trip for a few weeks. As soon as I have finished my business in London, I will personally inspect the situation at Wylington Manor."

Lord Leatham's smile was quite feral, and Mr. Johnston could not quite suppress a shudder at the sight of what was little more than bared fangs. If Creighton Trussell was indeed embezzling funds from the estate, then the good Lord have mercy upon him, because the poor fool could expect to receive none from the baron.

Anne Hemsworth descended from the coach at the Red Stag in Tavistock and efficiently directed the guard as to the removal of her luggage. The yard of the staging inn was bustling with hostlers unhitching the spent horses and bringing out the new team, with passengers embarking and debarking, and with sundry other people going about their business, all in the greatest of haste.

After the stage departed to continue its journey to Liskeard, a degree of calm gradually descended upon the yard, but no one appeared to inquire if she were being met or if she would require a room for the night. When five minutes of patient waiting stretched into ten, Anne decided to take matters into her own hands.

Waylaying the landlord as he hurried by, she inquired if anyone had arrived from Wylington Manor.

He eyed her impassively from the top of her bonnet to the tips of her half-boots, but she was quite used to receiving such thorough inspection, and it had been years since she had been discomposed by people's reaction to her unusual height.

"Another new governess, eh? Aye, Harry came with the gig nigh on an hour ago. Happen you'll find him in the taproom."

"And how may I recognize Harry?"

The landlord gave her a speculative look, and for a moment she was not sure he intended to answer.

"Just look for the man with the least hair on his head and the most on his chin, and that'll be the one you want." With a snort that might have been intended as a laugh, he turned away to deal with another guest.

Standing in the door of the taproom it was not hard, based on the landlord's description, to pick out the most likely candidate. The majority of the customers drinking their ale were clean-shaven, but one appeared not to have touched a razor in at least a sennight. Whether or not he was bald was not immediately apparent, since he wore a shabby cloth hat pulled down low over his forehead, but Anne was reasonably assured that she had the right man.

Approaching him where he sat at the bar, she heard the buzz of conversation around her gradually die down. The room was completely silent, all attention obviously on her, when she asked, "Are you Harry? The groom from Wylington Manor?"

He turned to look at her. "And what if I am?" he replied insolently, then spat in the sawdust at her feet.

"I am the new governess. I believe you have been sent to meet me."

"All in good time. I ain't done talking to my friends." He turned his back on her, and a low murmur of amusement rippled through the room.

Well, thought Anne, as Aunt Sidonia always said, start as you mean to go on. With lightning speed, she grasped the groom's ear firmly and hoisted him off the bench.

"Ow, ow, let go my ear! Whatcher think yer doing? Ow, ow, let go!"

"I find I much prefer to leave at once." Amid equal numbers of catcalls and cheers from the other patrons, she dragged the recalcitrant groom stumbling and protesting across the room and out the door. By the time they reached the yard, he was half running to keep up with her stride, in a futile effort to ease the pressure on his ear.

She did not release him until they had crossed the sill into the stables. "Now, harness up the horse and let us be on our way."

Rubbing his sore ear, he backed away from her. "And if I don't? Whatcher plannin' to do then? Harness up by yourself?" There was naked hostility in his expression, but then she had never found popularity worth the price one had to pay.

She took one step toward him, but he darted away before she could grab his ear again. In matters of strength, she knew she had the advantage, but she declined to make herself look foolish by chasing him around the stables.

Luckily, he was not indispensable, although he appeared to think he was. There was only one gig presently in the stable, so that presented no problem, but trying to guess which horse was the correct one was a more difficult matter.

Turning to the man whose livery proclaimed him the head hostler at the inn, she asked in an authoritative voice, "Which horse belongs to the Marquess of Wylington?"

The man nodded in the direction of a sleek roan placidly chewing a mouthful of hay, but otherwise he made no move to help her. Nor did any of the other men who were standing around appreciating the humor of her predicament, although one of them snickered, causing Harry to guffaw openly.

"They ain't none of the others going to help you none neither, so don't think they will. They're my friends." Harry taunted her from a safe position behind a phaeton.

Well, he who laughs last, she thought. Untying the horse, she quickly and efficiently harnessed it to the gig and led it out into the yard, where she recovered her luggage and effortlessly tossed it up into the vehicle. Then climbing onto the driver's seat, she proceeded on her journey without further delay. She made the turn out of the courtyard before it belatedly occurred to Harry that he was being left with no transportation.

She could hear him calling for her to wait, but she did not bother to look back, nor did she check her pace, which was perhaps a bit reckless for the crowded streets of the market town. She was a good whip, however, and was determined to convince not only the groom but the townspeople as well, that she was not a person to trifle with.

Thanks to her informative chat with Miss Jennings, Anne was able to pick the correct road out of town, and by the time the last house had been left behind, so too had the sounds of Harry's pursuit.

For the primary residence of a marquess, it was not excessively large. Anne pulled the horse to a halt, the better to survey Wylington Manor. Of uncertain architectural design, it sprawled in the sun, giving the impression of immense age. A regular indentation around the central portion of the building was evidence of an earlier moat, and behind the house the moor stretched away, bleak, desolate, and timeless.

Even while she watched, a cloud passed overhead, blotting out the sun, and the manor became at once forbidding and downright sinister. It was a good thing she was blessed with a practical disposition rather than a nervous one, or she would be quick to imagine the manor filled with villainous relatives, treacherous servants, and of course, the requisite ghost, more than likely stalking the battlements at midnight with his head tucked securely under his arm. Or under her arm, of course, if it were the female variety of unearthly apparition.

Indeed, it appeared to be the sort of house where secret passageways were the norm, and where sliding panels concealed hidden rooms filled with dusty bones. The library was certain to contain books of ancient magic, interspersed, of course, with fake books containing ornate keys or cryptic treasure maps in their hollowed-out cores.

The sun reappeared after its short absence, and once again the manor looked perfectly normal, concealing nothing more dreadful behind its ivy-covered facade than two ''hell-born boys'' and a gaggle of poorly supervised servants.

Clucking to her horse, Anne drove along the broad, curved drive to the front door. From past experience she knew it was vital to establish her standing in the household from the very beginning. So far, wherever she had been employed, she had never used the servants' entrance, nor did she intend to start now.

Tying the horse's reins to a hitching ring, she boldly mounted the flat, wide steps to the main door, where, using the lion's-head knocker, she loudly announced her arrival.

After a short wait, she pounded again, and this time was rewarded when the door creaked slowly open. Have the hinges oiled and the door knocker properly polished, she thought, beginning a mental list of tasks to be accomplished.

The butler, if indeed he was such, stared at her out of red-rimmed, bloodshot eyes, and it did not require a whiff of his overpowering breath to inform her he had been imbibing strong spirits rather heavily. Third, dry out the butler, she added to her list.

"I am Miss Anne Hemsworth. Mr. Trussell has engaged me to be the new governess." Without waiting for a reaction from him, she sailed past the befuddled man, drawing off her gloves even while she continued to instruct him. "Please inform the housekeeper of my arrival and tell her I expect to see her *at once.*"

He gawked up at her as if she were a figment of his imagination, or more likely, an hallucination whose origins might well be attributed to the consumption of far too many bottles of smuggled French brandy.

She waited while he rubbed his eyes and then goggled up at her again without apparent comprehension. "I am the new governess." With more patience than she had shown the groom, she looked down at him and repeated herself, this time speaking loudly and enunciating every word clearly. "Send the housekeeper here to me at once."

Finally her words seemed to penetrate the alcoholic haze in his brain. "The housekeeper? You want to see Mrs. Plimtree?"

"Yes, fetch Mrs. Plimtree." Anne sat down on an immense chair of medieval design, which appeared totally incongruous next to a delicately carved table holding a cracked Venetian glass vase containing the dismal remains of what may or may not have once been roses. The parquetry surface of the table had been damaged by water leaking from the vase, and the corners of many of the individual pieces of inlaid wood were curling up.

The butler shuffled his feet beside her, but Anne stoically ignored his continued presence, and finally he went away. Some time later a painfully thin woman appeared in the hallway, a ring of keys at her waist proclaiming her to be the housekeeper.

"If you are the new governess, you ought to have come 'round to the servants' door," the woman began querulously, but Anne cut her short.

"You may show me to my room and then have my luggage brought up. I shall require hot water immediately and a cup of tea in precisely twenty-five minutes." A duchess could not have been more regal or more haughty, and the housekeeper, although not precisely cowed, began to sound a bit more respectful.

"Well, then, I'll just have Harry fetch your things in at once."

"Harry has been detained in town. From somewhere he seems to have acquired the absurd notion that he is being paid good wages to drink ale with his friends. In this he will find that he is grossly in error."

So saying, Anne rose slowly to her feet, and by the time she had straightened to her full height, the housekeeper's mouth was hanging open, her eyes were virtually popping out of her head, and her hands were twisting her apron, which in Anne's opinion could have been vastly improved by the judicious application of soap and water.

Twenty minutes later there was a very loud knock at the door of Anne's room. Opening it, she did not find the tea she had ordered, but in place of the maid, two slightly grubby boys stood in the corridor. They were obviously not expecting to find someone as tall as she was, since their gazes were firmly fixed at about the level of her waist. Slowly their eyes traveled up to meet hers.

They regarded her with blank looks, then turned to each other and Anne had the feeling they were engaging in some form of unspoken communication. From what she could see, they were as alike as two peas in a pod—tousled blond hair above guileless green eyes.

They lifted their faces to her again, and Anne had to admit

the two of them were appealing. If one discounted the dirt, they might easily have served as models for a painting of cherubs by Raphael.

"Are you the new governess?" the boy on the left asked.

"Yes, I am Miss Anne Hemsworth. You may call me Anne."

"I am Lord Anthony," the boy on the right said. "And this is my brother Andrew, Lord Wylington."

The boy on the left turned to his brother. "I thought you were Andrew, and I was Anthony." His look of puzzlement was every bit as false as it was meant to be appealing.

"You're right. I do believe I am Andrew."

"No, wait. I think you had it correct the first time."

"Oh, dear."

They looked at her expectantly. She let them wait. After a long pause they shot each other a quick look, then the one on the right asked, "Aren't you going to tell us we are little men now, old enough to know which of us is which?"

"It does not really matter, does it?" Anne looked down at them calmly.

"Of course it matters," the one on the left said. "One of us is Lord Wylington . . ."

"And the other one isn't," his brother finished for him.

"But since I have no way of telling the two of you apart, at least this early in our acquaintance, I shall simply call you both Anthony on Mondays, Wednesdays, and Fridays, and on Tuesdays, Thursdays and Saturdays I shall call you both Andrew."

"And what about on Sunday?" the one on the right asked, receiving an elbow in his ribs from his brother, apparently for allowing his curiosity to get the best of him.

"Oh, by this Sunday or the next I shall doubtless know which one of you is which."

They exchanged speaking looks, then the one on the left asked hopefully, "Would you like to go for a walk on the moors with us? It is such a beautiful day and we are so tired of being cooped up in the house."

They both smiled angelically up at her.

Chapter Two

DEMETRIUS BAINETON, VISCOUNT THORVERTON, stood in the window of his club gazing disconsolately down at the passers-by. Behind him the room was singularly devoid of anyone under the age of seventy. It was hardly surprising, since there was a prize fight scheduled for the morrow some fifty miles distant from London.

Now that he had one precious day of freedom, Demetrius was finding it decidedly unrewarding to be at loose ends. If only he were home in Devon, taking care of his stud. With forty mares and an equal number of colts and fillies either already born or due to drop any day, there would be no possibility of time hanging heavy on his hands.

Catching sight of a man striding along through the crowds, his boredom vanished. Could it possibly be Leatham? The last Demetrius had heard, his neighbor was halfway around the world. But who else in London towered so tall above the crowds? No other gentleman whom Demetrius had ever encountered.

Bronson Roebuck felt a hand touch his arm and a familiar voice sounded behind him.

"Leatham, well met!"

"Thorverton, what the devil are you doing in London? Do not tell me you have entrusted the care of your precious horses to your cousin Mallory?"

"Lawrence is a good man and capable of managing the stud without me."

Bronson smiled. "I know that, and Mallory knows that, but you have never before been willing to admit you were not totally indispensable."

A shadow crossed his young friend's face. "I am spending the Season here in London with my fiancée and her mother.

The wedding is scheduled for a week from tomorrow. I hope you will be able to attend.''

For a man about to take the plunge into matrimony, Thorverton did not appear to be looking forward to his upcoming nuptials with anything approaching the eagerness one might expect from a young bridegroom who has won the hand of his chosen lady. "It is Diana Fairgrove, I presume.''

"Of course. It has been an understood thing since we were in leading strings. We have been sweethearts forever.''

With difficulty, Bronson was able to control his curiosity. "I am on my way to Manton's for a little target practice. Would you care to accompany me?''

"Manton's," his friend sighed. "Of course, I would be happy to go with you. It seems an age since I have been there.'' They walked in silence for a while, then Demetrius abruptly asked, "Why have you never married, Leatham? Excuse me, that was rude of me. You need not answer.''

"On the contrary, I will be happy to answer. You know I travel a lot.''

"And a woman would not wish to be exposed to the dangers you encounter.''

"No, that is not precisely the case. My father was also a great one for exploring strange parts of the world, and he married. To be sure, he was not home often. But with me it is really quite simple. I have been to exotic lands, seen wondrous sights, matched wits with truly ingenious barbarians—and in all my travels I have never found a woman who was the least bit entertaining except when she was in bed. To make matters worse, compared to some of the innovative foreign beauties I have dallied with, the average Englishwoman is too much a lady even to hold my interest when she is between the sheets. In short, the idea of being leg-shackled does not interest me in the least.''

Beside him Demetrius smiled ruefully. "And I thought there was something wrong with me. It is not that I do not love Diana . . . or at least, I have always felt a strong affection for her, which is the most one can hope for. But until this spring I had never before been in her company for more than an occasional evening.''

A heavy lorry rumbled by, forcing them to pause in their conversation until it had passed.

"And now?" Bronson asked.

"Now I have discovered that Diana is thoroughly accustomed to being the center of her parents' attention."

"Spoiled, in a word."

Demetrius gave a short laugh, which contained very little in the way of good humor. "Beyond belief. I am expected to devote my every waking moment to her entertainment. She apparently feels my whole reason for being on this earth is to keep her from languishing in boredom. My greatest delight should be in helping her decide the color of a ribbon or the tilt of a bonnet. I tell you, Leatham, you would not believe the tears, the pouts, and the sulks if I do not compliment her every hour. And she takes to her bed if I so much as hint that I might wish to engage in any activity she is not also interested in."

Bronson looked around. "And yet I do not see the fair Diana now."

"I have been granted an unexpected furlough for one day only. Quite extraordinary, really. 'Tis the first time I have had to myself in over two months. And more than likely the last hours of freedom I shall have during this lifetime."

"Surely it will not be so bad once you are married. She will not wish to sit in your pocket forever. I cannot picture her following you about in the stables like a puppy dog, for example."

"That was my most serious blunder. By coming to London at the height of the foaling season, I have apparently 'proved' that Lawrence can run the stud without me, and I am therefore to consider myself free to spend the entire year escorting Diana around the countryside from one house party to the next, only dropping in at Thorverton Hall for a day or two from time to time."

"Good God. Can you not . . . no, I suppose you cannot simply call off the wedding."

"No." There was a long pause. Finally Demetrius sighed. "Honor is sometimes a heavy burden, is it not? There are times when I think I would prefer to be a complete cad."

* * *

"You are a complete cad." Rosemary Pierce-Smythe leaned back against her pillows and made no effort to hide her displeasure behind dimples and fluttering eyelashes. Creighton Trussell was bought and paid for, body and soul, although he appeared not to be fully cognizant of the fact. "I am perfectly willing to frank your losses at the table and on the turf, but I am strangely unwilling to support your mistress."

"But I have no mistress. Only you, my dearest darling, and I have never thought of you in such crude terms. You are the only love of my life, and—"

"I am not the fool you seem to think I am." She cut his excuses short. "I have had you followed, my good sir, so let us be done with all pretenses."

She waited, but he made no further effort to continue his denials. Good. Now to make sure he knew exactly who held the end of his leash. "You will give that tart her congé, after which you will form no relationship with any other woman, whether professional or amateur. If you do, be sure I shall discover it."

"I think the time has come, madame, to end *this* liaison instead." He bowed curtly. "It has been a pleasure, but it is no longer worth the money you expend on my behalf."

"I am afraid it is not that easy," she said. "I have not actually discharged your debts, as I have led you to believe. I have merely bought them up from your other creditors. At the moment I hold your vowels to the tune of fifty-five thousand pounds."

He blanched, and for a moment she thought he was going to faint. It would seem he was beginning to realize exactly how much freedom he had sold away with his gaming.

"This is preposterous. I begin to suspect, madame, that despite the outward trappings of a lady, you have the heart of a usurer."

"Whereas you, my gullible love, have deliberately set out to make me believe that you desired my company only because of a deep and undying passion. Were you perhaps attempting to dupe me out of my money? Rest assured, I have a strong dislike for being duped. Were I to think, even for a moment, that such were the case, I am afraid I would be forced to have you brought before a magistrate and thrown into debtors' prison. Assuming, of course, you did not have the money to redeem your vowels.''

He wavered, but in the end cowardice won out, and he took the hand she held out to him and kissed it.

Unfortunately for him, Rosemary thought to herself, he had not had the courage to call her bluff. Had he but known it, she would have done everything in her power to prevent a scandal, rather than have caused one. It was all very well to take a much younger man for a lover, but nothing must interfere with her daughter's chance for marriage with a member of the peerage.

After he dismissed his mistress would be time enough to make it clear to him exactly why she had loosened her purse strings to such an extent. She had deliberately let him think it was because she had conceived a grand passion for him, but actually it was because of his connections in society. It was unfortunate that he had no title himself and was therefore ineligible for her daughter, but even so, he was not only the uncle of the Marquess of Wylington, but also the grandson of the Earl of Bardeswythe. With the proper coercion, he could open all the doors of the *haut ton* for her and her dear daughter Rosabelle.

In the meantime, there was no harm in enjoying his love making, which had proven to be far more imaginative than anything her late husband had been capable of.

"Come, come, my dear boy. I am a generous woman and I forgive you for your little lapse in judgment. But now you must show me that you are truly repentant.''

Creighton Trussell was astounded to realize this faded beauty actually expected him to ignore the scene that had just taken place as if it had never happened. Ecod, what did the woman expect? That she could bawl him out like a schoolboy, treat him like some demmed gigolo, and then expect him to perform in bed?

While he hesitated, her smile became colder, and he could hear the ominous words echo in his mind: fifty-five thousand pounds . . . debtors' prison. She would do it, too. The widow of a rich cit, she had not the delicacy of mind that characterized a true lady.

With no further delay he went to the window and drew the heavy draperies closed, then returned to where she waited and slid between the sheets. He was cold through and through, and the heat from her body had no power to warm him.

In desperation he closed his eyes and did his best to pretend she was not a plump widow from somewhere in Yorkshire, but a tall, incredibly well-endowed governess named Miss Hemsworth. His imagination proved equal to the task, and he was thankful to be able to satisfy the widow as to his continued devotion.

The mist was beginning to rise from the moor, although it was as yet too wispy to present a serious problem. Anne turned slowly around, scanning the horizon in all directions. There was no sign of any man-made object, whether path or shed or building. Stones jutted out of the ground at awkward angles, waiting patiently as they had done for centuries.

The twins had completely vanished. Anne sat down on the nearest stone, which had been shaped by the wind into a convenient seat. "Well, well, well, here I am, alone on the moor. Whatever shall I do?" Her voice was a bit louder than usual. "I could, of course, have the vapors and sit here all night, crying my eyes out, but that would be a bit uncomfortable, not to mention cold. On the other hand, I suppose I could retrace our steps."

There was the merest sound of scuffling, not enough to tell the direction it was coming from or determine whether it was made by a small animal or a ten-year-old boy.

"But since we have been walking in circles for the last hour, and since it is now nearly teatime, I think I might as well return directly to Wylington Manor." So saying, she rose to her feet and set off.

Walking south for about a hundred yards she topped a small rise and saw the chimneys of the manor house. Proceeding another fifty yards in that direction, she was joined by two boys, one on either side of her. She said nothing to indicate she was aware of their presence.

Finally, the one on her right spoke. "How did you know which way to go?"

"Skanadajiwah, who has lived for several years with my great-aunt Sidonia, is a Mohawk Indian. He taught me how to avoid getting lost. It would have been more difficult today, of course, if the sky had been overcast, but even so there are signs to watch for."

"Would you . . ."

"Could you teach us how you did it?"

"Well, I suppose, considering that I am your governess, I am actually expected to teach you any number of useful things."

There was a sigh from the boy on her right, echoed by the boy on her left.

"Did Skanadawija—"

"Skanada*ji*wah," she corrected.

"Yes, did he teach you any other things? *Useful* things."

"What kind of things are you interested in? Things like how to build a snare and catch rabbits? How to dry meat into jerky so that you can carry a week's worth of food in a small pouch? How to make a bow and arrows? How to tell whether bad weather is coming? How to ride a horse bareback? How to throw a tomahawk? How to catch fish without a fishhook or net? Do you mean those kinds of things?"

One boy slid his hand into her left one, then the other boy took her right hand. "How did your aunt come to have an Indian living with her?"

"Oh, she wintered over with his tribe many years ago, and when she returned to England, she invited them to come and visit her. I do not suppose she ever expected any of them to cross the ocean, since they are superstitious about such things, but one day she opened her door and there he stood. Apparently he likes England, because he has never mentioned returning home."

"But why was she living with a tribe of Indians?"

"Her husband was a government agent, sent out to Canada for some purpose. Shortly after they arrived, the settlement he was assigned to was attacked by Indians—not Mohawks, of course, since they are our allies, but a band of Hurons, who are the mortal enemies of all the Iroquois tribes."

"Why did her husband not protect her?"

"He was too busy saving his own skin. When the soldiers

arrived a few hours later, they found him hiding in a barrel. I would imagine he looked a bit ridiculous covered with cornmeal, but he was uninjured.''

"I do not understand. A man's duty is to protect his women. I think he should have been whipped for acting in such a cowardly way.''

"And do you agree?'' Anne asked the other twin.

"Of course I agree. It was a most dishonorable thing to do.''

"Then what is your opinion of a man who would lead a woman into the wilderness and then abandon her to her fate?''

"He should be hanged by the neck until dead,'' one twin replied, at the same time the other said with bloodthirsty relish, "He should be taken before a firing squad and shot.''

They looked up at her for approval, but she merely said, "And what do you think should be the punishment for two boys who lead an old woman out onto Dartmoor and abandon her, then derive amusement from her panic?''

There was a long silence, then one of the twins ventured to say, "You are not really all that old.''

"And you did not panic, not even for a minute,'' the other one added.

"I was referring to Miss Jennings. She is old enough to be your mother, and I believe she was terrified out of her mind.''

"Oh.''

"Yes, oh,'' Anne said firmly. "What do you think should be the punishment for men who acted in such a cowardly manner?''

There was an even longer silence. Then one twin said tentatively, "We are not actually men.''

"Yes, we are only just turned ten,'' his brother added.

"I see,'' Anne said thoughtfully. "Then what you are saying, is that the seedling of a thorn tree, when it is grown to full height, will magically lose its thorns and turn into a solid English oak?''

They contemplated this idea for a while, and then one twin said firmly, "There was no real danger. We did not actually go off and leave Miss Jennings.''

"No,'' the other twin added. "We were just hiding behind the rocks. We would not have let her become truly lost, so it is not as bad as letting one's wife be captured by Indians.''

Both twins looked up at her hopefully to see if she would accept that excuse, and Anne was interested to note that there was no sign of their earlier fake angelic smiles on their faces.

"So, being afraid for your life, as you were, you hid behind the rocks?"

"Oh, we were never afraid."

"We just thought it would be funny."

Anne stopped dead in her tracks and dropped the boys' hands. "Funny? You think scaring women is funny? And do you also think it is funny to pull wings off butterflies and tie tin cans to puppy dogs' tails?"

There was no answer. "Tell me, do either of you know what it is called when someone finds amusement in another's pain?"

"Mean," one of the twins said softly, his eyes now downcast.

"Malicious," the other one said, moving close enough to his brother that their shoulders touched, as if needing comfort from physical contact with his twin. "Are you going to whip us?" he asked finally. "I do not think Uncle Bronson will like it if you have us hanged or shot."

"Since you are old enough to understand right from wrong, you are also old enough to figure out what you can do to correct what you did."

"But we can't correct it. Miss Jennings is gone," one twin blurted out.

Anne made no comment; she just stood there waiting patiently.

"But I am sure we can think of something," the other twin finally said with resignation in his voice. "We are really very ingenious."

"Yes," his brother agreed. "Most resourceful. You did not happen to talk to Miss Sidwell before you came here, did you?"

"No, I did not. Should I have?" Anne asked, struggling to keep a smile off her face.

"Oh, no, that was quite unnecessary," the other twin hurried to assure her.

"I would invite you in, Leatham, but I am not yet a member of the family, and I would not like to impose unduly upon my host's hospitality. At this hour the servants have most likely retired.''

It was well after midnight and the two men were strolling; home after an evening of conviviality. They were still several doors away from the Fairgrove residence when it became obvious something was amiss there. Every window in the house blazed with light.

"Good God, someone must be ill." Demetrius dashed up the steps two at a time.

His curiosity getting the better of him, Bronson took the liberty of following, albeit more sedately. Inside, everything was total confusion. Servants were rushing about, but to what purpose was not immediately apparent. The majority of activity, however, appeared to be focused on a room to the right of the entrance.

"What the deuce?" Demetrius was almost knocked over by a footman hurrying out the front door on some urgent assignment. "I say, Leatham, it looks as if they have all run mad."

"Try in here. Perhaps you may find someone in authority."

The sight that met their eyes when they pushed open the door to the anteroom was enough to make the bravest man turn coward. Sprawling half on and half off the settee was a comfortably stout lady of middling age, in the throes of the most extreme hysteria. Behind her, like a Greek chorus, three maids stood in a row, weeping and wringing their hands. Hovering over her, a white-haired man was patting her hand ineffectually while tears streamed unchecked down his cheeks.

Demetrius showed his true mettle by advancing into the room, but Bronson thought it more prudent to remain by the door. In his opinion, the woman resembled nothing so much as a whale he had once seen floundering on the beach in Greenland, whereas the man, whose gray hair was in sad disarray, looked very like a tired spaniel uncomfortably decked out in evening clothes.

Catching sight of the newcomers, the women began to wail even louder, and Bronson took an involuntary step backward.

"What has happened? Is something wrong with Diana?"

At Demetrius's question, both of the older people began talking at the same time, each apparently trying to outshout the other. The lady hoisted herself up enough to grasp Demetrius by the lapels of his coat, pulling his face down until it nearly touched hers. She seemed to be trying to deny all responsibility for what had happened. Either that or she was indicating a desire to put a period to her existence, it was not completely clear to Bronson.

Finally the old gentleman thrust a letter into Demetrius's hand. With the lady still dangling from his coat he endeavored to read it. His cry of "No, it cannot be!" was so loud, it momentarily shocked everyone into silence. Pulling free of the woman's grasp, Demetrius turned and dashed from the anteroom.

Bronson followed his friend across the hall into a second room, which appeared to be a gentleman's study. Demetrius was bent over, his back to the door, clutching the edge of the desk so hard his knuckles were white.

Bronson was deeply concerned at the apparent tragedy. Spotting some decanters on a small side table, he asked, "May I offer you some brandy?"

His friend's shoulders shook, and in a strangled voice he said, "Just shut the door. Please."

Closing the door, Bronson decided that brandy was definitely called for, whether his friend wished it or not.

"I did not love her enough," Demetrius choked out. "And she . . . and she . . ." He seemed unable to go on.

Good God, surely the chit had not committed suicide? Bronson held out the glass of brandy to his friend. "Drink this, and do not blame yourself for what has happened."

Demetrius turned toward him, his face reddened by his effort to control his emotion. Then laughter burst out explosively. He clapped his hand to his mouth to hide the sound, while with the other arm he hugged his ribs, shaking all over.

Tossing off the brandy himself, Bronson waited for his friend to stop laughing enough to explain.

"She eloped . . . this afternoon . . . with Hazelmore . . . They were married by special license. . . . They are on their way to Italy for their honeymoon. He . . . he . . ." Demetrius was again laughing too hard to continue.

Bronson filled a second glass and thrust it into his friend's hand.

Demetrius finally managed to drink some of it. Then, wiping the tears from his eyes, he said in a calmer voice, "He wrote a sonnet to her right ear and an ode to her left eyebrow, and he sleeps every night with a rose from her nosegay tucked under his pillow. She is sorry to break my heart, but he threatened to throw himself from London Bridge if she went through with our wedding. Oh, I am undone." Laying his hand dramatically on his forehead, Demetrius fell backward into a leather-covered chair.

"The gods sometimes take pity on fools," murmured Bronson. "But might I suggest we depart this house, ere your un-in-laws decide that it is your responsibility to follow hotfoot after the eloping pair and rescue Diana?"

"Ecod, you may be right. By morning it will be too late to do anything but send an announcement to the *Gazette,* after which I plan to flee like the craven coward I am back to Devon. But for tonight, may I take refuge with you?"

"Of course, dunderhead, need you ask? Although the accommodations are not as grand as here, most of the rooms being in Holland covers, the company is unexceptional and not prone to having the vapors."

"On a night like this I would be happy to sleep on a dirt floor under a sod roof. But now that I think on it, I feel not the least bit sleepy. In fact, I am quite rejuvenated. I am for celebrating my last-minute reprieve. Are you with me?"

"Till the cock crows."

One of the twins is left-handed, Anne realized with dawning satisfaction. The three of them were seated cross-legged on the ground inside a rough circle of stones, busily occupied with making snares to catch rabbits. Both twins were engrossed in their efforts, and their movements were amazingly identical, except reversed. It was like seeing one boy sitting beside a mirror.

"Anne?" the right-handed twin asked without looking up from his work. "You never told us who rescued your Aunt Sidonia from the Indians."

"Oh, she rescued herself. She managed to steal a tomahawk and kill her captor. Then she walked over two hundred miles through the forest, crossing innumerable streams, eating berries and trapping small animals for food, until she finally arrived at the village where Skanadajiwah's tribe lived. By that time it was too late in the fall for her to continue on to the nearest English settlement, so she remained with them until spring.''

"But that is impossible. You are making that up," the left-handed twin said with assurance.

"Oh? Pray tell me why I must be making it up."

His brother looked up from his knotting and explained. "Women can't do things like that."

"And how did you arrive at that conclusion?"

"Well," he hesitated, then turned to his twin. "You explain, Drew."

Aha, Anne thought. The left-handed one is Andrew, Lord Wylington, which means the right-handed one is his brother, Lord Anthony. Now I just have to learn which one is which when they are not doing anything with their hands.

"There's nothing to explain," said Andrew. "Everyone knows it is a fact."

"Before Columbus discovered the New World, everyone 'knew' the world was flat. It was a fact."

"I have the feeling we are about to have another lesson. You argue with her this time, Tony."

"Coward," his brother hissed at him before laying down his snare and looking directly at Anne. "Very well, I shall explain. Women cannot do things like rescuing themselves from Indians because they are weaker than men."

"I am a woman. Does that make me weaker than men?"

"But you are an exception. Most women are not as strong as men."

"So, you think, for example, that the Reverend Goodman Thirsk, since he is a man, is stronger than, oh, let us say Kate, the washerwoman?"

"You are talking your way into a corner, Tony," Andrew whispered with great glee.

"But I can talk my way out again. Pay attention, and you will learn something." He took a deep breath, then faced Anne squarely. "Most women are weaker than most men, and most men are smarter than most women. And," he added triumphantly, "the lesson you are trying to teach us today is to avoid absolutes, because no matter what the rule, there is always an exception."

Anne shook her head. "No, the lesson today is about judging other people. What is the correct word for judging someone before you know anything about that person?"

The twins stared at her blankly.

"I shall give you a clue. What is the prefix that means 'before'?"

"Pre-," Anthony said quickly. "Pre-judge . . ."

"Prejudice," Andrew blurted out triumphantly.

"Exactly. And now I shall tell you an absolute rule to follow. Any time someone tells you that all of a group of people who share one characteristic also share all other characteristics, please be careful not to fall into the trap of believing them."

"Like when someone says all Americans are uncultured?" Anthony asked.

"Exactly." Anne nodded her approval.

"Or all Jews are misers?" Andrew added.

"Or all Gypsies will steal you blind?"

The boys began to get into the spirit of the game.

"Or all French soldiers are cowards?"

"And all English soldiers are brave?"

"Or all women are useless except when they are flat on their backs?"

Anne's hands stopped their automatic movements, and the snare she had been making dropped into her lap. She, who prided herself on being unshockable, was shocked to her core. Something of her emotions must have registered on her face, because Anthony added by way of explanation, "Uncle Bronson said that."

She was instantly so enraged that an adult, a grown man—a man purporting, moreover, to be a gentleman—should have said such a disgusting thing to an impressionable child, that for a moment she could not speak. Finally she managed to ask in a relatively calm, albeit wooden, tone of voice, "Your uncle said that to you?"

The twins regarded each other solemnly, then with downcast eyes confessed, "Well, actually—"

"He didn't exactly know—"

"That we were listening."

"We were—"

"Eavesdropping."

"I see. And do you share your uncle's opinion of women? Or can you perhaps think of other ways in which women are useful?"

"Well, Mrs. Plimtree is useful. She tells the maids what to do."

"And the maids keep the rooms clean. More or less."

"And Mrs. Stevens cooks food for everyone in the house."

"And you teach us our lessons, even though some of them I'm not sure we want to learn."

"And Nanny Gooch has been taking care of you since you were babies. Do not forget her," Anne pointed out.

"No, she hasn't." This time it was the twins who looked shocked.

"She hasn't? Has she neglected you in some way?"

"No, but Nanny Barlow took care of us when we were babies. But she went away after our parents died, and so Nanny Gooch came to live with us because a long time ago she was our mother's nurse."

"And she is so old, she mostly takes naps in her rocking chair."

"But we don't mind, because we are quite old enough to take care of ourselves."

"And we don't really need a nanny anymore."

"I see," Anne said. That would explain why the twins showed no particular affection for the woman who should have been like a mother to them. But nothing could explain away the totally prejudiced remark made by Lord Leatham.

"Well, if you are about done with making your snares, I shall show you how to determine the proper place to set them." It would be best to get the boys' minds off such subjects as the usefulness of women, because if she did not, Anne was likely to expound on the proper punishment for a man who was so prejudiced, so stupid, so bigoted, so . . .

She could not think of a word bad enough to describe a man like Lord Leatham. She wondered what answer he would give if *he* were called upon to justify his very existence. It was too bad she was not likely to have the opportunity to ask him that question herself.

Chapter Three

"NO, HARRY, I DARE NOT. She might find out." Sally, the upstairs maid, who was usually agreeably inclined toward a roll in the hay, had the audacity to resist this time when Harry tried to pull her into his arms.

"She, she, I'm getting rather tired of that blasted woman."

"Aye, I can believe you're tired. Made you walk all the way from town, or so I heard."

"I'll get even with her for that, see if I don't. Who does she think she is, telling everyone here what to do?"

"Miss Hemsworth is Quality, that's what she is. You just have to listen to her talk to know she ain't like us."

"She's a freak, that's what she is, and no matter how well born she is, she's nothing but the governess, which makes her a servant just like us, so by what authority is she bossing the rest of us around, making us all shave every day? Why she even took the keys to the wine cellar away from old Chorley, and as the butler, it's his responsibility to take care of the liquor."

"Well, his idea of taking care of the brandy was guzzling it down as fast as he could. Regular old tippler, he was, usually so soused he couldn't walk straight."

"That ain't the point. The point is, who gave her the right to interfere in other folks' business? Like you—why do you care if she does catch you having a tumble in the hay? It's not as though everyone here don't know already how quick you are to spread your legs."

"Harry, you know, you're right. She got no business saying who I can cuddle. It's my own business to decide who I want to kiss and who I don't want to kiss."

"That's more like it. Come here and—"

With all the force in her arm, Sally slapped him across the face, almost knocking him off his feet. "And I say I ain't going to have no more to do with you, Harry. You're a lazy good-for-nothing and a sorry excuse for a man. Miss Hemsworth says I can do anything I set my mind to, even learn to read, so I don't need you. I can do better than you."

"You? Learn to read? That's a laugh."

Before he realized what she was about, Sally had made his second cheek sting like the first. Then, sticking her nose into the air, she turned and walked back to the house.

Both hands pressed to his face, which still stung from the slaps, Harry watched the maid disappear from sight. That was one more account he had to settle with Miss High-and-Mighty Hemsworth, who was no better'n him, no matter what airs she gave herself. By the time he finished making a fool out of her, all the rest of the servants would realize it, too.

It had been a long evening. Bronson had dined privately with Lord Grenville and Mr. Fox, who had quizzed him for hours about the slave trade in Africa. He had been able to give them much detailed information, which they proposed using in Parliament, where it appeared the anti-slave-trade bill might soon be passed.

They had tried to persuade him to remain in London and take his seat in the House of Lords, where they could count on his vote, but he had declined. Although he had been in London less than a month, he was already starting to feel the boredom he always felt when he remained long in one locale.

Arriving finally at the town house belonging to his wards, which he normally used as his residence for the few days a year he had business to conduct in London, Bronson was met at the door by his manservant, Daws, who traveled with him and took on whatever role was required, whether that of valet, groom, or even butler.

Taking his top hat and cane, Daws said in an undertone, "There is a man waiting to see you."

"At this hour? The devil you say." It was past two in the morning, and Bronson was not in the mood to play the convivial host.

"He didn't give his name, but I believe he's the same Bow Street runner what you dealt with earlier. He's been waiting since ten o'clock."

After his long hours of intense discussion on weighty political issues, Bronson was not in the mood to consider the relatively trivial problems connected with his guardianship. "Ask him if he can return tomorrow—no, wait, I shall see him tonight. It must be important for him to have waited this long."

Bronson entered the anteroom and saw that his valet had been right in his assumption. "Mr. Black, what can I do for you?"

"It's more like what I have to report to you. Came across something else smokey and thought it might tie in with your interests."

Pouring out two glasses of brandy, Bronson offered one to the other man. "Proceed."

"I found out this evening that Trussell hired a new governess for those two wards of yours."

"And? There is nothing strange about that. In general, I leave the hiring of the servants up to him, since I am so frequently out of the country."

"Well, it happens that this time, contrary to what is normal, he only interviewed one candidate for the post."

"One candidate? I see nothing suspicious in that. Perhaps he was satisfied with her credentials and saw no need to waste his time with further interviews?"

"Aye, p'rhaps. Or p'rhaps he was intending to install an accomplice in Wylington Manor. Right handy that would be."

"What makes you think there is anything . . . smokey, I believe you termed it, about this person?"

"Not so sure she's respectable. Got a face what would get her on the boards at Drury Lane just for the asking. And a figure that would get her off again just as quick as the gen'lemen got a glimpse of her. So why'd a woman like that want to earn twenty pounds a year trying to cram a little education into some brat's head?"

It appeared to Bronson that her career choice tended to prove her respectability, rather than cast doubt on it. "I assume you have more, or you would not be troubling me at this hour of the morning?"

"Course I've got more. I discovered Trussell sold his lease on that little house in Mayfair to some banker, who took possession of it lock, stock, and barrel. Included in the furnishings was the red-haired bird of paradise. And Trussell has packed up his things and skipped out without paying his landlord a shilling on account.''

"From what you say, it would be just as logical to assume that he is running off to Gretna Green with a rich heiress, in which case I can only wish him the best of luck.''

"On the contrary, he caught the evening stage and appears to be heading for Devon, where that so-called governess is already installed, ready to hand, if you get my meaning?''

"This is all rather far-fetched. You are implying that Trussell has established his new mistress in Wylington Manor and is passing her off as a governess? On the face of it, it is too preposterous to believe.'' The Bow Street runner continued to stare at him stoically, so Bronson decided he would have to play out the game. "Very well, what is this woman's name, and what do you know of her background?''

Satisfied that he was being taken seriously, the runner pulled out his occurrence book and made a great show of flipping through the pages. "I been checking into things, you understand, just on the chance that you'd still be interested in having a little investigating done. The woman's name is—'' he scanned another page, then seemed to find what he was looking for, "—Anne Hemsworth, and her references would appear to be impeccable.''

"Then I fail to see what grounds you have for further suspicions.''

"You're a fine gentleman, m'lord, but I've been in this business since before you cut your eyeteeth. I said her references *would appear* to be impeccable because I learned long ago that anything what can be written and signed can be forged. Why I could tell you tales . . .''

Ceasing to listen closely to whatever story the runner felt called upon to relate, Bronson rubbed his forehead wearily. Really, when one thought about it, the whole case against the governess was unbelievably flimsy, like a huge, carefully constructed house of cards, which one breath of reality would more than likely topple to the ground. He opened his mouth to tell the runner that he was not interested in paying any money out for an investigation into the background of any Miss

Hemsworth, when he suddenly realized he had heard that name before.

In what connection, he could not immediately recall, but there was an overtone of unsavoriness that lingered in his mind. Abruptly, he reversed his decision and wrote out a bank draft and handed it to the runner.

"I shall be leaving in two days for Devon. Even if you are not finished with the investigation into the governess's background, I wish you to come here and give me a partial report of what you have learned before I depart."

The runner folded the bank draft into a small square and tucked it down into an inside pocket of his overcoat. "As you say, m'lord. I shall see you in forty-eight hours' time."

I have likely thrown away ten pounds, Bronson thought as he wearily climbed the stairs to his room. *My solicitor would be sure to say I am chasing after shadows. If only I could remember in what connection I have heard the name Hemsworth.*

But even when he awoke in the morning, he could not.

Something was wrong. Anne could not tell where she was getting that impression, but the feeling was too strong to ignore. Aunt Sidonia's words came back to her. "What people are inclined to dismiss as a woman's intuition is usually based on something she has heard or seen, or discrepancies that the woman has observed in the back of her mind without even being aware of them. The trick is to become aware, so that one does not have to be dependent upon the whims of intuition."

Without appearing to, Anne quickly catalogued her surroundings. The day was beautiful, with none of the signs that would herald an unexpected storm. The twins were already on their horses, and her horse, a great black beast, stood saddled and ready for her to mount.

Based on its appearance, she might assume that she was being tricked into riding a vicious or even an unbroken horse, except that she had been riding on the same animal twice before, and although spirited, he had been beautifully trained and had presented no problem at all for a proficient rider such as herself.

Extending the area of her attention, she looked around the

stable yard. Two stable boys were brushing down a pair of carriage horses, another was scrubbing the cobblestones, and Harry, the groom with whom she'd had the slight contretemps upon her arrival in Tavistock, was cleaning tack . . . and studiously ignoring her. The other three boys could not keep from occasionally glancing with curiosity at the riding party, but Harry kept his eyes firmly fixed on the bridle in his hands, as if he were completely alone. He looked not only totally preoccupied with his work, but also rather smug.

Anne rechecked her mount. Perhaps a loose cinch? She tugged at it, but it appeared to be firm.

On the other hand, the horse seemed not to approve completely of what she had done. Just for a moment, he showed the whites of his eyes.

"Hurry up, Anne. What is taking you so long? Mr. Mallory is expecting us within the hour. He sent over a note saying Dancer's Darling had the prettiest colt born day before yesterday, and he is letting us name it," one of the twins said impatiently.

She looked across the yard again. The three stable boys had stopped their work and were looking at her in open puzzlement, but Harry still kept his eyes resolutely fixed on his task and evinced not the slightest curiosity as to why she was standing and staring at her horse instead of mounting.

"I have decided that today I prefer to ride bareback," she announced with decision.

At her words Harry came to life, springing to his feet and rushing to her side. "Allow me to assist you in unsaddling your horse," he said hurriedly, reaching for the cinch.

"No, no, I am quite capable of fending for myself. Please return to your other job."

He hesitated, as if uncertain how to proceed.

"Now," she ordered coldly, and he walked back across the yard, throwing her a look that was openly angry.

The saddle, when she removed it, seemed to be in perfect condition, as did the cinch. Instead of pulling off the saddle blanket, however, she merely flipped it over on the horse's back. Stuck to the underside of it was a short section of cane from a bramble bush.

"Oh, I say, Tony, you didn't—"

"Course I didn't, Drew. That's a childish prank."

"Right. Then who did? You there, Harry," the Marquess of Wylington called imperiously. "Who saddled this horse today?"

"I couldn't rightly say, m'lord," the groom replied. "I was too busy with my own work to notice."

The three stable boys became totally preoccupied with their work.

"Well someone has tried to play a vicious trick on a lady—"

"Intending to hurt her. And whoever that person is, he is mean—"

"And malicious—"

"And a rotten coward, who deserves a beating."

No one in the stable yard moved a muscle.

Finally Anne said quietly, "I believe I might as well wait until another day to ride bareback." Removing the thorny branch from the blanket, she saddled her horse again, mounted it without assistance, and led the way out of the stable yard.

Confound it, did that overgrown female have eyes in the back of her head? How could she have known about the thorns? More than likely she had bribed someone in the stables to spy for her. In disgust at the failure of his grand plan, Harry threw down the cloth he had been using and carried the bridle into the tack room and hung it up.

Well, she might have caught on to his trick today, but there would be other days. She could not always be on her guard.

Emerging from the tack room, he stopped abruptly in his tracks. All the grooms and stable boys employed on the estate were gathered in a semicircle around him.

"We know who saddled Miss Hemsworth's horse today," said Patrick, the groom with the most seniority.

"So, what if I did?" Harry knew he could brazen his way out of this tight spot the way he had always done.

"It was a mean thing to do," one of the youngest stable boys spoke up.

"Don't talk that way to your betters, you sniveling little brat. No one cares what your opinion is."

One of the other grooms spoke up. ''Well, you see, Harry, we've decided Joe here can talk to you any way he likes, because he ain't a coward—''

''And you is,'' Patrick finished. ''And like his lordship just said, cowards deserve to be beaten.''

''When pigs fly!'' Harry felt the sweat run down his back, but he kept up his show of bravado.

Muggs, the strongest and normally the most even-tempered of the grooms, moved foward. ''And we've decided to give you what you deserve.''

Abandoning all pretense of bravery, Harry turned his back and scrabbled desperately for the handle to the tack room door. He found it too late.

One broken nose, two black eyes, three loose teeth, and four bruised ribs later, Harry agreed that he would never again make the slightest attempt to harm Miss Hemsworth or in any way be less than respectful to her.

He was quite sincere and meant every word of his promise. He was not, after all, completely stupid.

Fifty-five thousand pounds, and what did he have to show for it? A few new clothes on his back and not enough brass left in his pocket to afford to travel post. Creighton Trussell, having been forced to ride for hours elbow-to-elbow with his own valet, and in the company of a fat farmer and his even fatter wife, a clergyman, and a motherly woman who kept smiling at him, scowled out the window of the stage and cursed his own misfortune.

Blackmailed, by Jove! How had it come to this? It had seemed such a golden opportunity when he had met that wretched widow and she had proven to be such an easy mark. He should have known there would be something havey-cavey about anyone he encountered in what was little more than a gambling hell.

It was the outside of enough! She claimed connections with all the best families, but even with her money she could not pry open the doors of society. Yet she expected him to introduce her and her daughter to all and sundry.

Confound it, the woman had windmills in her head if she thought she could compel him to comply with her demands.

No, if she continued on her course, she would find she had sadly misjudged her man. No matter how deep she had sunk her claws into him, he would find a way to escape her clutches.

The easiest solution would be if he could "borrow" the necessary funds from his nephews' estate—but even that recourse was denied him, the twins' own maternal uncle, because their father had been fit to appoint Lord Leatham as sole guardian, and *he* was nothing more than a second cousin.

It was a disgusting arrangement. Leatham was absent from the country more days than he was in England, and while he was gone anything could happen to the estate without his knowing of it. Except he always seemed to find out. It was doubtful if a groom could pilfer a cup of oats without Leatham's discovering it. That man should have been a demmed accountant, such a head he had for figures, and a memory for details like a steel trap. Probably knew to the penny what the income from the estate was, and the cost of each item purchased down to the last tallow candle for the smallest housemaid.

It was to be regretted that Leatham had not simply vanished permanently on one of his trips to heathen parts, never to return. Then, after a suitable delay, Creighton could have had the courts appoint him guardian, since he was, after all, the twins' nearest relative.

Staring out the window, he let the motion of the stage lull him into a light doze. When a halt was made to change horses, he awoke with the answer to all his problems staring him in the face. His plan was not perfect, depending as it did upon Leatham's presence at Wylington Manor, but something could be worked out.

It was indeed fortunate that the baron was in England, so chances were good that before he left her shores again, Leatham would make a quick visit to Devon. With a little judicious planning, Creighton decided, that short visit could be turned into a long visit, and that long visit turned into . . . what? Public disgrace for Leatham? At the very least. And perhaps . . . dare he dream? Transportation for Leatham?

It all depended on proper planning. Creighton settled down to serious consideration of details and methods, and well before the stage arrived in Tavistock, he was quite pleased with himself and not the least bit worried about the widow and her demands.

Mr. Black laboriously consulted his occurrence book before beginning his report. "I have not been able in the short time available, to track down any of the previous employers of the woman in question."

Bronson suppressed his impatience with the way the runner was couching everything in obscure terms, as if he were investigating someone's cheating wife or mistress, which he was probably more accustomed to doing.

"Working through sources that appear to be accurate, I have ascertained that the subject has been employed as governess on three previous occasions."

Undoubtedly the runner had merely gone to the employment service patronized by Creighton and asked some lowly assistant for the information.

"To my regret, none of the three families are presently in London, and since you requested an immediate report, I have postponed traveling to their country residences to inquire further into the particularities of her employment with them."

The man paused to consult his notebook again, and Bronson surreptitiously looked at his watch. Much more of this man's pompous attempt to sound self-important, and the runner would find himself out on the street with no one paying him to go anywhere and speak to anyone.

"I have had more success with tracing her origins, however. She has been using an alias—"

At that word, Bronson lost all his detachment and boredom and listened to every word the runner was saying.

"She is in reality Lady Gloriana Hemsworth, daughter of the fifth Earl of Faussley. In case you are not familiar with him, m'lord, he was shot in a duel some twenty-odd years ago."

"I know of the man," Bronson replied.

"It would appear that he was caught out—"

"You do not need to continue. I am well aware of the details of the earl's manner of life." As well as his reputation and what he had done to acquire it. Bronson picked up his pen and again wrote out a bank draft, this time sufficient to cover not only the runner's fee, but also his travel expenses. "I will expect written reports from you weekly, and I will not be satisfied with untoward delays in this investigation."

Without bothering to ring for Daws, Bronson showed the runner out personally. Hellfire and damnation, Faussley's daughter ensconced in Wylington Manor. It did not bear thinking about. And Creighton, who was responsible for putting her there, was on his way to join her. Curse the man for the fool he was.

While preparing for bed, Bronson brooded about the news he had learned this evening. Based on Mr. Black's description of her physical attractions, plus his own knowledge of Creighton's taste in women, added to her bad blood, Bronson was amazed that the woman had managed to fool her previous employers. Or perhaps she had not fooled them at all.

More than likely, she had managed to obtain and keep her positions by assuming a horizontal position when in the presence of the master of the house. His lips curled into a smile when he contemplated what was in store for her once he took charge personally at Wylington Manor.

It was too bad that English law discouraged branding whores, but with his connections in government, he could probably arrange to have her transported. There was a shortage of women in Australia, so she would probably adjust easily. She might even prosper on that continent, but there was nothing Bronson could do to prevent that, except curse her black heart.

"Excuse me, my lady."

Lady Letitia looked up from perusing the morning paper and saw her butler standing deferentially beside the table. "Yes, Owens?"

"There is a *person* here to see you."

"At this hour? Is it not a bit early for morning callers, or am I mistaken about the time?"

"I do not think this is a social visit, my lady."

"Then who, pray, is this person and what is the nature of his business?"

"He says his name is Mr. Black, and as to the nature of his business, he purports to be a Bow Street runner."

"Indeed?" Lady Letitia stifled a laugh. "Then by all means, show the rogue in."

"Madame?"

"Come, come, Owens, show this Mr. Black in. And then tell Cook I am having a guest for breakfast. Be sure that she sends up a bottle of port and a thick beefsteak, rare."

With a very un-butlerish mutter, Owens went to do as he was directed, and only minutes later he returned and announced with exaggerated formality, "Mr. Black is here, my lady."

"Felix, you rascal!" Lady Letitia clapped her hands in approval.

"Behold, my dear, you see before you what the well-dressed runner is wearing this year." The Honorable Felix Sommerton, younger brother of Viscount Sommervale, held his arms out to the side and pirouetted gracefully around so that Lady Letitia could admire his costume.

His trousers may have been brown at one time, his waistcoat was mouse-colored, and the buttons on his jacket were totally mismatched. Over it all, despite the clement weather, he wore a greatcoat that looked as if it had started life in a noble household but had sunk to a mean estate.

"But you are dressed perfectly for the part. No one would suspect that you are an imposter. I admire your resourcefulness."

Having displayed his "finery," Felix took a seat next to his friend. "My only regret is that I have waited so long to find my true calling. Would that I had known twenty years ago how entertaining it is to be a runner."

"Do not take all the credit, my dear. Please keep in mind that you were not required to ferret out any of the information you passed on to Lord Leatham. I provided you with your script, if you please."

"And you must not belittle my triumph. Is an actor less worthy because his words have been given to him by the Bard himself? Is Kean any less a Hamlet because he struts and frets upon the stage for only a few short hours? Life's but an illusion, my pet, and I am become the master of illusion."

"By that I take it you have succeeded?"

"Can you doubt it? And you are wrong when you assume

that I have no talent for digging up evidence. For your information, I tested the effectiveness of my disguise by spending one whole afternoon trailing the suspect, Mr. Creighton Trussell.'' Pulling his well-worn "occurrence" book out of his pocket, he read aloud, "After leaving his club, the suspect went directly to the house of a certain Mrs. Pierce-Smythe, a widow from Yorkshire—"

"Let me see that!"

Before he could stop her, Lady Letitia snatched the little notebook out of his hand. "This is a laundry list."

"Got it from my valet. Went to buy a notebook in a stationers, but they were all shiny and new. Wouldn't have fit with my role as experienced runner. But tell me, pray, are you going to feed me now that I have danced to your tune?"

She reassured him that his breakfast had already been ordered, but her mind was not on his continuing prattle.

So Trussell was seeing Mrs. Pierce-Smythe, she mused. This was the kind of unexpected coincidence that kept her self-appointed job as matchmaker from being boring.

Perhaps she should go down to Devon herself, just to make sure her plans did not go awry? But no, she had too many other irons in the fire. Such as introducing dear Felix to Amelia Carlisle, who had finally become bored with provincial life and allowed herself to be coaxed back to London.

Chapter Four

IT WAS A QUIET Sunday afternoon and Anne was sitting in her room catching up on her correspondence.

> Dear Aunt Sidonia:
>   Things have settled down here very nicely. Having done their best on the day of my arrival to lose me on the moor, which achieved them nothing but an hour and a half of brisk exercise, the twins have come to accept me wholeheartedly. I find them quite the most intelligent of any of the children I have ever taught, and I believe even you would find them of interest to talk to. In some ways they are wise beyond their years and seem almost like small adults, but at other times I am reminded that they are indeed still quite young children. They have both been blessed with a more than adequate supply of natural wit and gumption, although I have noticed Andrew is the more aggressive when it comes to debating a point of logic, and Anthony is the quickest to react to a physical challenge.
>   The servants have not been as easy to manage, but in general they are beginning to toe the line . . .

She became aware that she was no longer alone and looked up to see the twins standing beside her.

"Excuse me, Anne, but we have been thinking."

"Yes, Andrew?"

"We thought perhaps we might write letters to the other governesses," Andrew explained, "and apologize for the tricks we played on them."

"If you think that might help?" Anthony added.

"It is certainly a start in the right direction. Would you like me to give you some notepaper?"

"Yes, please," they said in unison.

She handed them each several sheets of stationery. "Andrew, you may sit at that little table by the window, and I think if you pull up another chair, Anthony, there will be room for you to write there, too."

The boys hastened to comply with her suggestion, then discovered almost at once that they also needed quills and ink, which Anne was also able to supply. For a while there was no sound in the room but the scritch-scratch of the three pens.

> There is one groom who has been the most open in his resentment of my taking authority in the management of the household, but as someone has seen fit to give him two black eyes as well as assorted bruises, I do not think I shall have more trouble with him. And no, I was not the one who administered the thrashing. My days of fisticuffs are long behind me, as I have found words to be more effective weapons . . .

"Did you need something else, Anthony?" How long he had been standing by her shoulder, she did not know, but she shifted the papers on her escritoire so that he could not see what she had written. He did not, however, appear to be interested in the letter she was composing. Andrew was also staring at her intently from his seat by the window.

"We were wondering . . ." Anthony looked at his brother, as if needing support, and Andrew crossed the room to stand shoulder to shoulder with him.

"Are you having trouble figuring out how to express your apologies?"

They shook their heads.

"Are you worried that I shall read your letters and find out the extent of your mischief? You need not be. I am no more in favor of reading other people's mail than I am of eavesdropping."

Again it appeared that she had not guessed what was bothering them.

Finally Andrew spoke again. "You can tell us apart—which one of us is which," he said bluntly.

"Can't you?" Anthony made it into a question.

She nodded. "You are Anthony, and you are Andrew." She did not bother to ask if she had identified them correctly. She knew she had, although she could not pick out a single physical difference that made it possible for her to do so.

Anthony reached out a hand and touched her shyly on the shoulder. "No one else has ever been able to do that except Nanny Barlow."

"And Uncle Creighton fired her after our parents died."

Fired? Anne thought to herself. They had said their first nanny was gone, but *fired*? To the boys she asked merely, "Can none of the other servants?"

"Nope," Andrew said.

"Surely your guardian and your uncle can tell you apart?"

They shook their heads.

"But your parents could when they were alive?"

They continued to shake their heads.

Merciful heavens, had no one spent any time with them at all? Or had they just not cared? "If none of the adults can tell one of you from the other, then how do you know which one of you is which? What I mean to say is, someone must know because someone must have told you."

"When we were born, our father was afraid we might get accidently switched, so he tattooed the bottom of my foot, to be sure that I inherited the title and the estate, since I am twenty-three minutes older than Tony. I'll show you." Andrew sat down on the floor and pulled off his right shoe and sock, then held his foot up for her inspection. "#1" was crudely tattooed on it in blue.

To say that Anne was appalled was putting it too mildly. Enraged was not even adequate to express her feelings. Merciful heavens, it was unbelievable, that one little boy should have had his worth as a human being reduced to twenty-three minutes, to being the next in line for a title, was the stupidest thing she had ever experienced in her life. And the damage to the other little boy, who could only conclude that he was not worth even that much . . . and then to have put a mark on the child as if he were a piece of china!

"Anne, don't cry."

She had not even been aware that tears were streaming down her cheeks until Andrew said that. In seconds, both boys were in her arms, and it was impossible to tell who was hugging whom the tightest.

The tears were over as quickly as they had begun, and when

she was again able to talk, Anne decided that she had to show the twins the same trust they had shown her. "If you will promise never, ever to tell anyone, I will tell you a secret of mine."

Without hesitation they promised.

"My father was an earl, so I should really be called Lady Gloriana Hemsworth. And there is more you should know," Anne continued. "When I was about five, my father died, and some relatives came and took my mother and me to live with them. They did not know us at all or care about us in any way. They merely wanted to be able to brag that they had a real countess and an earl's daughter living with them."

The twins looked at one another, then they both laughed. "I think having an Indian living with us—"

"Would be more fun than having an earl's daughter."

"Yes, well, you are stuck with the earl's daughter," Anne retorted with a smile.

"Lady Gloriana." Andrew said tentatively, as if trying it out. Then he laughed as if he had made a joke.

"Lady Glo-o-o-o-or-r-r-r-iana." Anthony made it sound even more ridiculous, then dodged her attempt to tickle him.

Later that night when she was lying in bed reviewing the day's activities, Anne brought out her mental list of defects in Lord Leatham's character and added to it the fact that he had not been interested enough in his wards to get to know them as individuals.

The list had become quite long, since it seemed as if every day she discovered something worse about him to add to it. So far, however, she had not been able to discover a single redeeming virtue that Lord Leatham possessed. Lord Least-in-Sight, she felt would be a more appropriate name, and so she decided to call him in the privacy of her own mind.

His employer was up to no good, of that Wyke was sure. Having pockets to let and being forced to borrow the Reverend Goodman Thirsk's shabby one-horse gig to drive from Tavistock to Wylington Manor should have put Trussell in a disagreeable mood. Indeed, simply being in the country was usually enough in and of itself to guarantee foul temper on Trussell's part. Instead, he was smiling to himself and even occasionally chuckling out loud.

The valet had no intention of interfering with whatever dishonest machinations Trussell was plotting. On the contrary, while being careful to keep himself technically innocent of any wrongdoing, Wyke was not about to pass up an opportunity to make a little extra from Trussell's misconduct.

Until recently, Wyke's opportunities had been limited to little more than small change. An occasional bottle of brandy had gone out the back door or a tradesman had paid a small surcharge to be informed when Trussell was in the funds so that he could present his bill in person with some reasonable expectation of being paid.

To Wyke's delight, when the lusty widow, as he had dubbed her, had come upon the scene, she had been amazingly free with her brass. Not only had she been prepared to come down heavy to secure Trussell's "services," but she had also been willing to pay Wyke handsomely for private information about his employer.

Wyke had been more than happy to oblige. Revealing the existence of Trussell's mistress, for example, had netted him the equivalent of two years' wages. Rather than squandering his windfall the way his employer had done, Wyke had prudently invested all his misbegotten gains in the Funds, and he was well on his way to having a tidy nest egg, assuming the widow's purse and Trussell's stamina both held out.

Having debated long with himself as to whether he should inform the widow of Trussell's flight from London, he had finally decided to do so. But it had also occurred to him that she would undoubtedly pay more if he gave her ample opportunity to become truly frantic before he revealed where her hired lover had bolted to.

If pushed, he could insist that he had not known their destination before they arrived, and so had felt it best to delay writing her until he had more concrete information. But he doubted she would feel obliged to quiz him about the delay.

Wyke could only hope that she would not decide Devon was too far away and abandon her blackmail attempts. Perhaps as an added inducement, he ought to mention that there were other titled bachelors in the neighborhood? Only as a last resort, he decided, since other than Thorverton, all of them were either still too young or already in their dotage.

Of more immediate importance was discovering what kind of deviousness Trussell was planning, which was making him so cheerful. Although one could not get blood from a turnip, or riches from a man who was standing up to his neck in the river Tick, assuming that his employer could indeed come by some funds dishonestly, Wyke discovered in himself no particular aversion to trying a spot of blackmail himself—anonymously, to be sure.

"This is going to be a wonderful summer," Anthony said.

"The best summer of our lives," Andrew affirmed. "Tomorrow can we go over to Thorverton Hall and see the new colts and fillies again?"

"You may send a note over this evening and inquire if it would be convenient for us to visit." Anne and the boys were taking tea in the garden after a long day of fishing. Besides the usual scones with whortleberry preserves on the side, the pasties, and the pink-iced buns, in the center of the tray was a large bowl of fresh strawberries and clotted cream.

"Someone has discovered my Achilles' heel. Who told the cook we wanted strawberries and cream again? Is one of you trying to see to it that I become so stout I am unable to move?"

Neither of the twins would admit having had a hand in it, although both of them were grinning their heads off.

"What's an Achilles' heel?" Andrew asked.

"Have you never heard the story of Achilles?" Anne helped herself to a large portion of the fruit and cream, then began to relate the story of the invincible—almost—Greek hero. By the time she finished her story, nothing remained in her bowl but one fat, luscious strawberry. Ah, well, she thought, all good things must come to an end.

She popped it into her mouth and bit down, releasing the juicy sweetness that blended so well with the smooth tartness of the cream. Looking up, she saw a short man mincing his way across the terrace toward them, but the sun was behind him, making it difficult for her to recognize him.

When she did, she realized that the wonderful summer she and the twins had been anticipating had suffered a severe setback. The lecherous uncle, who Mrs. Wiggins had assured her was technically *not* her actual employer, had come to Devon.

"Good afternoon, twins." Nominally he was speaking to his nephews, but all his attention was focused on Anne—or rather, that part of her visible above the tabletop and below her neck. Since she was sitting down, he could not even be excused on the grounds that she was too tall for him to meet her eyes directly.

"Good afternoon, Uncle Creighton." The boys responded in unison, but evinced no other interest in their uncle. Instead, they developed an apparent fascination with the crumbs left on their plates.

"It is a beautiful day, is it not?" No one replied to Trussell's question.

"If you will excuse us . . ."

"We must be going."

The twins were already sliding sideways out of their chairs, although they did glance at Anne, their eyes asking silently for permission, which she gave with a nod.

After they scampered off, Trussell promptly seated himself in one of the chairs they had vacated and smirked at her. "I hope the twins have not been up to any mischief? Boys will be boys, you know, and one must make allowances for high spirits."

Anne was debating with herself how quickly she could make her own excuses to quit his company.

"Knowing how reluctant you were to take this position, I felt it behooved me to come here and check up on you in person. If the twins are causing you any problems, do not hesitate to ask my assistance." He reached out and patted her hand in what he appeared to think was an avuncular fashion. "I should not wish for anyone here to cause you the slightest distress."

The man was a veritable maw-worm. Offering her his help, indeed. Trying to turn her up sweet so he could hop in her bed was more like it. Men were such fools, always underestimating a female's intelligence, treating most of them as if they were backward children.

"Would you like some tea?" she said politely, knowing the pot had grown quite cold.

"No, no, my *appetite* cannot be satisfied so easily." Already forgetting his role as potential rescuer of a damsel in distress, his smirk changed to a leer.

Odious man. Was his heavy-handed attempt at a double-entendre supposed to make her develop an uncontrollable passion for him?

For the first time in years, she regretted her decision to use reason as a means of persuading others around to her point of view. Right now she would like to feel her fist flatten his nose. It would be such an efficient, such a precise way of letting him know her opinion of his character.

But she had outgrown such behavior. Although it was so tempting—perhaps too much indulgence in clotted cream inclined one toward physical violence? She smiled at the thought, realizing too late that Trussell would misinterpret her look as one of interest in him. He reached for her hand again, but she snatched it away in time.

Unexpectedly, his attention shifted from her. Then she heard footsteps on the gravel path, and she also turned to see who was coming.

"Excuse me, Miss Hemsworth." Beside her, Sally bobbed a quick curtsy. "Not wanting to interrupt your tea nor nothing like that, but Cook says she's a mind to speak with you at once."

With thankfulness that she did not have to invent a trumped-up excuse to end her so utterly delightful and intellectually stimulating conversation with the maw-worm, Anne rose to her feet and looked down at Trussell. "If you will excuse me." Without waiting to be excused, she strode rapidly toward the back of the house.

She had no sooner entered the kitchen, than she was pounced on by two boys.

"We rescued you," Anthony crowed with delight.

"Didn't our plan work well? I thought of it," Andrew added with a grin. "But Anthony was the one who asked Sally to help."

"We didn't want to just abandon you—"

"Come quick now, before he finds us—"

"We know some great places to hide—"

"We'll show you—"

Each one grabbing one of her hands, they dragged her away into the bowels of the house for an impromptu game of hide-and-seek, with Trussell being "it," even though he had not been informed of the role he was supposed to play.

Creighton poured the last of the brandy out of the decanter and stared morosely at his glass, which was only half full. Having renewed his acquaintanceship with Miss Hemsworth of the glorious bosom—albeit for only a few brief, fleeting moments—he had somehow not managed to catch up with her again.

When he checked in the schoolroom, he was told she was in the nursery; when he checked in the nursery, he was told she had returned to her own room, but her room was empty. She was not in the library, not in the kitchen, not in the stables. In a burst of optimism at the thought that she might have anticipated his wishes, he had even checked his own room, but the bed was empty.

He drained the last of his potion, then stared at the dregs in his glass. An evening of solitary drinking had only served to focus his attention on the elusive Miss Hemsworth. Having had her in his thoughts all those hours made it seem entirely reasonable to his brandy-soaked brain that she had likewise been thinking about him. She was undoubtedly getting impatient waiting for him.

Staggering to his feet, he tried to remember where he had put her. The corridor outside his room was dark, but it never occurred to him to light a candle. Although his path was somewhat erratic, his search was systematic. He opened every bedroom door along the corridor, cheerfully convinced that sooner or later he would find her waiting in bed for him.

To his delight, it was sooner rather than later, and she was indeed waiting for him. Opening the door to her room, he found her sitting up in bed reading a book.

Perhaps he should apologize for being so late? No, better just to get on with it.

"What the deuce are you doing in my bedroom?" Anne was astounded at the intrusion into her privacy. That Trussell was drunk was obvious from the careful way he was moving, as if balanced on a very narrow ledge.

"S-s-s-." He was having difficulties getting his tongue to work properly. Under other circumstances Anne might have found it amusing. But not late in the evening in her bedroom.

"S-s-sorry, my dear," he finally managed to get out, before smiling at her like an idiot.

Strangely enough, she felt herself to be at a disadvantage. She had never had much experience dealing with drunks, although somewhere she had heard that one should humor them.

Humor them? Before she realized his intentions, Trussell had taken off his robe and was folding it carefully. All he wore under it was a nightshirt, which exposed his bony knees and skimpy calves.

Distracted for a moment by the realization that his valet must use sawdust to fill out his stockings, Anne was caught off guard when the drunken lecher pounced, landing directly on top of her, the fumes of his breath making her nauseated and his hands—

How dare he!

With a bellow that Aunt Sidonia had once likened to that of a wounded bull moose, Anne tried to throw him onto the floor. With one hand trapped beneath the covers, she was somewhat handicapped. Unfortunately, those same covers provided her little protection from Trussell's groping hands.

One-handed she could not quite best him, even in his drunken state. But she brought up her knee sharply, heard his grunt of pain, then managed to shift his dead weight enough to liberate her other arm, and after that there was no contest.

In less than a minute, he was lying face down and she was straddling his legs. She had both of his arms twisted behind his back.

"Do you think she means to smother him?" A young voice spoke beside the bed.

"Probably," his brother replied with obvious relish.

Still feeling the effects of the strong emotion of the last few moments, Anne turned her head and saw the twins standing by her bed watching with detached interest.

"Why are you two out of bed?"

"We heard a noise. A *loud* noise," Anthony clarified.

"Do you need any help?" Andrew asked. "We know a place where you could hide the body."

"And no one would ever find it, not in a hundred years," his brother said.

Her attention thus being called to the fact that Trussell's squirms were becoming more feeble, she eased up on the pressure enough that he was able to turn his head and take great gasping breaths.

"You boys can go back to bed. I can handle your uncle quite well."

They dawdled on the way out, giving her ample opportunity to call them back if she changed her mind, but she did not. Once they were gone, she climbed off Trussell's back without releasing his arms, then pulled him off the bed, only to discover his legs would no longer support him. She was not sure if it was from the effects of the brandy or from being half smothered, but it mattered not. In either case, there was nothing for her to do but drag him bodily back down the corridor to his own room.

Men! Aunt Sidonia was right—they were nothing but unnecessary encumbrances. She heaved her present encumbrance through the door of his room and with satisfaction watched his unsuccessful efforts to get up. Leaving him crumpled in a heap on the carpet, she went to check on the twins.

They were in bed but not asleep. "Did you hit him?"

"I do not hit people," Anne replied sternly. "I reason with them. Violence solves nothing."

"We saw you reasoning his arms behind his back." Andrew chuckled.

"I was merely getting his attention."

It was undoubtedly only because it was the middle of the night that this remark seemed so funny, but the boys began to laugh, and finally Anne felt the anger drain out of her too. Kissing them good night once again, she returned to her room, where she took the precaution of locking her door behind her. After a moment of reflection, she also locked the French windows, which opened onto a little balcony.

Not that Trussell was any match for her, even sober. But she had no desire to have her sleep interrupted.

Creighton did not awaken until well after noon. When he did, every muscle in his body ached, as if he had been run over by a team of horses and a stagecoach. In comparison, the hangover from the large amount of brandy he had consumed the evening before was negligible.

When he moved even slightly, his shoulders felt as if his arms had been wrenched out of their sockets the day before. Moreover, his back was stiff, his legs—well, it did not pay to itemize every ache. If there was one part of his body that did not hurt, he could not identify it.

Responding to his feeble cries for help, Wyke came into the room and went directly to the window to pull open the heavy drapes.

"No," Creighton barely managed to croak out in time. "No light."

Wyke approached the bed and stood patiently waiting. "Do you wish a bath?" the valet asked finally.

"I want to know what happened last night." Even his jaw hurt, so Creighton did his best to speak with a minimum of movement.

"I have no idea what occurred. I helped you prepare for bed, then at your direction, fetched you another bottle of brandy and took myself off to my cot in the dressing room. At about two of the clock, I heard a thump and came in and found you lying on the floor. You were incoherent, so I assisted you to bed."

"And that is all you know?"

"Except . . . well, this morning the governess returned your robe, all neatly folded."

Wyke gave him a sly, knowing look, and Creighton seized the candlestick off the bedside table and hurled it at the valet.

It missed, but came sufficiently close that Wyke correctly perceived it as an indication that his services were not wanted at the present time.

Shutting his eyes, Creighton thought back over the previous night. With Wyke's explanation to jog his memory, he found he could remember most of what had happened. Enough, anyway, to know that the new governess had not only rejected him, but had treated him with mockery and blatant disrespect. And his nephews had witnessed it, yet had done nothing to help him.

Fury warred with pain, and fury won. Trussell forced himself to rise from his bed. Calling for his valet, he berated him for not being on hand when needed. Unfortunately, cursing his valet the whole time Wyke was helping him get dressed did little to alleviate his anger. Creighton was still coldly furious by the time he entered the morning room and found Miss Hemsworth and her charges blithely eating a cold repast and showing no sign that they were the least bit repentant for the trouble they had caused him.

"For conduct unbecoming a governess, you are fired," he said, noticing with satisfaction the horrified looks on the twins' faces. "You will pack your things and be ready to leave in the morning. Do not expect to get a character from me, either."

She stared at him coldly. If she begged him nicely, he was prepared to reconsider, but she was not acting the least bit repentant.

"As you are not my official employer, I believe I shall remain here until I receive my notice from Lord Leatham." So saying, she turned her back on him and began talking to the twins as if he were no longer in the room.

"There is no need to wait. I have full authority from Leatham to hire and fire employees!" His voice had risen too high. That blasted woman was enough to make a saint lose patience. "You will leave at once—today—within the hour!" He stamped his foot.

Without bothering to look at him, she said firmly, "When you show me a written power-of-attorney from Lord Leatham, I shall be happy to pack my things."

His hands were itching to grab that woman's neck and

squeeze. Never had he felt such an urge to silence a woman by throttling her! "I do not need written authorization. No one has ever questioned my right to hire and fire."

She merely stood up, smiled down at him in a patronizing way, and moved toward where he stood blocking the door. At the last possible moment, remembering how easily she had handled him the night before, he moved aside.

Not that he was afraid of her, of course. Sober, he was sure he could wrestle her to the ground. If he wanted to, which he did not. She was too unnatural a woman for him to have the slightest interest in her, and so he would tell her. She was, after all, freakishly tall, which he had been willing to overlook before. But no longer.

Chapter Five

"WE'VE GOT TO DO SOMETHING, DREW." Anthony sat in bed hugging his knees, imagining what it would be like if Anne left. Even thinking about it made his stomach hurt.

"We already did. We stole the letter Uncle Creighton wrote and burned it." Andrew got out of bed and started dressing himself.

"But after a while, when he doesn't get an answer from Uncle Bronson, he'll write another."

"By that time we'll have thought of something else. Just because we've been behaving good as gold for Anne, doesn't mean we can't think any more. We're still in-gen-i-ous." Andrew picked up a pillow and threw it at his brother.

Anthony caught it, then tossed it aside and got out of bed, too. "Yeah. It'll be fun, too. I miss playing tricks on people."

"But it's better with Anne here."

"Of course. I never want her to leave. And I won't let Uncle Bronson make her. I'll write him my own letter and explain what really happened . . ." He stopped with his shirt half on and half off, because his brother began pounding him on the back.

"See, see, I told you we'd think of something! We'll write our own letter. But we have to be careful and keep it a secret, because Uncle Creighton would have a fit if he found out, and even Anne might forbid us to interfere if she knew what we were doing."

"Why would she do that?"

"Because it's funny about ladies. It's all right for an upstairs maid like Sally to kiss the footmen and grooms and get her clothes all messed up, but if a lady is caught kissing a man, or even if the man is kissing her, or even if it looks as if they *might* have been kissing, then she has to marry him." Tying his last shoe, he stood up and went to the door, where he waited for Anthony to put his own shoes on.

"That's nonsense."

" 'Struth. Collier Baineton told me, and he's almost eighteen. He knows all about rules for ladies."

They started down the corridor together.

"Is Anne a lady?"

"Course she's a lady. She's Lady Gloriana, remember?"

"I remember. I just wasn't sure if the rules count for her since she's our governess."

"I'm not sure. But we'd better keep our letter secret from everyone, just in case."

"We can post it ourselves in Tavistock. All we have to do is think of a reason for going into town." The bad feeling was gone from his insides, and Anthony grinned at his brother.

"Hold on, what's this?" Andrew caught his arm.

The door to Uncle Bronson's room was open, and Anthony looked past his brother's shoulder into the room. Seeing Sally inside, they entered.

"What are you doing in here?"

She gave a little jump, then spun around, scowling when she saw who it was. "Oh, it's you two. I wish you'd stop sneaking up on a body like that."

"We didn't do it on purpose." This time, anyway, Anthony thought. But next time, maybe. He wondered what Anne's opinion would be if they didn't do anything very bad, just a little "boo" every now and then to watch the maids jump. Somehow he didn't think she'd approve.

"Well, clear on out of here now, I've got to get this room ready. Old Chorley got a letter from Lord Leatham saying he's arriving here this afternoon."

Anthony looked at his brother in dismay. The bad feeling was twisting up his insides again. With a curt motion of his head, Andrew indicated they should leave.

By unspoken agreement they changed their direction. Instead of going to the morning room to join Anne, they went to the formal dining room, found the proper carved oak leaf, twisted it, then went through the hidden door that swung noiselessly open.

Pulling the door shut behind them, they moved swiftly along the low-ceilinged passageway and down the steep, twisting stairs. They did not speak until they came to the door at the other end, which opened into a small empty room behind the wine cellar. No one could enter except through the outer room, which was kept locked, or through the secret corridor, which no one knew about except them, so they knew they would not be disturbed.

It was all Anthony could do not to cry. But he didn't want his brother to think he was a baby, so he blinked back his tears.

"The thing to do is get rid of Anne." Andrew said, a scowl on his face.

"What? I don't want to get rid of her, and I thought you wanted her to stay here, too."

"Not permanently. Just temporarily. Just until after we have a chance to tell Uncle Bronson our side of the story. We might be able to get him to listen if we can talk to him first—"

"Before Uncle Creighton talks to him?"

"No, that doesn't matter. Before Uncle Bronson tells Anne to pack and get out, is what I mean. After he tells her she's fired, then even if we convince him she's innocent, it won't matter. Because once he gives the order, he won't want to change his mind. Grown-ups are funny that way. They don't want anyone to think they've made a mistake. Even when everyone knows they have. That's what happened to Nanny Barlow, remember?"

"Course I remember. Uncle Creighton fired her for stealing his watch, and even when he found out later it was her father's watch, and his watch was under some papers on his desk, he still didn't do anything to fetch her back, not even when you cried."

"I didn't cry, you cried."

"Well, one of us cried, it doesn't really matter which one. What matters is stopping Uncle Bronson from firing Anne."

The twins were late in joining her, but Anne was not worried. They were indeed used to fending for themselves, especially when it came to satisfying their bottomless appetites. When they did finally appear, they ignored the kippers and back bacon, which meant Sally had probably taken a tray up to the nursery, or the boys had simply gone down to the kitchen and wheedled what they wanted out of the cook.

Laying down her own napkin, she stood up. "So, shall we go hiking on the moor today? Or would you prefer to ride over to see how the new colts are getting on? Or what would you like?"

"We have been talking it over," Andrew announced. "And we realized you have not had even a half day off since you got here."

"So we have decided you should have the whole day off today. You can even ride into Tavistock if you wish. I am sure you could use some new ribbons."

"Or a bonnet or something. We can stay here and work on our lessons while you're gone."

The boys' attempt to look innocent was so phony, Anne did not believe for a minute that they were not up to some mischief.

"But I would not want to leave you two all alone."

"And why not?" Andrew's look of indignation was remarkably realistic. "Are you implying we are incapable of taking care of ourselves? We got along on our own just fine before you came. We are not *babies*, you know," he said with great scorn in his voice.

She looked from one to the other of them. "Why do I get the feeling you are trying to deceive me?"

Just for a moment she thought Anthony looked guilty, but then he smiled angelically, which made her even more certain they were up to something. "Now I wonder what sort of mischief you could be planning? Have you perhaps decided to bedevil your Uncle Creighton?" The idea had appeal, even for Anne. For the last several days Trussell had been making snide comments about her under his breath every time their paths crossed, and all she could do was pretend not to hear.

"Really, Anne, we promise to be good," Andrew said easily. "And we always keep our promises."

"Yes," his twin added. "We truly only want you to have a little holiday."

It was tempting. It really was. As much as she loved the boys and enjoyed being with them, she had been rather isolated here at Wylington Manor, with no one to talk to except the boys and the servants. If she took the entire day, she could call first on Lady Thorverton, who had been feeling poorly, and then afterward visit Mrs. Thirsk in Tavistock. And a little browsing in the shops would be fun, even though she could not think of anything she particularly needed.

But could she trust the twins? That was the question that was still not answered to her satisfaction. "Do you promise you are not planning some kind of mischief?"

"We promise that we are not going to do anything mean or malicious."

"But we don't have to be nice to Uncle Creighton, do we?" Anthony asked. "I mean, it will be enough if we just sort of avoid him, won't it?"

That did not sound as if whatever they were planning would be too bad.

"I guess you don't trust us," Andrew said flatly.

"Before I decide," she said, "I want you to come with me. We shall have a small lesson, just a very quick one, and then, perhaps, I shall take the day off."

With the boys following her, she descended to the servants' level, where she fetched a fresh egg out of the larder and showed it to them. "For the purpose of our lesson today, this is not merely a hen's egg. This egg is a symbol of my trust in you. If you break the trust—" She dropped the egg onto the stone floor, and the kitchen cat hurried over and started licking up the spilled yoke. "Now, Andrew, please put it back the way it was before it got broken."

"I can't," he said.

"How about you, Anthony?"

The other boy shook his head.

"Do you understand what happens when you break your word? You destroy your reputation as someone who can be trusted, and it is virtually impossible to regain that trust."

They both nodded. "We promise—"

"That we are not going to get into trouble—"

"While you're gone, or do anything—"

"Mean or malicious."

They were no longer smiling angelically, which was a good sign as far as Anne was concerned.

"Very well, then I will trust you to stay out of trouble until I get back."

They looked at one another, but she could not read on their faces what they were thinking.

"You don't need to hurry back."

"You can be gone all day."

"We can even put ourselves to bed—"

"If you're very, very late."

"I will not be that late. I shall stop for a while at Thorverton Hall to visit Lady Thorverton, and then I shall ride on into Tavistock. I will plan to be back by teatime," she said with a smile.

An hour later, when she was riding her favorite horse away from the manor, she wondered if perchance the boys' oath had been couched in ambiguous terms that had slipped by her—if, in fact, she would be met by disaster upon her return, with the boys swearing that they had followed their promise to the letter, but that it had not included . . . what?

"It isn't exactly breaking our promise, is it Drew?" The twins were walking down the road in the direction of Tavistock. They were planning to stop when they reached the edge of the estate and wait for Uncle Bronson to come.

"Course it isn't. She didn't say anything at all about not talking to Uncle Bronson. Nor did she ask if he was coming today."

"But we are planning to tell him something she wants us to keep secret."

"We are *assuming* that she wouldn't want anyone to know that Uncle Creighton tried to climb into her bed, but she has never *said* that we are to keep it a secret. She can't blame us for doing something she never told us not to do."

"And it's not being malicious, because we are just trying to help her."

"Right. The worst she can do is say we should have asked

her, but then she never told us we had to ask her for permission to talk to Uncle Bronson.''

"Even so, maybe we should have told her Uncle Bronson was coming today?''

"That's Chorley's responsibility.''

"But Chorley found the bottle of brandy we left on the front hall table.''

"We cannot be held responsible for Chorley's weakness in drinking from it, can we?''

"Only if Anne finds out.''

"If she asks us directly, did we sneak down a secret passageway into the back of the wine cellar and remove a bottle of brandy and deliberately leave it where Chorley could find it so that he would get too drunk to remember to tell Anne that Uncle Bronson is coming,'' he paused for a breath, "then of course, we will have to tell her the truth.''

"I think it's unlikely she will ask us that.'' Anthony grinned at his brother. "Race you to the gate!''

They were both off like a flash, although by the time they reached the remains of the ancient stone gate that marked the edge of the Wylington estate, neither one paid any attention to who had gotten there first.

Someone was shouting in a high-pitched voice, and Bronson reined in his horse. At first he could not determine where the sound was coming from, until he spotted two small boys, sitting each of them atop a stone pillar, looking like grubby little gargoyles.

"Uncle Bronson, we've been waiting for you.''

His wards. He should have known. Without worrying unduly, he watched them scramble down from their perches. As agile as the monkeys he had seen in the jungles of South America, the twins were just as fearless. In any event, he could not afford to let himself worry just because they were climbing around on stone pillars that were undoubtedly weakened by age until they could collapse at any moment, in the process likely crushing one or the other of the boys.

That was what the governess was paid for—to do his worrying

for him, and to restrain his wards from the more death-defying feats. Except the governess so recently hired by Trussell was nowhere in sight. She did not appear to take her duties seriously, but then he had expected nothing better.

Deftly lifting one twin up behind him, he swung the other one up in front of him, then signaled his horse to continue at a walk in the direction of the house and stables.

"We have something very important to tell you, Uncle Bronson—"

"About Anne—"

"Our governess—" As usual, both boys were talking at the same time.

"Uncle Creighton wants you to fire her—"

"Because she wouldn't let him kiss her—"

"But it was all his fault—"

"So we think Anne should stay—"

"And you should kick Uncle Creighton out of the house—"

Kissing her accomplice in front of the boys—it was beyond belief. The sooner he got rid of her the better. "Just where were they kissing?"

"In Anne's bed—"

"Except they weren't kissing—"

"They were wrestling—"

"But Anne was stronger—"

"So she sat on Uncle Creighton—"

"He was moaning."

The devil take that woman! Bronson could picture it quite clearly—the lovemaking, which the boys in their innocence thought was wrestling. He just bet Creighton was moaning—moaning with pleasure.

"How did you happen to see all this?" He was proud of himself for staying so calm, but he did not want to upset the boys any more than they obviously were already.

"Oh, Anne made a lot of noise—"

"So we went to see what was wrong—"

"But she said she didn't need any help—"

"And she sent us back to bed."

I'll just bet she did, Bronson thought.

"She says from now on, she's going to lock the door."

A little late for that, now that she had already let the boys see what kind of light skirt she was.

"The next day Uncle Creighton said she was fired—"

"But Anne says she doesn't work for him—"

"She works for you, but you're not going to fire her—"

"Are you, Uncle Bronson?"

So, there was a falling out among thieves. "When did all this happen?"

"Four nights ago."

Since so much time had elapsed and the governess was still in residence, it would appear that the conspirators had gotten over their lovers' quarrel. "I will need to talk to Miss Hemsworth and your Uncle Creighton and see what they have to say before I make up my mind." He felt the twin in front of him take a deep breath, as if preparing to argue further. "And that is all I am willing to promise at this time," he added, not sure he could control his temper if the boys began relating more nefarious doings at midnight.

Arriving at the stables, he swung the boys down before dismounting himself. "Now then, perhaps I might have a talk with your governess."

"She's not here."

"She took the day off."

Bronson felt like cursing, but he reminded himself that no matter how irresponsibly she was behaving, he could not become more angry with her, because he had already reached the limits of his temper. "So where did she go? And when will she be back?"

"She went to see Lady Thorverton."

"And she said she'd be back by teatime."

It was now eleven o'clock. He'd be hanged if he would wait around until she decided to show up. No, by all that was holy, he would drag her back by her hair, and *then* he would throw her out on her ear.

But first he would find Trussell and deal with him.

He found his wards' uncle sitting down to a late breakfast of coddled eggs and back bacon. The food smelled so good, Bronson filled his own plate. There was, after all, no point in ripping another man to shreds on an empty stomach.

"I hear from the boys that you have been having trouble with the new governess you hired," he said, deliberately keeping his voice cool.

Trussell turned white as a sheet, and for a moment it appeared he might faint, but then he made a recovery. "The boys talked to you? Oh, they probably exaggerated. It was nothing, really." He laughed rather sickly. "If you will excuse me; I am not feeling at all well." The dandy practically ran from the room.

Rather energetic for an invalid, Bronson thought. Finishing his own meal, he ordered a horse brought around from the stables, then set off to track down the missing governess.

He missed catching her at Thorverton Hall by three-quarters of an hour. She had taken lunch with them and had then set off for Tavistock.

Hoping to catch her before she got to town, where she could lose herself in the crowds, he put his horse to a gallop, but he met no one along the road until after it joined the main road from Tavistock to Plymouth. After that, there were any number of travelers to choose from.

Once he arrived in town, it did not take long to realize he had no idea what the errant Miss Hemsworth looked like, other than that, according to Mr. Black, she would do very nicely as an opera dancer.

Having had experience with opera dancers in his salad days, Bronson had a reasonably good idea of the type of woman he was looking for. He was also able to eliminate women with small children in tow, older women, farmer's wives, and so on, which narrowed the field considerably.

After an hour of looking, he had worked up enough thirst that he stopped in the Red Stag for a glass of ale. The landlord himself waited on him, and without thinking, Bronson asked him if he had seen his wards' new governess in town that day.

"Aye, she left her horse here an hour or two ago."

"Do you know which way she was headed?"

"Nope." The landlord was being uncommonly laconic.

"Did you happen to note what color of dress she was wearing? If I knew that, it would be easier to spot her in the crowd."

Someone behind him snickered, and he heard someone else say in an undertone, "Easier to spot—that's a good one."

Leaving the rest of his ale untouched, Bronson stalked out of the taproom without waiting for the landlord to give a more specific description of the missing governess. He had changed his mind about dragging her back to the Hall. Apparently she was wandering around town in a gown that was so indecent, he had best forget about seeing to it that she was suitably chastised, and simply concentrate on getting her back to London where she belonged.

Behind him he could hear loud laughter coming from the taproom, which only added to his feelings of rage.

Having enjoyed a nice cup of tea with the vicar's wife, who had shown a surprisingly motherly affection for "those two poor neglected children," Anne was now enjoying herself walking along the high street, looking into the shop windows, when someone coming out of the tobacconist's bumped into her.

"Excuse me," she heard a deep voice say. She looked up into a pair of dark brown eyes—such kind, intelligent eyes, it took her a moment to realize she was looking up instead of down. She stared at the man wordlessly, too overcome by his magnificence to utter a word.

For the first time in her life, she did what people had so often done to her—she looked him up and down, from head to toe and back again, shamelessly memorizing every detail of his physique: his broad chest and muscular shoulders, his narrow hips and shapely legs, his firm jaw and square chin. . . .

Then her eyes met his again, and she had the strangest feeling that they were communicating without words. The intensity of his look was so strong, she almost forgot that he was a stranger, that they had not been properly introduced.

Despite an inner shiver, undoubtedly occasioned by his forceful gaze, she could not feel the proper regret that she had allowed him to see her interest. Indeed, she doubted she could have hidden it, no matter how hard she might have tried.

Tipping his hat at her, he finally moved away, and as if in a trance, she continued in the opposite direction. She stopped in front of the next shop window and stared at the dusty apothecary jars with as much interest as if they were the latest bonnets from Paris. Then, unable to refrain any longer, she looked over her shoulder and saw the tall man still standing in front of the tobacconist's shop, watching her.

If she were of a romantic disposition rather than having a practical turn of mind, she would say that his hair was black as midnight, that his eyes were a rich mahogany, like dark Jamaican rum . . . and that she had met the man intended for her since the world first began turning . . . that the fates had decreed she would meet him on this street at this time, and that he would be a part of her life from this moment forward.

But unlike other young women in these modern times, she had not had her head stuffed full of such silly dreams. Instead, she'd had the inestimable good fortune to spend a few short years at Aunt Sidonia's side, which had cured her forever of the desire to throw herself into the arms of a man—to give control of her own life into the hands of a husband.

No, she was definitely too practical for such romantic nonsense. Risking a glance at the stranger again, she saw he was still watching her intently.

That he was a London man, she could not doubt from the cut of his jacket, although there was nothing of the dandy about him. Just thinking how ridiculous a man his size would look decked out in frills and furbelows made a smile creep out onto her face, which she realized only when he smiled back at her.

This time she was the first to turn away. She fully intended to continue on down the street, but after only a few steps, curiosity to know what he was doing—to find out if he was still looking at her—pulled her to a stop in front of the second shop. Yes, he was still watching her.

She was the most magnificent woman Bronson had ever encountered. Tall enough that he could converse with her without getting a crick in his neck, she also had lustrous brown hair and clear blue eyes. But it was not her beauty that attracted him. It was the intelligence, the humor, and the kindness in her eyes that he found so appealing—and so unexpected. Plus something else he had not yet identified.

For a moment he had been terrified by the fear that she might just be passing through town, but he was reassured when he noticed she was wearing a royal blue riding habit. Dressed like that, she could not have journeyed too far. Surely someone in town must know her—must be able to introduce him to her properly.

That was the last rational thought he had—at the insistence of his body, he ceased thinking and allowed himself merely to feel . . . to admire . . . to appreciate . . . to enjoy. He could not tear his gaze away from hers—her blue eyes were like a magnet, pulling him back to her. He could still vaguely hear the sound of the traffic, but it was virtually blotted out by the beating of his own heart.

Helpless to resist, he took a step toward her, trying to shake off a hand that was clutching his arm.

The hand refused to release him, and the voice that had been a minor irritation gradually became understandable words.

"Lord Leatham, please, I must speak with you."

Looking down at the woman who was clutching his arm, he knew at once who she had to be, namely the errant Miss Hemsworth. He could even see how she might successfully pass herself off as a governess, while still having the kind of looks that would attract a man like Trussell. For himself, he thought her a bit too fleshy, too overblown, and her prettiness was already beginning to fade.

"Please, Lord Leatham, I must talk to you. The landlord at the Red Stag told me you were in town. It is about Creighton Trussell. I realize he is no relation of yours, but as he is uncle to your wards—"

He gripped the woman's arms, not caring if he was leaving bruises. "I have no intention of listening to your excuses. As far as I am concerned, you and Trussell are equally guilty, and I want you out of town—no, out of this county—immediately. On the next stage, if possible."

She cringed away from him, still whining piteously at him. "But I have no money—"

He released her, then pulled out a handful of gold coins and flung them at her feet. "That will be enough to get you to London, after which you can peddle your wares in Covent Garden, where such as you belong."

The woman made no move to pick up the coins, but covered her face with her hands and began to weep.

"Don't talk to my mother that way. You're making her cry."

A little scrap of a boy kicked Bronson in the shins. It was not hard enough to hurt, but it was enough to startle him out of his fury. "Mother?" he repeated in a stunned voice. No one had said anything to him about the governess having a child.

Anne no longer had the slightest interest in staring at the tall man. No matter how magnificent his physique, he had proven to have feet of clay. And to think, he had even started to follow her before the other woman had detained him. Although the woman had spoken to him calmly, the man had responded by berating her, by shaking her even, reducing her finally to tears. Then he had shoved her away from him, only to have the boy come to her defense.

Turning her back on the pathetic tableau none of the other passers-by seemed to have noticed, Anne started walking briskly on up the street.

There was really only one way to interpret the scene she had just seen. Although dressed as a gentleman, the man clearly did not know the first thing about honor, and the woman had to be his cast-off mistress.

She must be, because otherwise, however harshly he might have spoken to her, *he would not have touched her person.* The way he had grabbed her arms denoted a degree of intimacy between the two of them that could not be explained away.

She gritted her teeth in an effort not to call curses down upon his head. Why, oh why could he not have been as wonderful as he had seemed at first?

"Men are useless encumbrances," Aunt Sidonia's words echoed in Anne's ears. "When you need them most, they will fail you. Put your trust in yourself, not in a man."

For a moment, overcome by nothing more than his sheer size, Anne had imagined she had found a man she could count on, who would not fail her. How laughable she would seem if her aunt could see her now. Taken in by a pair of broad shoulders and kind eyes. Kind eyes? There was no kindness in that man. He was the worst sort of male who walked the face of the earth—a user and discarder of women.

So why did she feel so much pain? Why were her eyes even

now filling with tears? She was not by nature a watering-pot. She had, in fact, always agreed with Aunt Sidonia that women who used tears to get their own way were silly widgeons, not worthy of the slightest respect.

Taking a handkerchief out of her reticule, Anne surreptitiously dried her cheeks, hoping no passers-by had seen her momentary loss of composure.

It was not pain; it could not be. It had to be sympathy for the poor woman, that was all it must be. It was definitely not disillusionment that the tall man had shown himself to be an irresponsible cad.

She could not be crying over him, because he had never been who she had thought he was—never! So she could not now feel as if he had betrayed her. The fact that she would never ever see the bounder again was something she should be rejoicing in, not weeping over.

So why was a stray tear still sliding down her cheek? And why was there such a lump in her throat that she doubted she could even speak? And why was there such an ache in her chest that she felt as if her heart were breaking?

The woman grabbed the boy and held him protectively in her arms, as if afraid Bronson would strike him back. "Come away, Adrian, come away."

"Wait!" Bronson again caught her arm, but this time he held it more gently, although still too firmly for her to pull away. Something was not right here. Something did not make sense. "What is your name?"

The woman was weeping too much to speak, so the boy answered for her. "Her name is Martha Miller and she is my mother." The boy drew himself up to his full height, reminding Bronson of a banty rooster. "And you, my lord, are no gentleman. Gentlemen do not make ladies cry."

Bronson was stunned speechless. Martha Miller. Not Anne Hemsworth. He had mistakenly accused a stranger of the most vile conduct, and then had ordered her to—

He cursed himself for his rashness. Was he the man who had frequently been praised for his ability to react calmly during any crisis? The only thing he had managed to do correctly during this contretemps was to keep his voice down, so that none of the passers-by had heard his accusations.

"Please, madame. Please forgive me. I mistook you for someone else entirely. I apologize for the things I said. They were not meant for you. I ask your pardon, and I will listen to whatever you have to tell me about Creighton Trussell."

It was a good ten minutes before he was able to find out from her that she was the daughter of a vicar just over the border in Cornwall, and that Trussell had seduced her while promising her marriage. But when she had told Trussell she was with child, he had laughed in her face and abandoned her immediately.

Her father had, of course, thrown her out, and she had been forced to support herself and her son by becoming a servant. But the old woman she had cooked for had died recently, and the heir had wasted no time in ordering her and her misbegotten son out of the house.

Miss Miller, however, was not asking for charity or even for simple justice. She just needed assistance in finding another job.

Thoroughly humbled, Bronson bent down and picked up the coins he had thrown in the dust. "I can only offer you my profound apologies, madame. I mistook you for someone else, but that is no excuse for the things I said to you. If you will consent to take this money, I shall do my best to find you honorable employment as soon as possible."

After more persuading, this time aided by the boy, who looked enough like the twins that Bronson saw no reason to doubt the woman was telling the truth, she finally accepted the money.

"Where are you staying?" he asked her.

"I had not thought that far in advance. I was trying to get to Wylington Manor, because I heard that Creighton was in residence, and he is so seldom there. But when they told me in the Red Stag that you were in town, I thought to approach you instead. I suppose I can stay there."

"I will tell the landlord to send me the bill, and I shall do my best to find you employment before the week is out."

"Oh, thank you, thank you."

To his dismay, the woman threw herself down on her knees, and seizing his hand, began to kiss it.

When he finally got her calmed down and she set off with

her son for the inn, Bronson turned and looked back up the street. In his imagination, he could still see the unknown lady standing there looking at him, still feel the incredible pull to go to her.

She was no longer there, of course, which did not surprise him in view of the way he had just acted. He, who never explained his actions to anyone, now felt a compulsion to find the tall, beautiful lady with the magnetic blue eyes and explain everything to her—not just about Trussell's mistress, but about all of it.

He wanted to tell her his suspicions about Trussell, to tell her about the runner's report on the governess's background. He wanted to tell her the whole story about Demetrius being jilted. He wanted to see her smile again—hear her laugh—he wanted to laugh with her.

What was surprising was that no matter how he covered the town, up one street and down the next, peering into each shop window, always scanning the crowds, he could not catch even a glimpse of her.

Finally it grew late and he knew he must abandon his search, or he would finish his ride home in darkness. Returning to the Red Stag, he inquired of the landlord, who informed him the governess had collected her horse and departed hours ago.

The governess. It was, in a way, her fault that he had lost the unknown lady. For Bronson, that thought, coming as it did at the end of a very long day, seemed sufficient justification for transporting Miss Hemsworth to Australia, even without her other various and assorted crimes.

Chapter Six

"WE TRANSLATED TWO extra chapters of Cicero while you were gone," Andrew said.

"Without even being asked," Anthony added.

"And we had the cook fix clotted cream especially for you." Andrew looked at her appealingly, but Anne did not return his smile.

Sitting at the table in the schoolroom, Anne continued to drink her tea and eat what was obviously a peace offering from the twins. She did not, however, say a single word to ease the twins' consciences. Her tacit disapproval of their earlier actions had its effect: Neither of the twins had touched his pasties or saffron cakes, and they were both letting their own tea grow cold.

Finally Andrew said, "We are sorry that we sent you into town without telling you Uncle Bronson was coming."

"But it was not really a mean thing to do. We just did it to try to help you," Anthony added. "We thought if we told him about Uncle Creighton first, before he had a chance to fire you, then maybe he would believe us and not send you away."

"And we never actually lied. We never told you anything that was not true."

Anne looked directly at the twins for the first time since she had arrived at the house to find the servants in a turmoil over Lord Leatham's arrival. She had been doubly shocked to discover that he had been expected, and that no one had bothered to inform her of that fact.

"I have only one question." At least she now had their undivided attention. "You say that you did not lie to me. Did you at any time, however, suspect that you might be tricking me by what you were not telling me? Or did you in your hearts, in fact, actually *know* that you were deceiving me, no matter how you managed to justify it to yourselves?"

There was a long silence while the twins looked at each other, then back at her. "Yes," they said in mournful unison. "We knew."

Anne continued to eat her clotted cream, but it might as well have been cold porridge, for all the enjoyment she derived from it.

"Does this mean you will never trust us again?" Andrew asked.

"Like the broken egg can't be put back together again?" Anthony added.

"I do not know," Anne replied honestly. "Do you plan to be trustworthy or devious? Will I still have to guard against the things you do not say? Do you plan to be honest with yourselves, or do you plan to come up with excuses and justifications to do things you know in your heart are wrong?" It was the surreptitious sniffle that got to her the most, although she was not sure which twin had lost control to that extent.

"We promise that you can trust us in the future," Andrew said.

"Please forgive us—please!" Anthony entreated.

"Very well, I forgive you, but that is not to say you shall go unpunished. For your deliberate deceitfulness, you may spend the rest of the day in your room."

One would have thought she had offered them a special treat, the way they thanked her. Then, after hugging and kissing her, their normal hearty appetites reasserted themselves, and they cheerfully gobbled up the food remaining on the tea tray.

Watching them eat, she realized how much she would miss them. Their attempts to help had been inspired by affection, of that she had no doubt. It was unfortunate that their efforts had been in vain, but Anne knew enough about the role governesses and companions played to realize that Lord Leatham would take Trussell's word over hers any day. Virtually every governess she knew who had the slightest pretension to beauty—and indeed many who could honestly only be described as quite, quite plain—had a story to tell about a "gentleman" in the household accosting her.

It mattered not if the gentleman were twenty or seventy, the results were the same. The lady of the household was either jealous or protective, depending on her relationship with the "gentleman," and the governess/companion invariably lost her position.

Well, now she had her own story to tell, Anne thought with a smile, and although being thrown out on her ear was not to be desired, Mrs. Wiggins was adept at minimizing the repercussions of such a blot on a governess's record. This dismissal would, therefore, not unduly affect Anne's chances of obtaining another satisfactory position.

It was the twins who would suffer, especially Anthony. Having finally given their trust to an adult, they would be devastated when she was sent away. On the other hand, considering the total indifference of their guardian, she did not think such an argument would carry weight with Lord Leatham.

But life was as it was, and wishing did not alter circumstances. There was nothing for it but to start packing.

Rising to her feet she headed for the door, where she paused. The most shocking thought had occurred to her. Patrick, the head groom, had said Lord Leatham had gone into Tavistock looking for her. . . . There was that man she had been attracted to in town. . . . No, he could not have been Lord Least-in-Sight!

But then again, the man in town, now that she thought about it, could be said to bear a resemblance to the boys, especially the shape of the eyes. . . .

The mere idea that the tall man—that user and discarder of women—could be Lord Leatham was so appalling, she did not even wish to know for sure if, by some wild chance, her suspicions were correct. Admitting her own cowardice, she reached for the door handle.

But, on the other hand, how could she endure wondering if it were true? Just the mere possibility that they could be one and the same man—just the thought of such an unmitigated disaster—the very idea would torment her until she knew for sure. Turning back, she asked the twins one last question. "How tall is your Uncle Bronson?"

"Oh, tall. Really, really tall."

" 'Bout the tallest person in the whole world, probably."

As quickly as possible, Anne made her way to her room, her thoughts in such a turmoil, she was shaking all over. She should have known the minute he grabbed that woman's arms—on the street, right out in public view—she should have known he was Lord Leatham, whose low opinion of women was unequaled, that much she had learned from the twins.

She should have known—Anne threw herself face down on the bed and hit her pillow over and over again. She should have known—how could she ever have been attracted to such a man, even momentarily?

To compound her horror, she burst out crying, like the veriest watering-pot. In spite of her best efforts to stop, she was forced to bury her face in the pillow to muffle the sound of her sobs.

The sooner she left Devon and returned to Aunt Sidonia, the better. A few days of exposure to her great-aunt's no nonsense ways and Anne knew she would be cured of these emotional outbursts.

Bronson had ample time to think during the ride back to Wylington Manor, and his thoughts stayed firmly centered around the three women who had affected his actions during the course of the day: First, the woman he had sought after; second, the woman he had found; and third, the woman who had found him. Each of them had taught him something unexpected about himself.

The governess had taught him that he was not actually the patient man he had long prided himself on being. It had been an insane idea to go chasing after her on the spur of the moment instead of waiting for her to return. Never before had he acted so . . . so out of control.

Control? Martha Miller had shown him an even more unpalatable side of himself. He, who had always been careful to show women the proper respect, had attacked an innocent woman—a woman who, moreover, had come to him for help—and he had reduced her to tears. The demeaning things he had said to her in his anger had served only to demean himself—the degrading things he had accused her of doing and then suggested she continue doing, only reflected back unfavorably upon him. He did not recognize the picture of himself he saw, nor did he like it.

If he had observed another man acting in a similar manner, Bronson would have considered him to be a conceited, arrogant oaf, and he would not have hesitated a moment to call such a man to account.

On the other hand, every time Bronson's thoughts came back to the tall woman with the magnificent brown hair and magnetic blue eyes, he felt even more of a shock at his reaction. "Know thyself," had always been his motto, and until today he had thought he did.

He had thought he was not like other men—not so weak as to fall under the spell of a woman and make a fool of himself. Women played only a very minor role in his life. Indeed, sometimes for months at a time they were totally absent from his life and not missed even for a moment. If he had been asked—and indeed, Thorverton had asked him—he would have said that in general, women bored him.

So how was it possible that he could have taken one look into this woman's eyes and felt as if there were a bond between them? A bond he had never felt for any other woman—indeed, not even for his parents or his best friends?

Why had he felt an actual physical pain in his chest when he realized she had vanished? A pain that had died down to a dull ache, but that was still there? Why had he spent the afternoon wandering the streets of Tavistock like a fool trying to find her again? And why was he even now racking his brain to figure out whom he might ask about her?

Why did he now feel a deeper need to grieve at the thought of never seeing her again than he had felt when his own father and mother had died? Why, when he had never even spoken a word to her, did a life without her at his side seem so empty and desolate?

None of it made sense, and being a sensible man, he determined again to put all thoughts of her out of his mind. But having made that decision at least five times since he left town, and having been unable to abide by it, he had to accept that it might be impossible to forget her. And that in turn made him question whether or not he really was superior to his fellow men, who were so quick to lose their dignity by throwing themselves at the feet of women and allowing themselves to be trod upon.

Had he just seemed immune to such weaknesses because he had never really been seriously tempted?

Resolutely pushing thoughts of the woman, if not out of his mind, then at least to the back of his mind, he considered again the problem of the governess. Once he admitted to himself that he could act hastily—and today was the first day that seemed possibly true—then he was forced to admit that he had not done a very thorough job of investigating the situation at Wylington Manor.

In spite of what the Bible said about the sins of the fathers being visited upon the sons, when he considered the runner's report rationally, Bronson did not feel he had been fair in assuming that Faussley's daughter was cut from the same cloth he was. And the testimony of ten-year-old boys, no matter how intelligent, was also not perhaps the most reliable evidence. Although now that he thought of it, the twins seemed to have an uncommonly high regard for Miss Hemsworth.

Riding into the stable yard, Bronson dismounted and turned his horse over to one of the lads. Then recognizing one of the older grooms, he signaled with his hand.

"Yes, m'lord?"

"Patrick, is it not? I wish to ask you a question or two. About the twins and their new governess."

"Miss Hemsworth? She's a fine rider. Can handle any nag we've got in the stables, but treats them gentle like. Not one to ruin the tenderest mouth."

"I am not so much interested in knowing how she sits a horse, as I am in knowing what the other servants think of her."

"Well, I know in the stables there are some of the lads who are not too happy to have her here. In their opinion, she's a bad influence on the maids."

"A bad influence?" Could it be possible that his initial opinion of Miss Hemsworth was correct? "In what way?"

Patrick laughed. "Well, she's been putting ideas into their head 'bout the proper way for a lady to act. Not that the maids are ladies, mind you, but they've been getting the notion they can be just as good as ladies. For myself, I've had a good chuckle. Being married, I was never one to chase the girls, and a proper skinning my old woman would give me if she caught me rolling in the hay with some flighty young thing. But some of the others, well, they're a bit put out. Even Sally has got her knees locked together tight as anything, and she was never all that particular. Seems Miss Hemsworth is teaching her to read, and she's got ambitions now, our Sal does.''

Not wishing to hear all the particulars about the frustrations of the grooms and stable boys, Bronson soon excused himself and headed toward his room to change. Passing the door to Trussell's bedroom, he met Wyke coming out and decided on the spur of the moment to question the valet about the events at midnight four nights past.

"Miss Hemsworth? Well, I cannot say for sure what happened that evening, as I was not an eye witness to the events. Mr. Trussell was drinking heavily when I retired to my cot in the dressing room, but about two in the morning I was awakened by a loud thump, followed by a door slamming. I found Mr. Trussell passed out on the floor in a heap, so I put him to bed. The next morning Miss Hemsworth returned Mr. Trussell's robe to me. And that is all I know for a fact.''

"But you have thought about the probable events of that evening, have you not?''

"Well, I hesitate to discuss . . .''

A sharp look from Bronson was all it took for Wyke to overcome any scruples about idle speculation.

"I have assumed that Mr. Trussell, regrettably bolstered by the courage he found in the bottom of the brandy bottle, sought out Miss Hemsworth in her room and made improper advances, which she naturally rejected. From his condition by the time I found him, namely unable to walk or even to sit up without assistance, I would also have to assume that she carried him back to his room, and the noise I heard was her dropping him on the floor.''

"Carrying him?'' An idea sprang full-grown into Bronson's brain—an idea too horrible to contemplate.

"I could almost wish she had remained a moment or two, as I had the devil's own time hoisting him into bed.''

No, Miss Hemsworth could not be the tall woman with the magnetic blue eyes. The idea was preposterous!

But Bronson had a growing conviction, however appalling, that he had met the governess on the street in Tavistock. Everything fit—the riding habit the tall woman had been wearing, the remark he had overheard in the Red Stag about the governess being easy to spot, the fact that she was strong enough to carry Trussell . . .

"Is something wrong, m'lord? You look ill. Do you require some assistance?"

Waving off Wyke's concern, Bronson retreated on shaking legs to his own room, where he sat on his bed and contemplated his future, which had suddenly become murky.

One half of him was insisting he seek out Miss Hemsworth immediately, to see if she was indeed the tall woman who had fascinated him.

The other half of him was just as fervently urging him to flee from her while his freedom was still intact.

Unable to sit still, he began pacing, and *nemesis* was the word that immediately popped into his head. Of all the people to have observed him make an ass of himself with Trussell's discarded mistress, why had it been Miss Hemsworth?

But this was patently ridiculous. He had not met his fate on the streets of Tavistock, of all places. If he had indeed noticed Miss Hemsworth in town, it was merely because she was a fine figure of a woman. She did not have any power—natural or supernatural—over him.

Although she might prove to be an interesting person to talk to—for a day or two, at least—he would stay in Devon only long enough to make sure Miss Hemsworth was adequate as a companion for the twins. Then, assuming he did not find out Trussell was stealing from the estate, Bronson would set out on his postponed journey to the Far East. Alone. The way he always preferred to be.

The only reason he now left his room to seek out the twins was because he was still not positive Miss Hemsworth was the proper person to have them in charge.

He found the twins in their room, again alone. "Miss Hemsworth has not returned from Tavistock?"

"Oh, hello, Uncle Bronson. No, she's back. She was mad as hops because we tricked her into going to town when we knew you would be coming—" one of them said.

"And we didn't tell her you were expected," the other one concluded.

"I wonder if you boys can do something for me?" Bronson asked.

"Of course!" They jumped up off the floor where they had been playing with their lead soldiers. "Oh wait, we can't go anywhere."

"Cannot?"

"Anne is making us stay in our room—"

"As punishment—"

"Because we were not exactly honest with her."

"She says telling part of the truth is not the same as being truthful."

"Well, what I want can be done just as well here as anywhere else. I would like you to show me just how your Uncle Creighton and Miss Hemsworth were 'wrestling.' "

It took the boys a moment to sort out which one should play the role of Trussell and which one Miss Hemsworth, but finally one of them was lying face down on the bed, the other sitting on his legs. "She had both his arms pushed up behind his back, like this."

"Ow! Don't twist them so much!"

"But Uncle Creighton couldn't talk, because his face was shoved down into the pillow—"

Bronson quickly stopped the twin on top from smothering his brother. "So then what happened?"

"We wanted to help—"

"We were going to tell her where she could hide the body—"

"But she sent us back to bed—"

"Except we dawdled long enough to see her carrying Uncle Creighton back to his own room."

"Then she came and tucked us in a few minutes later."

The twin underneath managed to throw his brother off his back, and he then sat up and asked worriedly, "You do believe us, don't you, Uncle Bronson? We don't want you to send Anne away."

"Please, Uncle Bronson, it was not Anne's fault, in spite of what Uncle Creighton said when he told her she was fired."

"If anyone had unbecoming conduct, it was Uncle Creighton."

"He was the one who was drunk and in the wrong room."

"And we don't want Anne to leave, ever—"

"It's important. Really and truly important."

"Because we love her, you see."

"And we don't want her to go."

Bronson contemplated his wards, who had variously been described by governesses as hell-born brats, devil's spawn, and worse. "Yes, your demonstration of the midnight wrestling match has made it quite clear to me who was at fault. I only have one last question." There was no more doubt in Bronson's mind, but it was better to tie up loose ends. "How big is Miss Hemsworth?"

"Oh, *big*—"

"But not fat—"

"No, not fat, although she does stick out in front—"

"But she can't help that, 'cause she's a woman."

"Mostly she's just tall—"

The one boy stood on the bed and held his hand up to Bronson's mouth. "About this tall, prob'ly."

"Yeah, about that tall. And strong."

"She can do anything."

The boys looked at him expectantly. "She sounds . . . formidable," was all Bronson could think of to say.

"Oh, she is," the boys affirmed, then proceeded to tell him about Anne's more impressive talents, such as being able to roam the moor without getting lost and to ride bareback, which reminded them about the prickles under the saddle blanket, so they told him that story as well as others.

If the boys were to be believed, Miss Hemsworth was fearless, with nerves of steel. She was as athletic as a top-of-the-trees Corinthian, so intelligent and well-educated she was able to discourse logically on any topic, and it often seemed she had eyes in the back of her head, since nothing escaped her notice.

What made it especially daunting was that Bronson was well aware that he himself had on more than one occasion been praised in just such glowing terms. But to hear a female described thusly . . .

"So she has no weakness, this new governess of yours?"

"We do know her Achilles' heel—"

"Yes," his brother added promptly, "she loves clotted cream

with strawberries, better than anything else in the whole wide world.''

Leaving the twins to serve out the rest of their sentence, Bronson descended to the main floor, his thoughts bedeviled. The mere mention of clotted cream called forth a tantalizing image of Miss Hemsworth's clear complexion; ripe strawberries made him think of her lips; touching a finger lightly to his own lips, he wondered if she were indeed that tall.

He had not long to wonder. Entering the library with the intention of reviewing the bailiff's accounts, he found the elusive Miss Hemsworth already there, perched halfway up a polished walnut ladder, apparently with the intention of returning a book to the top-most shelf.

Her ankles were as trim as the rest of her was well-endowed, and by the time Bronson finally lifted his eyes to meet hers, he had to admit he had earned her look of icy disapproval. Blast the woman! He'd be hanged if he would apologize to her before they'd even been properly introduced.

''I trust we still have footmen, whose job it is to climb about on ladders?''

With a regal tilt of her head, she replied, ''I am perfectly capable of managing for myself, without the aid of any *man*.'' Then, without giving him a chance to play the gentleman, she proved her point by descending unaided from her perch.

They were standing too close . . . and the twins had been right. If he leaned forward just a trifle, his lips would touch her forehead, which was presently creased with annoyance. He had, indeed, only to tilt his face down slightly for his mouth to meet hers . . . since her chin was already tilted up at a most belligerent angle.

Looking down into her blue eyes, which in spite of the anger they held were still most fetching, Bronson felt an irrational desire to apologize for his own failings and to make excuses for the shortcomings of his fellow men. It was with difficulty that he resisted the urge to grovel at her feet.

So this was what drove other men to make fools of themselves, the rational part of his mind observed. This readiness to pay any price, to give up everything else in life, in order to bask within the magic circle of a woman's charms. And not any woman would do. It had to be one single, specific, irresistible, indispensable—

"If there is nothing else, my lord, I have other things to do."

She started to step around him, but he caught her by the arm. He could not let her vanish again, not yet, not after he had spent so many hours looking for her.

"Unhand me, my lord!" Her rage was palpable. "I have already been accosted by one 'gentleman' in this household, and I do not intend to repeat the experience."

"Are you accusing me of wanting to kiss you . . ." His voice trailed off when he realized he was indeed thinking about her soft lips and wondering how they would feel touching his.

"Do you deny it? If you do, I shall have to assume I am in the presence of a liar."

"Miss Hemsworth, do calm down. There are things we need to discuss." Bronson cast around wildly in his mind, trying to think of an excuse to keep her in the room. "About your job—"

"There is nothing to discuss. If you will kindly release my arm, which you are bruising, I shall finish my packing and be ready to leave by morning."

"Now *you* are lying. I am not hurting your arm in the slightest. Admit it."

For a moment she looked away, but then she again met his gaze squarely. "No, you are not hurting me. But I am, as a matter of principle, opposed to the use of physical force in any and all situations."

He looked down into her eyes and felt again the strong pull of attraction. His free hand came up of its own volition and cupped her cheek, then without conscious decision, he leaned toward her. She sighed softly just before their lips met.

It was the most chaste kiss he had ever shared with a woman, and yet the most satisfying. Lifting his head slightly he looked down into eyes that mirrored the confusion he felt.

Chapter Seven

"I SHOULD NOT HAVE DONE THAT," Lord Leatham murmured, finally releasing her arm.

"No, you should not have done that," Anne murmured back. Try as she might, she could not bring herself to move away from him. His eyes held her where she was, and she even had to tuck her hand behind her back to keep it from coming up to touch his cheek—her own body was turning traitor on her.

I should have suspected there was more to it than Aunt Sidonia explained, she thought, *else there would not be so many babies born into this world.*

His eyes appeared to darken, and she realized if she did not move away, he was going to kiss her again.

Unfortunately, curiosity had always been her one besetting sin, and now she wanted nothing more than a chance to explore the strange sensations that had been aroused with that one light touch of Lord Leatham's lips against hers. After all, she tried to rationalize, if she were to be fired for conduct unbecoming, she might as well experience what she was already accused of having indulged in.

But it was only a momentary temptation. Before his mouth could again make contact with hers, she reminded herself of her responsibilities and obligations, and that was enough to make her turn her head away and avoid the second kiss, which Lord Leatham ended up bestowing on her ear.

To her surprise, she discovered that appendage was also quite highly sensitive and in some undefined way connected to her knees, which now gave every indication of wanting to buckle beneath her.

Lord Leatham growled something wordless under his breath and Anne realized that sometime when she had not been paying strict enough attention, he had managed to place both his hands on her waist, and he was now halfway supporting her.

112   *Charlotte Louise Dolan*

Only by resolutely forcing herself to remember the scene with the woman and the child in Tavistock was Anne able to gather enough gumption to step out of his arms.

What she would have done if he had refused to unhand her, she did not know. It was a little late to proclaim her modesty by slapping his face. What on earth had gotten into her? Why had she acted in such an uncharacteristic manner, like the veriest romp of an upstairs maid?

For a moment her eyes again met Lord Leatham's, and she recognized that she was still in danger of succumbing to his potent charms. In spite of her efforts to hold onto it, the image of the other woman was fading away—banished by Lord Leatham's smile. He was indeed a most accomplished rake.

Distance. That was what she needed. Enough distance between them that she would not be tempted to . . . her mind shied away from the thought of yet another kiss.

She needed to escape to her own room . . . to pack . . . to remove herself from Wylington Manor . . . from the near presence of Lord Leatham.

But the attraction between them was too strong to allow her to follow the proper course. Instead of bolting through the door, she found herself walking calmly to one of the leather-covered chairs, where she seated herself as sedately as possible, considering the fact that her cheeks now felt so hot, she had to be either blushing bright red or coming down with a fever. "I believe you had something you wished to discuss with me?" Her voice was unnaturally low and husky.

Lord Leatham's only reply was to shut the heavy oaken door, ensuring their privacy in the quiet, shadowed room and giving her the strange feeling that she had still not really escaped from his embrace.

Had he turned the key in the old-fashioned lock and then thrown himself down upon her to ravish her, not even that would have surprised her, so right did it feel to be alone with him.

Instead of acting in such a rakish way, however, he left the door unlocked, then crossed the room to seat himself rather prosaically on the matching chair beside hers. She was left with the unanswered question of whether or not she would have resisted or aided in such a ravishment.

It was only when she noticed his hand shaking slightly that she realized he was as affected by the kisses as she had been, and she was able to regain a little of her usual self-assurance.

"I believe you mentioned my job?"

"You need have no fears for your job. In spite of the reports I have had about you, I find, after suitable investigation, that you are, in my opinion, the proper person to be in charge of the twins for the summer."

For a moment she was rendered totally speechless by his gall, his totally unmitigated gall at having actually investigated *her,* whose morals were above reproach—or at least whose morals *had* been above reproach—when he himself was a cad and a rake, who littered the countryside with his discarded mistresses. Added to which was his knowing *smirk* now that he had managed to—to corrupt her into conduct unbecoming a governess!

When she recovered from her initial shock, it was not only anger at him that brought her to her feet, but anger at herself for having behaved like a weak, mindless female. How could she have forgotten, even momentarily, the long mental list she had been composing concerning Lord Leatham's failings and shortcomings?

"I, on the other hand, after investigating you, do not feel that you are the proper person to be the twins' guardian."

Likewise springing to his feet, Lord Leatham faced her, transformed in a flash from the suave seducer back into the heartless cad who had so shamelessly shaken a woman on the streets of Tavistock.

"How dare you question my honesty where the boys are concerned? If someone has been dipping sticky fingers into the boys' money, it is Trussell, not me. I have always been scrupulously correct when managing the estate."

For a moment Anne was so blinded with rage, it was all she could do to resist the urge to draw his cork. "It is so typical of a *man,*" she invested the word with every bit of the scorn she had learned from Aunt Sidonia, "to think only of money and property and estates. But a child raised in a castle without love and attention is poorer than one raised in a hovel if he finds love there."

"What are you blathering about? My wards are not being neglected in any way."

They were virtually nose to nose now, but Anne felt not the slightest desire to resume exploring the strange phenomenon of kissing. She did, to be sure, feel a strong urge to place her fingers around Lord Leatham's throat, but only to throttle the arrogant baron. "I do not blather, my lord. And no matter how you may try to deny it, the twins have been severely neglected."

"Neglected? That is utter nonsense. If you would make such rash charges, you must be prepared to prove them."

"I shall have no difficulty in doing so."

All Anne's rage was replaced by satisfaction. Seating herself once again in her chair, she smiled up at Lord Leatham, whose male pride had caused him to fall into her trap. Yes, indeed, words and reason were more powerful than physical force, and soon he would have to admit defeat at the hands of a mere woman. A *useless* woman, as he had been known to categorize all of her sex.

"Then, my lord, I challenge you to tell the boys apart."

"Tell them apart?" he parroted, obviously shaken out of his complaisance by her challenge.

"Yes," she repeated, feeling quite smug. "All you have to do to prove that you have not neglected the twins, is to tell me which one is Andrew and which one is Anthony."

Never had Bronson felt such a strong urge to forget his upbringing as a gentleman.

He had no desire to hit the infuriating woman, however. What he felt was a need to kiss her into submission—into accepting his dominance as a male.

The thought was so unexpected and so out of character for him, he began to prowl the room, unable to control his restlessness enough to sit down.

"Well, my lord? Do you accept my challenge?"

With difficulty, he pulled his mind off the memory of Miss Hemsworth's trim waist and focused on the subject at hand, namely the twins and his supposed neglect of them. Without stopping to think it through, he said, "I have not been around the twins long enough to—"

Her laughter interrupted him, and he did not need to have her point out that he had just proved her correct. But she did anyway.

"You are proving my case for me," she said, smug self-satisfaction in her voice.

Stung not so much by her laugh as by the truth of her accusations, he said in his own defense, "In spite of my supposed neglect, you will find that the twins are quite fond of me. And in any case, it has not been necessary for me to be in constant attendance in Wylington Manor. The boys have been too young and have not had a need for my presence. Children below a certain age do not need adults other than their nanny and a governess. I am sure that Nanny Barlow can tell Anthony from Andrew."

His pacing had by now taken him around the room until he was standing directly behind the governess, so he could not see the expression on her face. Her tone, however, was acid enough to convey her feelings. "Nanny Barlow undoubtedly can, wherever she may be. But since you fired her years ago, she need hardly be brought into this conversation."

Rising to her feet, Miss Hemsworth turned to face him, and despite her unfeminine propensity for arguing like a man, he could see deep hurt in her eyes when she said accusingly, "I think, my lord, that if you *investigate,* as you seem to be so fond of doing, you will find that there is no one in this household, other than myself, who can tell which twin is which. And at this time, there is little I can do to correct the years of neglect, since I have only been hired until the end of the summer. In fact, the longer I stay, the more painful it will be for the twins when I do leave, so I would as lief pack my bags now and depart. But you need not worry about ensuring the proper succession. The present marquess is suitably branded."

With those words she walked briskly to the door and jerked it open, but he caught up with her before she could make good her escape.

Grabbing her again by the arm, he spun her around to face him. "What the deuce are you talking about, branded?"

"On the bottom of the foot. Did you not know? But then, there seem to be so many things you do not know." She jerked her arm away from his now nerveless fingers. "I suggest it is high time you make the acquaintance of your wards and apprise yourself of what is going on in your absence."

This time he let her go. Watching her climb the stairs, her back absolutely radiating indignation, his thoughts remained on the shocking things she had told him.

No one in the household could tell which twin was which . . . branded . . . no, it was all too preposterous. Miss Hemsworth must have her facts wrong. Surely Nanny Barlow had not been fired—pensioned off, perhaps, when the twins became too much for her to handle, but not fired.

There was a slight noise beside him and Bronson turned to see Chorley standing deferentially a few feet away. Earlier in the day the butler had been quite mellow, but from the suffering expression now on his face, he appeared to be paying for his earlier indulgence with a giant hangover.

"Yes?"

"Begging your pardon, m'lord, but Braithwaite is waiting in your study to discuss the estate accounts as you requested."

"I have not yet had time to go over the books. Tell him I will send word in a day or two."

"As you wish, m'lord."

The butler turned away, but Bronson called him back.

"One question, Chorley. Can you tell which twin is Lord Wylington?"

"No, sir."

"Can anyone in the household?"

"Miss Hemsworth appears to be able to do so."

"I meant other than her."

"Can't say that anyone can, m'lord. But then, it doesn't really matter, does it? The marquess is marked on his foot, so there is no danger that the younger lad will be able to lay claim to the estate when they arrive at the age of one-and-twenty."

"Marked?" Bronson fought to suppress the memory of a party of slave traders he had come upon while traveling along the coast of Africa. They had been engaged in branding their captives, and the screams and smell of burning flesh had haunted him for months afterward. "Who did such a thing?"

"Why your cousin, the late marquess. He tattooed the first-born babe on the bottom of his foot. And a good thing, too, since those lads are as alike as two peas in a pod."

Bronson closed his eyes momentarily. Tattooed, not branded. Thank goodness for small favors. "One more thing, Chorley, and then you may take my message to Braithwaite. Was Nanny Barlow pensioned off?"

The butler stiffened perceptibly. "Pensioned off? Fired, she was, with no reference, and at her age, too. All because she dared to cross Mr. Trussell."

The look the butler gave him made it quite clear that Miss Hemsworth was not the only one who held Bronson responsible for all that went on in Wylington Manor.

He resisted the urge to explain himself to a servant. Not that there was a suitable explanation. He could hardly excuse himself on the grounds that it had been Trussell who had done the actual firing, since he, Bronson, had given Trussell the authority to hire and fire the servants. Nor, knowing Trussell's weak character as he did, should he have assumed the twins' uncle would not abuse such authority.

But it was hard, nevertheless, to resist the impulse to explain. Never before had Bronson's conduct been found wanting, and now, in the space of less than an hour, two different people had virtually accused him of failing to fulfill his obligations. He was not in the least pleased with their opinion of his character.

"But if you leave, who'll teach me to read?"

Anne looked at Sally, who was supposed to be helping with the packing, but who instead was expending all her energies on trying to dissuade Anne from her course. They had been going around and around the same arguments for at least half an hour, and it was beginning to give Anne a headache.

"I have told you already, I have no recourse but to leave."

"But you told me that a lady can do anything she sets her mind to. Does that mean you don't want to stay?"

"Whether I want to or not has nothing to do with the case. Circumstances are such that I can no longer stay here, and that is that." Anne folded her best Sunday dress and laid it in her portmanteau.

"But it wasn't your fault that Trussell came to your room. Everyone knows it wasn't, and we're all willing to vouch for that if m'lord don't believe you. You ain't the kind of female to let men kiss you."

Sally was wrong in her opinion, but Anne could hardly tell her that she apparently was that kind. She had stood there in the library and let Lord Leatham kiss her not once, but twice. It was the second kiss that made it impossible for her to beg to be allowed to stay.

If she so much as hinted that she might reconsider her decision to leave Wylington Manor, Lord Leatham would undoubtedly try to persuade her to stay by kissing her again. Her hands trembled at the thought, but her mind remained resolute.

"Are you going to help me pack, or are you going to stand there arguing all night?"

"Neither." Sally marched to the door and jerked it open. "If you're set on leaving the rest of us to try an' handle them twins, don't expect me or anyone else in this household to help you pack. And I 'spect you'll be having to walk to Tavistock, too, 'cause I don't think anyone's going to drive you, neither. You may have charmed those boys into being good as gold, but 'thout you here, they're positively heathenish."

With that parting shot the maid was gone, leaving Anne to her thoughts.

Talk about cutting off your nose to spite your face! Anne threw down a stack of neatly folded handkerchiefs and began to pace back and forth in her room. How on earth had she managed to get herself into such a predicament? She had been prepared to humble herself, to beg for another chance, even to admit she had been in the wrong—even though everything that had happened had been Trussell's fault from start to finish.

In short, she had been ready to do or say anything in order to stay on as the twins' governess.

Instead of which, in what was obviously a fit of insanity caused by too much kissing, she had told Lord Leatham that she was leaving. Apparently she had sounded convincing, because he had made not the slightest effort to persuade her to remain.

Even if she now ignored the kisses and acted as if they had never happened, there was no way she could seek Lord Leatham out and say she had changed her mind, could she please stay on until the end of the summer?

All that would accomplish would be to prove to him that she was a typical fickle female—moody, hysterical, unpredictable—totally unsuited to taking care of two young boys. Any claims she might have to authority in the household would be thoroughly undermined, even if Lord Leatham did not try to kiss her again.

No, there was nothing for it but to retreat in ignominy to Aunt Sidonia's. Not that she would be able to tell her aunt what had happened here in Devon.

Oh, Lord, what a muddle everything was in. Well, at least she would have plenty of time on the stagecoach to think up a good story to explain why she had, for the first time in her career, lost a perfectly good position.

For a moment, she could hear in her mind an echo of the speech she had made to the boys about always telling the truth, and she wished with all her heart that she could go back and start the day over again.

The entire situation, as bad as it was already, continued to deteriorate. After an hour of staring at the estate books and seeing only angry blue eyes in place of columns of neat figures, Bronson gave up and retired to his own room, where he found Daws waiting.

His normally taciturn valet had, however, become uncharacteristically loquacious, but then after such a day, why should Bronson expect anyone to be acting in a normal manner?

"The general belief belowstairs seems to be that if you lets that governess quit, the twins are going to make life a merry hell for everyone. And it would appear that finding a replacement for her is not going to be an easy task. You should have thought of that before you fired her."

"I did not fire her!"

There was dead silence in the room following his outburst. Daws stared at him, but Bronson could not read the expression on his manservant's face.

"She quit," he added finally.

Daws gave a low whistle. "Then, m'lord, you've got yourself in a powerful bad position. I've been hearing tales about the mischief those two used to get into before Miss Hemsworth came to take charge of them. Why once they hid in the house for a full sennight and no one could find them. The woman who was supposed to be governess at the time enlisted the aid of all the servants indoor and out, but it was like chasing a will-o'-the-wisp. Food would disappear, and they heard footsteps at night, but no one caught sight of the twins. 'Tis a big house, but even when Braithwaite was called in to organize a proper search, they never found out where they'd been staying all those days. Yes, if I was you, I'd find a way to persuade Miss Hemsworth to stay on."

"I would if I could, but I cannot," Bronson replied baldly, unable to explain about the two kisses. If it were just a matter of convincing Miss Hemsworth that he really did have the boys' best interests at heart, it would be a simple matter. But how to convince her he was not merely using the twins' welfare as a ruse to keep her around so that he would have an opportunity to seduce her?

Especially since the idea of Miss Hemsworth in his bed was so totally appealing?

"Then you're really in the suds, m'lord. Who's going to take care of them two little demons, I'd like to know? Ain't nobody in the household going to want to get near them. They're bound to be mad as hops, and they're trouble enough even when they're just in high spirits."

"I shall take charge of the boys myself."

Daws looked at him in astonishment, but he was no more surprised than Bronson himself. On the other hand, now that he thought it over, it was not such a bad idea. The twins could undoubtedly profit from a little man-to-man instruction before they went off to school at Harrow, where it would not do at all for a Roebuck to be thought a sissy. Family pride demanded they make a good showing.

"In fact, I shall go up to the schoolroom and explain the situation to the boys right now, before they hear about it from a servant."

"But we told you how necessary it is for Anne to stay."

Whichever twin it was, and Bronson had to admit he did not know if it was Anthony or Andrew, the boy made no effort to conceal his displeasure.

"It was not my fault." Bronson found himself becoming adept at making excuses. He had reached the point that he no longer felt the slightest surprise at such uncharacteristic behavior—acting totally out of character seemed to be normal for this day. "I did not tell her she was fired."

"Then why is she packing her bags?"

The other twin, either Andrew or Anthony, was equally indignant.

Why had Miss Hemsworth insisted upon leaving? She had babbled something about the twins being neglected, but that was surely no cause to abandon them herself—which left only the kisses he had forced on her. It was not surprising that a lady of the highest moral rectitude would refuse to stay under the same roof as a man who assaulted a woman on the streets of Tavistock and then repeated the offense in his own household.

"I am afraid it may—" Bronson stumbled over the words he had not had occasion to use in years, "—be my fault she is leaving."

"Then," one of the twins announced with surprising authority, "it is up to you to make amends."

"Yes. Anne says that if you do something wrong, then it is up to you to do something right, to do something constructive to fix the problem," the other twin explained. "You cannot simply pretend that being sorry for what you did is all that is necessary."

"If you have trouble figuring out what to do, we would be glad to help you think of something." One of the twins looked up at him calmly.

"Yes, we are very ingenious," the other one added.

The two of them looked at one another for a long moment, then back at him. "You might keep that in mind."

His tone of voice was quite bland and their smiles were now sweetly angelic, yet looking at them Bronson felt a strong urge to flee from the house, from Devon, and in fact from England itself. How had he ever, even for a minute, thought the boys might have trouble adjusting to Harrow?

The question now in his mind was whether Harrow was capable of surviving the twins.

"The thing of it is, m'lord, that they somehow got hold of my keys, because that morning, 'twas shortly before Michaelmas last, we woke up to find they'd locked us all in our rooms. What was we to do, I ask you? No one of us could get out and fetch the keys to unlock the doors, so we had to wait nearly till teatime before Mr. Braithwaite came to confer with Cook and discovered our plight. So you see, don't you, that you really must persuade Miss Hemsworth to stay on. Perhaps if you doubled her salary?"

"Yes, yes, Mrs. Plimtree. I have already said I shall do my best to see that the situation is arranged to everyone's satisfaction." Bronson opened the door of his study to signify that the interview was over, but standing outside in the hallway were several more servants waiting to interview him. With a sigh, he waved the next one in.

This was really not the way he preferred to start the day, especially since he had lain awake most of the night, reliving over and over again the events of the previous day.

"And then when they were nine, Miss Hemsworth, what did they do, but climb up the ivy on the wall all the way to the top floor, where they drew on my window with soot. When I pulled my curtains back the next morning, like I always do, there was this hideous grinning face staring in at me. Like to scare me to death, it did. Thought some fiend was there wanting to break in and murder us all in our beds. I 'bout had a seizure on the spot. Screamed so loud, the footmen all came running and Mr. Chorley even, and there I was in my nightclothes! I like to have died of embarrassment, Miss Hemsworth. Please, you can't go away and leave them two to their own devices. Why, when they were just nine and a half—"

The cook appeared ready to go on for hours describing in detail the twins' checkered pasts, so Anne attempted to fore-stall her. "I am sorry, Mrs. Stevens, but the matter is not for me to decide."

"—they hit on the idea of having a race, using Mr. Barrow's prize sows as their mounts. . . . "

"It had us all buffaloed, m'lord. Every time the wind was out of the northwest, it seemed as if the whole house was crying. Then the twins claimed they found a book in the library, which appeared to explain it. 'Twas all about how the first Marquess of Wylington had murdered his wife, and she was crying for revenge. I tell you, m'lord, the wailing was so unearthly, you'd ha' thought it was a dozen poor souls tormented in the fires of hell. Gave us the willies, it did, and several of us was thinking of handin' in our notice, so bad it was. It went on for weeks, with all of us ready to jump out of our skins, till the roofer came out from Tavistock to replace some slates that had come loose. He discovered someone had tied some pipes up to one of the chimneys in such a way that the wind would blow across them, like the way you can blow across a bottle."

Bronson looked at the footman, who appeared physically stalwart, but who was apparently easily spooked. "And you suspect the twins? I would not have thought they would be allowed out on the roof."

"But that's it. That's exactly what I've been telling you. 'Thout Miss Hemsworth, it ain't a question of what somebody allows the twins to do—them boys just do what they please and no one can stop them."

"Well, you need have no worries. I have decided to take over the day-to-day supervision of the twins myself."

The footman looked at him, opened his mouth as if to say something, then snapped it shut again. Rising to his feet, he left the room, shaking his head all the way.

Once the servant was gone, Bronson could not hold back his mirth. The twins had told him they were ingenious, but he had envisioned something more along the line of fixing buckets of water to fall on people's heads when they opened doors, or putting frogs in the maid's pockets, or snakes in the footmen's boots.

There was a light tap on the door, and Bronson wiped the smile from his face before calling out to whomever it was to come in. It was Chorley, the butler.

"Begging your pardon, m'lord, but I was hoping I might speak to you on Miss Hemsworth's behalf. You may perhaps be unaware of the fact that your wards are a trifle high-spirited."

If Bronson had been unaware of the extent of the twins' mischief before, he could definitely no longer claim ignorance as an excuse.

"It's not that I don't like the little marquess and his brother, whichever one is which, but it was rather upsetting last October when I discovered they'd taken apart the great clock."

"The clock?" Bronson hoped he was managing to keep his amusement from showing.

"The one that has always stood in the blue salon, m'lord, ever since your grandfather, God rest his soul, brought it back from France. No one is even allowed to wind it except me, but those two had not only taken it completely apart, but they had it halfway back together before anyone discovered what they were doing."

"The chickens was drunk, Miss Hemsworth. Them two devils had used one of my tubs to concoct a batch of home brew strong enough to knock your socks off," Kate the washerwoman explained to Anne.

"They said it was an excavation, m'lord, and they was going to find some Roman ruins. But it was nothin' more than a mammoth hole, m'lord. Took two of the undergard'ners three days to fill it in—"

Before the head gardener could continue, a groom pounded on the French doors, calling out frantically, "M'lord, m'lord, you got to come quick!"

Bronson opened the door just in time to hear a woman scream and men yelling. Rushing out into the courtyard, he saw a scullery maid point with horror at the roof of the east wing, before she fainted dead away.

Turning, he saw a sight that chilled his own blood.

One of the twins had climbed out an attic window onto the steep slate roof and had lost his footing. He was dangling from the eaves, and even while Bronson watched, he slipped a bit more.

Chapter Eight

YELLING AT THE BOY TO HANG ON, Bronson set off at a run, but before he had gone more than a few steps, the child lost his grip and fell, plummeting more than fifty feet to lie motionless on the paving stones.

Even though it was too late to help, Bronson did not check his headlong rush, hoping against hope that somehow the boy had survived the fall. In his heart, he knew there was no chance. Once before he had seen the sickening results of such a fall—in his mind's eye he could still see the mangled limbs, the blood, the contorted features, the sand—

The sand?

He looked down at the "corpse." There was no blood, only sand . . . and the remains of an old linen sheet, which had been stitched into a crude effigy and then dressed in an old suit of boy's clothing.

The servants who had followed Bronson now stood silently in a circle around the dummy, but they were not looking at the twins' handiwork; they were watching the twins' guardian to see what he would do.

Without a word he turned and entered the house by a side door, walking faster and faster through the maze of corridors. Taking the stairs two at a time, he wasted not a minute in getting to the schoolroom. He threw open the door and saw the twins sitting at their desks, apparently busily engaged with their lessons.

At the sound of his arrival, their heads turned in unison toward the door. "Have you persuaded Anne to stay?" one of them asked.

"Not yet," Bronson replied, unable to hold back a touch of admiration for their sangfroid even while he wished he were a proponent of corporal punishment.

"She hasn't left for London yet, has she?"

Bronson could hear the merest suggestion of anxiety in that twin's voice, and he had to remind himself that fiends though these boys might be on occasion, they were, in fact, still children. "No, she has not yet left."

"You might try clotted cream—"

"With strawberries."

She was a coward, there was no getting around it. Anne sat in the breakfast room listlessly stirring her cup of tea and postponing the moment she would have to say good-bye to the twins. She could already see the reproach in Andrew's eyes and the tears in Anthony's.

It was not as if she had long been a part of their lives; she had scarce been in Devon a month. So short a time really—a few weeks, no more. They would soon get over her, soon forget her—or so she had been trying to convince herself.

She was a coward and a hypocrite. If she were honest with herself, she would have to admit that time had nothing to do with the depth of emotion she felt for the boys, and she was sure they returned her love and affection in full measure. Her premature departure would destroy all the trust she had worked so hard to earn, and would negate all the lessons she had so cleverly interwoven with the fun.

But she had to leave Wylington Manor, had to leave Devon. She could not bear to stay under the same roof as Lord Least-in-Sight, that rake, that cad, that despoiler of women.

She was a coward and a hypocrite and a liar. No matter how hard she tried to pretend to herself, what she could not bear was the thought of never seeing Lord Leatham again.

Taking a sip of her tea, she found it stone-cold. Hardly surprising, since she had been sitting at the table for over an hour trying to stiffen her resolution.

The door opened, and she looked up, expecting to see one of the servants. Instead, Lord Leatham himself stood in the doorway. For a few moments she allowed herself the luxury of gazing at him, before she stood up to leave.

"Excuse me," she said. "I am finished with my packing and need only say my farewells to the twins."

"Sit down," he said curtly, striding over to the table.

"Please," he added in a more restrained voice when she remained standing.

She sat, and he took the seat opposite her.

"Since seven this morning I have been bombarded by tales of the twins' misbehavior. Every servant seems to have first-hand experience with their outrageous plots."

"They are very ingenious," Anne admitted. "I have also been hearing of their mischief. While I realize full well that they cannot be allowed to continue such activities, I still find it hard not to admire the cleverness that they have displayed."

Lord Leatham grimaced. "I have just discovered for myself that hearing about their pranks is not exactly the same as experiencing one first-hand."

"Oh, no, they did not—"

"Oh, yes, Miss Hemsworth, they did." In graphic detail Lord Leatham described what it was like to watch a "child" fall to his "death."

For the first time she noticed the ashen pallor of his countenance, and she realized he was, if anything, understating the horror and despair he had felt.

"I do hope, my lord, that you can dissuade the twins from doing such things in the future. They are truly not malicious. Perhaps if you explain to them—"

"Miss Hemsworth, do not be naive." Lord Leatham had regained his color nicely and now looked positively choleric. "The episode this morning was an object lesson in what I may expect if I allow you to resign your position. If you wish to give the boys the benefit of the doubt, you may call it a warning, but it was a threat, Miss Hemsworth, a *threat*. Do you understand threats?"

Anne looked across the table at the baron. He was glaring at her. "Are you threatening me, my lord?"

"No, Miss Hemsworth, I am not. I have been told that you are a woman of superior understanding, so you should recognize groveling when you see it."

She could not hold back a faint smile. The scowl on his face reminded her so much of the way the twins invariably looked when she told them it was time to put away their books and toys and make ready for bed. "Just so, my lord. You are groveling, and it was silly of me not to recognize it."

There was a light scratching at the door, and Lord Leatham went to open it. He returned bearing the largest bowl of strawberries and clotted cream that Anne had ever seen. It was more than enough to satisfy the appetites of at least five starving people.

"Here," he said, thumping it down on the table in front of her. "And this, in case you do not recognize it, is a bribe. And if that is not enough to persuade you, I shall also accept your challenge if you agree to stay."

"Challenge?"

"I shall endeavor to learn to tell which twin is which."

She had meant, almost from the first moment he appeared, to tell him she would stay, but apparently she hesitated too long with her answer. Before she could stop him, he was down on his knees beside her. A lock of his hair had fallen across his forehead, and she wanted nothing more than to brush it back into place.

"Well, Miss Hemsworth, you have brought me to my knees. I hope you are satisfied. You may name your price."

The first thought that popped into her head was the line from the fairy story: I want your firstborn son.

But Lord Leatham already had a son; she had seen the boy in Tavistock with his mother.

No longer feeling the slightest urge to smile, Anne said simply, "Very well, then, I shall stay until the end of the summer."

Lord Leatham rose with alacrity to his feet and brushed off his unmentionables, which were fawn-colored and fit very well over his muscular legs.

"I shall hold you to that, Miss Hemsworth. And now that the matter is settled, do not think that I shall allow you to play the role of fickle female all summer, blowing now hot and now cold. The matter is settled, once and for all."

With effort Anne pulled her attention off her contemplation of the baron's lower limbs. "I give you my word, my lord," she said, standing up and laying her napkin neatly on the table.

"And is your word good?"

Anne looked at him in disbelief. Surely he could not have said such an insulting thing? But he had, and now waited impatiently for an answer.

"If I were a man, I would call you out for such an insult."

"If you were a man, I would not question your word."

"And since you are a man, I would be a fool to put my reliance on anything you promised."

He now looked as angry as she felt. She could barely keep from screaming imprecations at him, and he looked as if he wanted nothing more than to throttle her.

"I assume that since I have now so *insulted* you, you shall fall back on your sex's favorite prerogative and change your mind about staying." His voice was laced with contempt.

"No, my lord," she responded in kind, "I shall not change my mind. In fact, there is nothing you can do now that will persuade me to leave the boys alone in the care of a man like you."

He started to say something more, but then he paused, and a slow smile spread over his face. "I shall hold you to that also, Miss Hemsworth."

An hour later there was a loud rapping at Anne's door, which she assumed must be the footman she had requested to come and fetch her again empty portmanteau and return it to storage. She was therefore caught off guard when she opened the door and found three lords smiling at her.

Lord Wylington and Lord Anthony had their usual angelic smiles. Lord Leatham's smile was more . . . devilish.

"Good morning, Anne, we were hoping—" Anthony said.

"We could ride over to Thorverton Hall—" Andrew continued.

"So that I can be introduced to the newest colts and fillies," Lord Leatham finished.

"Yes, of course you may ride over there. But do not stay too long. I shall expect you back here in time for lunch."

Three lords slowly shook their heads in unison.

"Only an hour ago you swore that you were never going to

leave the twins alone with me," Lord Leatham said in a silky voice. "You were not planning to break your vow so quickly, were you?"

Anne looked desperately at the twins for help, but they were openly grinning now. However had she, the very model of a clear-thinking, rational being, who remained calm no matter what the crisis, allowed her tongue to betray her into such a predicament?

"Well, Miss Hemsworth? Have you reached a decision?"

Declining to give him the satisfaction of hearing her object, she merely said, "I must change into my riding habit. I shall be ready in half an hour." Then she shut the bedroom door in Lord Leatham's face and leaned weakly against the cream-colored panels.

The two remaining months of summer stretched before her like an eternity—like a prison sentence to be endured, rather than an enjoyable interlude.

Then adjuring herself to show a little more gumption, she resolutely pushed herself away from the door, straightened her shoulders, and firmly resolved to win this battle of nerves with the arrogant Lord Least-in-Sight.

She was pulling on the heavy blue velvet skirt of her riding habit when it occurred to her that she would have to find a better nickname for Lord Leatham, since he had apparently decided to reverse his role and become Lord Always-Underfoot.

He would lose interest soon, she reassured herself while buttoning her jacket. As he himself had virtually admitted, the twins were not yet of an age to be of interest to an adult male, especially a man like Lord Leatham, who had traveled all over the world.

Sheer boredom would have him packing his bags within a week, two weeks at the most.

Anne looked in the mirror and then adjusted her hat at a more jaunty angle. In the meantime, as long as the arrogant baron was going to be underfoot, perhaps she could teach him a lesson or two about the dangers of underestimating the female of the species. Lord Leatham was considerably older than her usual pupils, she had to admit, but that would just make him more of a challenge. And she did relish a challenge.

With a smile of anticipation, she picked up her riding gloves and set out to meet her two—no, her three pupils.

Creighton stood at his window and watched the party ride away toward Thorverton Hall. The hoity-toity governess, who had acted as if she was too good for him, was now giving all her smiles to Leatham, that insufferable, conceited, arrogant baron.

Well, they were both going to receive their comeuppance— if not together, then separately. And there was a certain justice about it that made him smile.

The only problem with his plan, and it had been a serious flaw, was the probability that Leatham would run true to form and leave Devon after only a day or so. He, Creighton, had been racking his brain trying to think of a way to delay the baron's departure, but had come up with nothing.

Now, just when it had seemed that failure was inevitable, Leatham had announced he was staying at Wylington Manor for at least two months, and according to the servants, it was all because of the charms of the governess.

Apparently Leatham was expecting to enjoy a pleasant summmer dalliance with her, and it would appear she was not adverse to his advances.

Creighton's lips curled in a sneer. She might pretend to be a lady and above such things, but in the final analysis she could be bought with enough money.

Well, before the summer was over, he, Creighton, would be the one in charge at Wylington Manor—really in charge, and not just nominally in charge. And Miss Hemsworth, like all females of her ilk, would change her tune quickly enough when she saw which way the wind was blowing.

"How do you suppose they did it?" Bronson kept his horse at a steady trot beside the governess, while the twins rode a little ahead.

"How did they do what?" Miss Hemsworth turned her beautiful blue eyes toward him, a puzzled expression on her face.

"I can understand how the twins could use a rope to suspend

the dummy from the roof, but how did they make it fall at the appropriate time? Neither boy was visible anywhere near the effigy, so how did they manage to untie the rope?''

She smiled, and to Bronson it seemed that the sun had come out, even though the sky was still overcast. "They undoubtedly made an eye splice in the end of the rope and held it in place around the dummy with a toggle. Then when they jerked on the cord attached to the toggle, it would instantly release the rope. Last week I taught the boys splices and knots, you see.''

She began to laugh, and he felt his newly discovered temper start to flare.

"I am afraid I do not find it as amusing as you do.''

"No, no," she said. "I was not laughing about the trick with the dummy. It just occurred to me that this week we have been studying electricity.''

Bronson gave an involuntary jerk on the reins, causing his horse to rear. He quickly brought it back under control, to the obvious amusement of his riding companion. "Miss Hemsworth, has it occurred to you that it would be safer by far to limit your instruction to less dangerous subjects? Nature study, perhaps?''

"Oh, but we have not been neglecting that at all. We have started studying anatomy, for example.''

Bronson leaned over and caught the reins of her horse, pulling it to a stop. He was now so close to her, his leg brushed against her skirt. "Miss Hemsworth, I want to make myself very clear. It has never been my wish to arise some morning and discover that someone has raided the family vault to find specimens for anatomical study.''

The warmth had vanished from her voice and the laughter from her eyes when she answered him. "We have conducted very scientific dissections of a toad and a rabbit, my lord. I have not turned the boys into grave robbers. The twins have the finest minds of anyone I have ever met, coupled with a curiosity and a thirst for knowledge that is rarely found in anyone, old or young. It would appear that their former governesses were not the only ones who have underestimated their intelligence. You may decide to limit their education to memorizing Latin verbs,

my lord, and you may order me to avoid certain 'dangerous'
subjects, and you may even censor their reading and burn their
books, but your efforts will be in vain. They will learn, whether
you wish it or not.''

With that, she jerked her reins free from his grasp, and kicking
her horse into a gallop, she set off after the twins.

Blast that woman! He had no intention of censoring the boys'
reading material. All he was interested in was a little discretion
as to subject matter, a little enlightened self-interest, a little
. . . self-preservation. Suppose the boys decided they were
interested in learning how to make gunpowder—was she in
favor of helping them mix the saltpeter and charcoal?

Really, her arguments were nothing more than rationaliza-
tion, and so he would point out to her the next time he had a
moment alone with her.

He would also make it clear that running away from any
debate without giving one's opponent the opportunity for a
rebuttal was a cowardly thing to do—no, a *womanly* thing to
do. He smiled to himself when he considered what her reaction
would be if he accused her of arguing like a typical female.

Setting his horse to a gallop, he rapidly overtook the other
three riders. She did sit a horse well, he had to admit. The old
groom, Patrick, had been right about that. It was too bad she
could not control her temper and her tongue as well as she
controlled her mount.

She was, in fact, decidedly prickly, like a little hedgehog.
No, she was more like a mother hen, puffing up her feathers
at the least threat of danger to her two little chicks.

What would it be like to unruffle her feathers? To soothe away
her prickles? To give her further instructions in the gentle art
of kissing?

The rest of the way to Thorverton Hall he pushed out of his
mind all the serious subjects that had been occupying his
thoughts for the last several years, and allowed himself instead
to enjoy the familiar rolling hills of the moor, the cool breeze
in his face, and the feel of a good horse beneath him.

But most of all he found delight in observing Miss Hemsworth. Everything about her was perfection, from her straight

back to the way she held the reins, from the curve of her neck to the tilt of her chin.

He remembered also the frank appraisal she had given him in Tavistock . . . the way her lips had felt when he had kissed her . . . the swell of her hips when he had put his hands on her waist . . . the sigh she had uttered when he had kissed her on the ear. . . .

Even the way she had scolded him for his supposed neglect of the twins now seemed endearing instead of aggravating.

With a little patience on his part, he could win her trust. He could teach her to respect men, rather than to berate them. It would be a challenge, but before the summer was over, she would call him by his first name, rather than "my lord," and she would smile at him the way she smiled at the twins.

Arriving at Thorverton Hall, they bypassed the house and went directly to the stable block, where Lawrence Mallory came out to meet them.

"Morning, Leatham. Heard you were back. We were hoping you would manage to visit before you take off on your travels again. Demetrius just went up to the house, but I shall let him know you are here. Collier is around somewhere."

A gangling youth came dashing full tilt into the courtyard, and with shouts of glee, the twins scrambled off their horses and ran to meet him. Bronson realized with a shock that it was Collier. The little brother who had tagged along behind Demetrius was no longer little.

Had so many years really passed since Bronson had been at Thorverton Hall? For a moment he had the disconcerting feeling that Miss Hemsworth was correct, that he had not spent enough time recently in Devon.

He dismounted and went to help Miss Hemsworth, but Mallory was before him.

Bronson froze in his tracks, overcome with a burning rage at the sight of the other man's hands on Miss Hemsworth's waist.

"I tried that poultice you recommended, Anne, and it seems to be more efficacious than the one we had been using. Our only problem is that Daisy keeps trying to eat it."

"I warned you about that, Lawrence. And how is Dolly's fine son doing?" Without a backward look, the two of them strode off toward the row of stalls, calmly discussing horses.

Bronson could not believe what he was seeing. Miss Hemsworth, the man-hater, the radical feminist—Miss Hemsworth, who talked back, who argued, who criticized—Miss Hemsworth was being nothing but charming.

She was not berating Mallory or ordering him around; she was not tossing challenges in his face or upbraiding him for his supposed shortcomings.

Irrationally, what rankled the most was that she called Mallory by his first name, and at the same time allowed him to call her Anne. That was a privilege he, Bronson, desired above all else, and that it should have been granted to another man made him angry—no, it was not strictly anger he felt, but jealousy.

That hitherto unknown emotion now twisted his insides painfully; the strength of it made him feel weak.

"Ah, Leatham, I did not expect to see you again so soon. As you can see, I made good my escape from London and the matrimonial trap."

Bronson turned to see Demetrius approaching him. With effort he managed to act is if everything were normal. "Have you heard anything from the fair Diana?"

"Not directly, but her father wrote me a civil letter, apologizing for the 'inconvenience' I had been put to. And via my Uncle Humphrey I have heard that it is generally accepted that my heart is broken, and that I will never again look at another woman. And speaking of women, is that Anne's horse? Did she come with you?"

At the sound of Anne's name on still another man's lips, Bronson felt such a surge of jealousy that if he'd had an epée in his hand, he would have driven it through his friend's heart.

Creighton Trussell crouched on the little balcony, spying on the party of four seated below him on the terrace behind Wylington Manor.

He ground his teeth in rage at their failure to cooperate with him. Since the day after Leatham's arrival, the baron had never

THREE LORDS FOR LADY ANNE   137

left the twins' side except at night, when the boys were tucked in bed in the nursery.

It was almost as if he were deliberately doing his best to foil Creighton's plan.

But wait—Leatham was standing up. Now he was turning and walking toward the house. He was leaving the others. The moment was at hand.

Creighton fumbled in his pocket, the gun he had been forced to carry loaded for the last three days tangling itself in the fabric of his jacket.

Leatham disappeared from view below the balcony just as Creighton managed to extract the gun. With shaking hands, he pointed it through a small, round opening in the stone balustrade and aimed it in the general direction of the twins.

Shutting both his eyes, he pulled the trigger.

Chapter Nine

BRONSON HAD BARELY SEATED himself at his desk and picked up the first letter addressed to him when he heard a shot fired outside, followed immediately by a woman's scream.

Dear Lord, Anne—

Leaping to his feet he dashed back out onto the terrace, to be met by a scene of utter confusion and chaos. In the center of the broken crockery and spilled tea cakes, one of the maids lay lifeless on the ground. Miss Hemsworth and the twins were already at her side.

"Where was she hit?" Bronson asked, shoving one of the boys aside and kneeling by the stricken woman, checking her quickly for signs of blood.

"I do not believe she was, my lord," Miss Hemsworth replied calmly. "The bullet shattered the teapot on the table, which startled her so she screamed and fainted. In falling, she struck her head on one of the flagstones and has rendered herself quite senseless."

Other servants came running up, and Bronson instructed two of the footmen to carry the unfortunate maid back into the house. Then he turned his mind to the question of who had fired the shot . . . and at whom.

Wyke laid a carefully folded shirt in the proper drawer and picked up a pair of his master's boots that needed cleaning. Hearing someone enter the adjoining bedroom, he put the boots aside for later attention and went to see if his services were required.

The sight that met his eyes astounded him, but he managed to maintain an impassive mien. Trussell stood there, his back against the door, gasping for breath, his cravat in disarray and his coat mussed . . . and in his hand was a pistol.

Upon catching sight of his valet, Trussell gave a little shriek and dropped the pistol.

Whatever Wyke had suspected his master of plotting, it had nothing to do with guns. On the other hand, when opportunity knocked, as his dear mum had always said. . . .

Without losing his dignity, he approached the shaken man and bent and picked up the pistol from the floor. One whiff, and he knew it had been recently fired.

"You had better tell me what you have been doing," he said matter-of-factly, sliding the gun into his pocket.

His calm acceptance of the situation had its effect on Trussell, who stood up, smoothed his hair with one hand, straightened his jacket, and said, "I merely fired a shot at the twins."

Merely? thought Wyke. That was an understatement if he ever heard one. "To what end?" he asked.

"As you know, I have been a trifle short of funds recently, so I have come up with a plan to cast suspicion on Lord Leatham, so that—" here Trussell paused to catch his breath, "—so that I will be appointed guardian of the twins in his stead."

Wyke did not need any more explanation. The advantages that would accrue to Trussell and through Trussell to himself were obvious.

What was also obvious, was that as a conspirator Trussell was hopelessly inept. There was not a minute to be lost if this scheme had any chance of succeeding. Although he had not intended to become directly involved in Trussell's plotting, he had to take an active part now or Trussell's part in the shooting would be discovered, and all chance for later blackmail would be lost.

"Quickly, sir." Wyke grabbed his master and spun him around, then ruthlessly ripped the jacket off his back. Shoving the unresisting gentleman down into a chair, the valet wrapped a towel around his neck, picked up the shaving mug, and in minutes had slathered shaving soap all over the lower half of Trussell's face.

"What on earth—"

"Don't speak, sir, just do as I tell you. We must be sure to divert suspicion from you."

Trussell blanched, but made no further effort to resist or question what his valet was doing.

Using the back of the razor, Wyke quickly wiped most of the soapsuds from his master's face, then pulled him to his feet. "Hurry, go out and join the others on the terrace, quick, before they come looking for you."

"In my shirtsleeves?"

"Yes, of course in your shirtsleeves, now hurry—run, tell them you heard the shot."

"Oh, yes, of course, how clever of you." Trussell departed, if not at a run, then at least more briskly than usual.

Now the only remaining problem was the gun. Wyke took it out and inspected it. A dueling pistol, and quite expensive by the looks of it. He could only hope that Trussell had been smart enough not to use one he had purchased himself.

Shoving it into his pocket, Wyke cautiously opened the door to the hallway and checked to be sure he was not being observed. Then, as if he had not a care in the world, he sauntered casually toward the stairs.

When he reached Lord Leatham's study, he tapped gently on the door once, then a little louder the second time. Receiving no answer, he opened the door and peered cautiously inside. Empty. Perfect for his plan.

Hugging the edges of the room so that he could not be seen through the French doors by anyone looking in from outside, he circled the room. Then standing concealed behind the curtains, he took the pistol and carefully tossed it through the open doors and into one of the bushes.

That accomplished, he made haste to retrace his steps, emerging at last into the safety of the corridor. His heart was pounding but all his senses were alert.

A few minutes later he was out on the terrace mingling inconspicuously with the majority of the other servants, who were all preoccupied with the broken crockery and singulary uninterested in what should be their most important task, namely finding the gun.

He could not simply tell them to go look in the bushes, nor would it suit his plans to find the gun himself. For a moment he was stymied, but then he decided to try setting them an example, in hopes that they would follow his lead.

Deliberately picking the wrong bushes to look in, he made a great show of pushing branches aside, all the while being careful not to catch his sleeves on any twigs.

"And what do you think you're doing?"

Wyke turned to see Muggs, one of the grooms who had vastly more brawn than brain, glaring suspiciously at him. The perfect unsuspecting helper.

"It occurred to me that whoever fired the shot might have disposed of the gun by throwing it into the bushes."

It took a moment for that thought to penetrate the thick head of the groom, but then he reacted just as Wyke had hoped.

"Hey, Patrick, Will, Harry, the rest of you. Come help me look for the gun. 'Tis prob'ly in these bushes somewhere."

Quite casually, Wyke moved away from the area of the search, and he was standing next to his master when one of the young grooms called out, "Here it is. I found the gun."

"But that cannot—" Trussell started to say, but Wyke grabbed the towel around his master's neck and under the pretext of wiping the rest of the shaving soap from his face, managed to muffle whatever the idiot was about to say.

"People are talking, Leatham. I thought it best I ride over and tell you what is being said." Thorverton looked down at the glass of brandy in his hand, then continued. "They are saying you are the one who fired the shot."

"That is preposterous." Bronson paced his study, so angry he wanted to smash everything in sight. "I would never hurt anyone, least of all those boys."

"I believe you, and anyone who knows you would never suspect you of such a dastardly deed, but there are those in the neighborhood who do not know you except as a tall stranger who appears briefly and then vanishes just as quickly. They are the ones who are whispering that you have the most to gain if the twins meet with a fatal accident. Unfortunately, it is not only servants and tradesmen who are ready to believe the worst of you, but also some of the more socially prominent citizens.

It is unfortunate that your travels have kept you from becoming really well known in the district, or the gossip would never have spread to this extent."

"I see. So because I do not stay at home in Devon paying polite social calls, I am suspected of attempted murder? Pshaw!"

"You may scoff, but there are many who see nothing strange in the idea of a man murdering two children in cold blood so that he might inherit a title and a vast estate."

"I have a title and an estate already."

"But people are saying you are not satisfied with being the second Baron Leatham, that you wish to be the sixth Marquess of Wylington."

"That is total nonsense. However you look at it, such suspicions are not rational."

"But then, so few people are rational. I believe it is their own greed that makes them so willing to believe the worst of their fellow man. And you must not forget, you not only have a motive—"

"I have no motive," Bronson bellowed, releasing some of his aggressions by smashing a rose-colored vase off a little octagonal table with one swipe of his hand. He looked down at the shards on the rug and said in a shaken voice, "And besides, I am not prone to violence."

His friend glanced at him with sympathy, then continued calmly, "You do not only *appear* to have a legitimate motive, but the gun was proved to be one of the set of dueling pistols belonging to you—"

"Which I keep in my bedroom, the door to which is unlocked, so that anyone might have taken it at any time—"

"And the shot came from the general area of the house where you were known to be at the time it was fired."

The room was silent while Bronson continued to pace. Then he threw himself down in the chair next to his friend. "I am in the devil of a dilemma, is what you are saying. So what do you suggest I do about it?"

"I assume you have tried to discover who really fired the shot?"

"Of course. Everyone has an alibi, but they are all equally

unsubstantiated. Not only that, but no one else has a motive, however flimsy."

"There I would beg to differ with you. From the tales I have heard at the Red Stag, the twins have played some rather wild pranks on people. Perhaps a disgruntled servant?"

Bronson grimaced. "As strange as it may seem to an outsider, in spite of being the target of the twins' tricks, the servants all appear to have a genuine fondness for the boys. It would not surprise me at all if over their pints of ale they were actually bragging about the twins' ingenuity."

"But it would only require one servant who nursed a grudge . . ."

"Dear Lord."

"Have you thought of someone?"

"Yes—no—that is to say, no one connected with this affair. Just someone who is even now at the Red Stag waiting to hear from me—and who probably thinks I have forgotten all about her."

"Her?" A slow smile spread over Thorverton's face. "You have imported a female friend? You, who have no interest in women, or so you informed me not long ago in London."

"She is Trussell's discarded mistress," Bronson said flatly. "And the mother of his son. And the boy looks enough like the twins to be their brother, so there is no doubt that she is telling the truth."

Thorverton whistled. "That puts a different complexion on things. Although I fail to understand why it is up to you to settle Trussell's obligations."

"There is no obligation on my part, but I cannot help feeling sympathy for the poor woman. She is gently born and the daughter of a vicar, who of course set an example of proper Christian mercy by throwing her out of his house when he learned she was increasing. In any event, she is not asking for money from me. I merely promised I would try to find her a position. She has been supporting herself until now as a cook, but her former employer is deceased, leaving her with no references. You would not happen to know of anyone needing a cook, would you?"

"Who me? I could find positions for any number of grooms and stable lads among my acquaintances, but most of them care more about their horses' feed than about what they put in their own stomachs."

"You could have your mother ask around."

"Are you mad? To begin with, my mother is too self-centered to lift a finger to help anyone but herself. Secondly, the gossip about you is bad enough without adding to it. If it were to become known that you are involving yourself in this woman's affairs, everyone will assume that you are the father of the boy."

"I suppose this is not the time to tell you that I am paying her shot at the Red Stag?"

To Bronson's surprise, Thorverton began to laugh. "Oh, my, such an innocent you are, Leatham. How could you be so ignorant of the perils and pitfalls of society? You, of all the men I know, most need a wife to look after you. But since you are determined to remain a bachelor, I suggest you ask Anne for advice. You hired her through some employment agency in London, did you not? She is bound to have some connections who can help find a position for the poor woman."

Ask Miss Hemsworth? She was the last person Bronson would turn to. She had already judged him once and found him guilty of neglecting the twins. No, this was a matter to be handled privately by men. He would do what he should have done right from the first day, and ask his valet. Daws would know what to do.

"It is working. My plan is working beautifully."

Trussell was almost prancing around his bedroom in glee, as if he were responsible for the success of the fake assassination attempt instead of Wyke. The valet did not, however, bother to point out to his master who it was that had snatched victory out of defeat. It would not suit his purpose, namely blackmail at some future date, to emphasize that he, Wyke, was equally guilty as an accomplice after the fact.

"Now, then, Wyke, we must not let any grass grow under our feet. We must strike while the iron is hot, move to consolidate our position."

Merciful heavens, his master was truly dicked in the nob.

After their previous narrow escape, was he actually plotting fresh mischief?

"The first thing we are going to need for my new plan is ether, which I managed to procure in Tavistock yesterday." Trussell pulled a blue bottle out of his pocket and held it up proudly.

Ecod, the man was clearly insane. Wyke cast around wildly in his mind for a way to stop the fool before they both ended up swinging from Tyborn.

The widow. Yes, it was time to summon the wealthy widow to Devon. She could distract Trussell from any further scheming. He would be so busy trying to defend himself from her determined advances, he would have no time for plotting another disaster.

"I don't know, m'lord. It is a rare employer who will hire a woman with a child." Daws was showing a marked reluctance to come up with a solution to the problem of Martha Miller.

"She does not have to admit she is unmarried. She could say she is a widow," Bronson pointed out.

" 'Tis the child what is the problem, not the ring on her finger. Most rich folks don't want someone else's brat in their house, making noise and tracking in dirt. The only thing to do that I see is just hire her yourself."

"Hah! What a wonderful idea. I should bring her to Wylington Manor, where no one would dream of linking my name with hers. Really, Daws, I expected better from you."

His valet cast him an affronted look. "I said nothing about bringing her here. I was suggesting you hire her as cook at your *own* residence in Sidmouth. It is far enough away that no one would think to connect her with you—other than as an employee, of course."

"My residence?" It had been so many years since Bronson was in Sidmouth, he had almost forgotten he still owned a town house there.

"Not that you need a cook since you're never there, but it would be a fine place for a boy to grow up, so near the sea and all. And Mrs. Uglow, your housekeeper, is not a woman who would judge another person harshly. She has a goodly amount of true Christian charity.''

"I shall have to take your word for that." Bronson thought for a minute or two, but could find no flaw in his valet's proposal. "Very well, I shall do it." He quickly gave Daws directions for finding Martha Miller and escorting her and her son to Sidmouth.

Relieved to have that chore off his mind, he went to find the twins and Miss Hemsworth, secure in the knowledge that he had stopped any potential gossip.

Mrs. Pierce-Smythe sat propped up in bed sipping her morning chocolate and sorting listlessly through her mail. Nothing but tradesmen's accounts—no *billet-doux* from any cicisbeo, no gilt-edged invitation to attend any of the last-minute festivities being squeezed in before the end of the Season.

Toward the bottom of the stack, however, one envelope stood out from the others and caught her attention. Opening it, she scanned the short message quickly, then she rang for her maid. Tapping the letter against the fingers of her other hand, she contemplated this new information. Then a slow smile spread across her face.

"Zizette," she said when her maid finally appeared, "start packing immediately. We are leaving for Devon *tout de suite.*"

"*Oui, madame.*"

"And send John Coachman to me, also. I have something to discuss with him concerning the trip."

"*Comme vous voulez, madame,*" the maid replied, but she later told the cook, "She's at it again. Got 'er sights set on another titled gen'leman, the old bag does. She oughter be ashamed, at 'er age. Still an' all, I ain't never seen Devon yet. Per'aps I'll find me a rich young smuggler there, who'll give me a silk dress and a ring on my finger, you never know."

"There, now if you connect those two stars in Ursa Major and extend the imaginary line beyond them, you will come to a particularly bright star, and that is the North Star." Anne was lying on her back in the grass on a little hillock near Wylington

Manor, and her three companions were likewise horizontal, all four of their heads virtually touching and their bodies angled out like points on a compass. "Do you see the one I mean?" She pointed up at the starry heavens.

"I think so," one of the twins replied.

"I am almost positive I know which one it is," his brother remarked.

"If you are navigating a ship," Lord Leatham said in his deep voice, "you must do more than be almost positive, else you will likely run your ship aground on a reef. If you are interested in learning more, I have some star maps inside somewhere that you are welcome to study, and your father used to have a telescope, although I have not seen it for years."

One of the twins said, "We know where to find it."

There was a long silence after that remark, and Anne stifled a laugh. One thing she was thankful for: In the last few days Lord Leatham had learned not to question the boys too closely as to how they had acquired various bits and pieces of information. Ignorance, he had discovered, was more conducive to sound sleep, or so he had informed her privately.

"Look at the moon," one of the boys said. "It seems so close, as if we could reach out and touch it."

"Or go there," his brother added.

"Do you suppose if someone made a balloon big enough, he could float up to the moon?"

"Perhaps," the other twin allowed, "but it'd probably be better to use rockets."

"Rockets?" There was a note of incipient panic in Lord Leatham's voice.

Anne decided it was time to intervene. "Scientists say it is about two hundred and forty thousand miles to the moon. So at the rate of twenty miles per hour—"

"Which is about the fastest a human being has ever traveled—" Lord Leatham picked up on her cue.

"How long would it take to get to the moon?" she asked.

The boys mumbled to themselves for a minute, then one of them said, "About five hundred days."

"Plus another five hundred to get back," Anne pointed out.

"And no posting houses along the way," Lord Leatham

added. "Which means you would have to take all your food along with you."

"And water," Anne said.

There was a long silence while the boys contemplated this. "That's over three years," one of them said finally. "That's a long time."

"Speaking of time, it is now well past your bedtime." As much as she was enjoying the evening and the pleasant companionship, Anne knew she must not neglect her responsibilities as governess.

"Do you suppose, Uncle Bronson, that maybe tomorrow night, if we find the telescope—" One of the boys got up, his head tilted back, his gaze still on the heavens.

"And if it's not raining or too cloudy—" The other boy scrambled to his feet also.

"Maybe we could all come out here again—"

"And *look* at the moon. Please, Uncle Bronson?"

"I should like that, too," Anne admitted. "I have never seen the moon through a telescope."

Lord Leatham stood up and looked down at her. "What is this, Miss Hemsworth? Have we finally found some area where your knowledge is deficient?"

Feeling decidedly uncomfortable lying flat on her back while he was looming over her, Anne sat up. Lord Leatham reached down to assist her in getting to her feet, and the feel of his hand holding hers only increased her agitation. "I am sure I am not half as experienced as you are."

Realizing abruptly that her remark could be taken more than one way, she quickly attempted to clarify it. "That is to say, in your travels around the world, I am sure you have had many novel experiences."

"To be sure, Miss Hemsworth, undoubtedly you are correct in your assumption that I am more experienced than you are."

His words were conventionally polite and his voice sounded normal, but she was still left with the unsettling feeling that she had amused him. She looked up at his face, but since his back was to the moon, there was not enough light to see if he was smiling.

He further surprised her, however, by tucking her arm into his and escorting her down the hill. She started to point out to him that she was just as capable of descending a hill unaided as descending a ladder, but that only brought to mind what had happened in the library the last time she had refused his assistance. Somehow ladders and kissing seemed to have become indelibly linked in her mind.

On the other hand, she rationalized, although his assistance was not necessary, since she was hardly in danger of tumbling down the hill, it was indeed pleasant—in a companionable way, of course—to walk arm and arm with a man, or rather with a friend, she corrected herself quickly.

The boys ran helter-skelter down the slope ahead of them and vanished into the house, and she realized with dismay that she was alone with the baron. In the dark. With no one around to observe them—no one to overhear what they might say—except, if she would be honest with herself, what she was feeling was not exactly dismay.

Her heart began to race unaccountably fast, and she wondered if he could feel her pulse pounding in her wrist.

"I have succeeded in meeting the challenge you offered me, Miss Hemsworth," he said, his voice low enough that the boys would not have heard even if they had still been close by.

"Challenge?" For a moment she could not think what he was talking about.

"I can now tell which twin is which."

"Oh?" was all that she could think of to say. She felt vaguely disappointed that his thoughts were on such mundane matters.

"If you would like to test me?"

"That will not be necessary," she began, but he interrupted.

"Oh, but I insist on proving myself. I would not want you later to be able to throw it in my face that I have merely pretended to know."

Her indignation was instant, and she tried to retrieve her hand from his arm, but he refused to release it.

"No, Miss Hemsworth, you must strive not to be so overly sensitive. I meant no insult. I think, on the contrary, that I said what I did, not because I doubt your word, but only because

I wish to show off for you, and here you are trying to deny me that pleasure.''

"I would not wish to deny you pleasure, my lord," she blurted out without thinking. Then feeling herself blush, she looked up at his face, which was now well illuminated by the light coming from the windows.

It was as she had feared. He was smiling down at her. For the first time in her life, she wished her Aunt Sidonia had taught her some of the more normal female accomplishments—such as the proper way to conduct a casual flirtation with a man.

Lord Leatham made no effort to take advantage of her unfortunate choice of words, and for that she could only be grateful. When they reached the entrance to the house, he released her hand, and there was nothing improper in the way he held the door open for her and escorted her up the stairs. Irrational as she knew she was being, she could not bring herself to be thankful that he was staying within the bounds of propriety.

She was, in fact, still having a hard time keeping her mind off the subject of kissing. It was only with the greatest effort that she was able to avoid staring at his mouth.

Not that she was interested in him romantically, of course, since she did not have a romantic disposition. It was only that she did have a streak of scientific curiosity as strong as that of the twins, and this was one area of study where her education was woefully deficient.

As had become their custom during the last few days, Lord Leatham accompanied her to the nursery to tuck in the boys. After they were settled down, he told them the story of one of his adventures, this time an amusing episode that had occurred during the course of a long sea voyage.

Anne had to struggle to keep from smiling at the number of times he managed to call the twins by name—each time the right name with the right boy, of course. On the way back down the stairs, she congratulated him.

"You concede I have won the wager?"

"Indeed, my lord, you are a quick study."

"I only regret that we did not set any forfeit. But I am sure you will be a gracious loser and join me in the library for a drink to help me celebrate my victory. It is the least you can do," he added when she hesitated.

Even realizing the danger she was putting herself into, she could not resist the opportunity to banter with him. "No, my lord, it is the *most* I shall do."

"Touché, Miss Hemsworth." He smiled and held the door of the library open for her, allowing her to enter first.

We are only going to share one drink, she tried to convince herself. He is definitely not going to kiss me again.

Ignoring the settee as too dangerous, she seated herself in a wing-backed chair a little apart from the others and watched him pour from a cut-glass decanter. The room was shadowed, the night seemed hushed, and if she did not have a practical nature, she would say it was a very romantic setting—the leathery smell of the many books, the few candles like tiny stars, two goblets of ruby-red wine. . . .

"Here you are, Miss Hemsworth." He held her drink out to her.

And she must not forget her companion, she thought, because the gentleman was, after all, the most important element in any romantic scene. In this particular case, any lady would be satisfied to have such a tall, handsome, charming lord at her side. The mood was such that Anne was even able to put out of her mind, at least for the moment, how aggravating and arrogant Lord Leatham could be.

What she could not forget, unfortunately, was that he was her employer. And she was not a dainty, helpless, romantic heroine in a novel by Mrs. Radcliff; she was only the governess.

Taking the wine he was offering her, Anne breathed in its heady perfume and sampled the bouquet, but she did not find it the least bit intoxicating.

She was, after all, a most practical, very sensible, completely reliable, extremely resourceful, and always much-in-demand governess, but still and all—no, she was not the least bit romantically inclined.

"I have a problem, Miss Hemsworth, and I would like your advice."

Anne looked up into dark, intense eyes.

"I am trying to think of something to say that will get your hackles up, some remark guaranteed to put you in a taking. Perhaps you can suggest something suitably enraging."

"You wish to pick a quarrel with me, my lord? To what purpose?" Surely he did not prefer squabbling to this peaceful equanimity of spirit.

"Because, Miss Hemsworth, you are sitting there in isolated splendor, which makes it deuced hard for me to kiss you. If I can make you angry enough, you are sure to leap to your feet, which will make it so much easier for me to take you in my arms. But maybe I am making things more complicated than necessary. Perhaps all that is needed is a simple request."

He took the goblet from her now nerveless fingers and set it down on the table beside the chair, then held out his hand to her in silent invitation.

Still in shock, she stared up at him. "But why on earth would you want—" She stopped, so embarrassed she could feel the heat rise to her face.

"To kiss you?" He finished the question for her. "When I have undoubtedly kissed so many women during the course of my travels around the world? Is that what you were going to ask?"

"You go too far, my lord," she said angrily, "and I have no intention of sitting here and discussing kissing with you."

She stood up with the sole intention of leaving the room, but he stopped her with the lightest touch of his hand to her cheek. She willed her feet to move, to carry her away from him, but they remained obstinately still, as if rooted to the floor.

"And I have no intention of discussing kissing, either," he said with soft laughter in his voice. "No matter how adept the poet, the pleasure of a kiss is not to be found in words, but in the deed itself."

He stood too close, yet even while she watched, he leaned perceptibly closer. Her mind shrieked at her to flee while she still had the opportunity, but her heart pleaded with her to stay . . . just a little while . . . only long enough . . .

Both his hands now cradled her face, and she knew she should make some protest. Then his fingers slid around to caress her neck, and her eyes slowly drifted shut of their own accord. It had to be the sip of wine she had taken that was making her feel so light-headed. "This is conduct unbecoming a governess," she murmured. "I shall undoubtedly lose my position."

"Shhhh," he whispered. "You will find that your employer is very lenient in such matters."

His lips brushed softly against hers, and her knees weakened even more than when he had kissed her ear. She had not even enough strength to resist when he pulled her into his arms and held her with her head pressed against his chest. His heart was pounding loudly beneath her ear—

No, someone was pounding on the door. "My lord," she said faintly, "I do believe someone is trying to get your attention."

Lord Leatham added to her education by uttering a very colorful phrase, but then with a sigh, he released her and went to the door.

Without his support, her knees gave way and she sat back down with a plop in the chair he had so recently teased her out of.

Indeed, it would appear that Lord Leatham had been correct when he had warned her of the perils lurking in scientific experiments. Kissing would appear to be even more dangerous than rockets.

The low sound of voices reached her from the hallway, but she paid them no mind until one voice stood out quite clearly—a distinctive voice she recognized but could not believe she was hearing.

Tiptoeing to the door, which his lordship had left slightly ajar, she peered through the crack. At first she could see nothing but Lord Leatham's back, but then he moved slightly and she found herself staring directly at Dear Aunt Rosemary.

Chapter Ten

BRONSON KEPT HIS FACE carefully impassive while the woman rattled on with her story about her coachman having lost his way on the moor. She concluded her tale by explaining how one of the carriage wheels had struck a hidden stone in the dark and been broken, leaving herself and her daughter in what appeared to be desperate straits.

"Oh, I cannot tell you how thankful we were when we saw the lights of this house. I vow, 'twas like the Hand of Providence reaching down to save us. We are saved, my dear, sweet Rosabelle, we are saved, I said. Surely the good people who live in such a charming manor will not hesitate to offer us succor until our wheel can be fixed and our journey put forward." The woman fluttered her eyelashes at him, but behind the missish airs she was feigning, Bronson could see cold calculation and greed.

Admittedly, he might have found the account more believable if he had not already heard it on three other occasions, each time related with great pathos by a matchmaking mama with her simpering offspring in tow. It had been years since any of that sisterhood had set her sights on him, but apparently he was not yet so long in the tooth as to have completely lost his appeal as an eligible *parti*.

Although the chit being obliquely offered for his approval was comely enough in a china-doll sort of way, the mother was an unfortunate example of precisely how the daughter's superficial prettiness would with the passage of years become coarse and overblown. There was about the pair not the slightest hint of refinement, and in his mind Bronson categorized her as the wife, or perhaps widow, of a moneyed tradesman. In short, she displayed all the signs of being one of the mushroom class.

"I shall have the housekeeper prepare rooms for you," he

said curtly, wishing there were some way he could in good conscience turn them away from the door. But he had no doubts that the wheel really was broken, and the two females were stranded here, miles from any other habitation, though he doubted strongly that fate or misfortune had had a hand in the matter.

Like as not, Daws would discover by the light of day that the stone had been used to batter and break the wheel. It was not beyond the bounds of possibility that the stone had even been brought along in the carriage expressly for that purpose.

But these machinations would avail the travelers little. Mrs. Pierce-Smythe, as she called herself, would find it truly amazing how rapidly a wheel could be transported to Tavistock, and how ready the wheelwright would be to drop whatever he was doing to see to the needs of the Marquess of Wylington, ten years old though he might be.

Breakfast would have to be provided here for the two stranded wayfarers, but they would find themselves back in town in ample time to partake of the midday repast provided for hungry travelers at the Red Stag, or several of the employees at Wylington Manor would be looking for other jobs.

"Oh, thank you, my lord. I shall just instruct my servants to bring in our luggage, for if we are to be cast upon your hospitality, I know you would want us to be comfortable." She arched her eyebrows up in what was obviously intended to be a significant manner.

Having taken part in this melodrama three times previously, Bronson was familiar enough with the script to know his lines by heart, but sheer obstinacy and the knowledge that Miss Hemsworth was waiting for him in the library kept him from playing the genial host and politely ushering the pair of females into an anteroom where they could wait in comfort. Instead, he stood impassively in the hallway and watched while an impressive number of trunks, portmanteaus, and bandboxes were dragged in by four liveried grooms, their efforts directed by a lady's maid who spoke French with the most appalling Cockney accent.

Equally impressive was the flood of small talk that bombarded him. Although the young chit seemed to have as much conversation as a dressmaker's dummy, the older woman had an apparently inexhaustible supply of meaningless chatter, and he could fully understand why her husband might have found the grave a more restful place. For indeed, by the time Mrs. Plimtree arrived to show them to their rooms, the mother had confirmed that she was indeed a widow—from Yorkshire, but, she was quick to point out, originally from Lincolnshire, and related in some way Bronson could not quite grasp, to various minor gentry in that county, of whose existence he had until this evening been totally unaware.

He was hard put not to show his boredom with her continued explanations of the various and assorted ramifications of her purported pedigree, but he managed to stand his ground and murmur, "Just so," at the appropriate places. It was with great relief that he finally saw the backs of his uninvited guests vanish up the stairs in the wake of Mrs. Plimtree.

The library, when he finally returned to it, was empty. At some time during his absence, Miss Hemsworth had apparently exhausted her patience. Not that he blamed her—he knew exactly who to blame for the disruption of what should have been a very pleasant evening.

The curses that he then called down upon the heads of Mrs. and Miss Pierce-Smythe, he had picked up from an Egyptian camel driver, and they would have shocked even Daws, had he been in the room to hear them and had he understood Arabic.

Then putting the intruders completely out of his mind, Bronson poured himself a measure of brandy, threw himself down in the chair so recently occupied by the intriguing Miss Hemsworth, and let his thoughts drift back to the delightful kiss they had shared.

He had early on convinced himself that his reaction the first time he had kissed her had been induced by a combination of many things, beginning with his travel fatigue, added to the frustration of searching all over Tavistock for the elusive governess, then his unconscionable behavior when he met Martha Miller, and culminating in the discovery that he had been guilty of leaping to certain unfounded conclusions about the new governess.

As attractive as Miss Hemsworth was, he had found it easier to believe that it had been these extraneous events that had weakened his resistance to that point that a simple kiss—the mere touching of lips—had seemed to him to be more than it actually was. More than it could be, in fact.

In that he had erred. The kiss this evening had engendered in him an even stronger reaction—a burning desire to possess this woman. Until now, he had always felt that such intensity of emotion was nothing more than a flight of imagination on the part of poets, novelists, and callow youths.

It would appear that he still had something to learn about life—or at least about women.

Mrs. Pierce-Smythe dropped her genial manner as soon as the bedroom door was shut behind her. "Zizette, you will discover immediately which room belongs to Mr. Trussell."

"But ma'am, 'tis—"

"Zizette! I did not hire you to speak English."

"*Pardonez-moi, madame.* Eet ees *très* late, and perhaps the monsieur is already *dans son lit*—in hees bed."

There was a dead silence in the room, and the widow merely stared at her maid with a cold eye. Like a dead fish, was the way Zizette had once described that look to her sister Maggie, who was employed in a milliner's shop.

"*Très bien, madame,* I shall try to discover where Monsieur Trussell sleeps."

"And be discreet about it, Zizette. I do not wish to find myself thrown out in the cold after I have gone to so much effort to gain admittance to this house."

Anne stood just outside the circle of light emanating from the library windows and watched Lord Leatham sip his brandy. Drat the man! Unable to go through the hallway to reach the safety of her room, she had dashed out of the house in a panic, lest Lord Leatham take it into his head to usher her cousins into the library.

Unfortunately, although she had made two complete circuits around the manor, she had not found a single door that Chorley, in his newly sober and conscientious pursuit of his duties, had failed to secure tightly. The only way into the house was back through the French doors leading into the library.

But that option was also not viable, because Lord Leatham seemed determined to spend the night sitting in front of the fireplace in the library sipping brandy.

If he had not kissed her, she could simply go back into the library now with some excuse about having wanted to look at the starry heavens again.

But he had kissed her, and if she rejoined him, she had not the slightest doubt but what he would kiss her once more . . . or perhaps twice more . . . or thrice more . . . .

Summer though it was, the night air was on the cool side, and if she stood out here very long without so much as a scarf around her shoulders, she would likely catch a chill and die, and it would all be the baron's fault, because he had taken advantage of her.

She shivered and hugged her arms, which helped, but not enough. She could not keep from remembering how warm Lord Leatham's arms had been when he had wrapped them around her. "My lord," she murmured to herself, "if you do not take yourself off to bed soon, you will likely find me frozen solid by morning, because no matter how cold I become out here, I am going to resist the temptation, which I freely admit is tantalizing, to curl up on your lap."

As if he had heard her, Lord Leatham drained the last drops of brandy from his glass, stood up, stretched, and approached the windows.

Although she was sure she could not be seen from inside the room, Anne instinctively took several steps backward. Then she heard the distinctive click of a bolt being shot home, and she took an involuntary step forward.

Oh, no, he could not have done this to her! He could not have locked her out!

Even as she watched, all the candles but one were extinguished, and that one was picked up by Lord Leatham, who exited the room without a backward glance.

On the morrow, Bronson thought while climbing the stairs, he would first rid himself of his unwelcome guests, then pursue the matter of why Miss Hemsworth's kisses were so very potent—but he was forgetting the boys.

Perhaps he had best send the effusive Mrs. Pierce-Smythe and daughter cum baggage and servants on their way, then foist the twins off for an hour or two on some unsuspecting servant. . . .

No, none of the servants were that naive.

An interesting project, that was what he needed. Something to occupy the twins while he, Bronson, was occupied with Miss Hemsworth. Surely he could think of something intriguing enough. He must also have inherited an adequate measure of the ingenuity that had been allotted in such abundance to his young relatives.

On the other hand, if he failed to come up with a suitable idea, perhaps Daws could be persuaded—coerced?—into minding the twins. A bribe might be useful in that respect. . . .

Anne was ready to kick in one of the panes of glass in the French doors. It was not really a hopeless situation, of course. She could always pound on the kitchen door until she awakened one of the servants. Assuming, of course, that she was willing to make a spectacle of herself.

Which she was not about to do.

Abandoning her attempts to pick the lock on the French doors, she strode briskly around the house to the back and stared up at the window of her room. So near and yet so far. She could, of course, easily climb the ivy to her little balcony, where she would doubtless also be unable to pick the lock, since she had carefully secured it days ago, immediately after the abortive attempt by Trussell to climb into her bed.

To the best of her knowledge, he had never made the least effort to scale the heights of her balcony, so the only one she had locked out was herself.

Curses on all men! Aunt Sidonia was correct when she said all men were useless encumbrances.

But even if there were no unlocked doors, there must be an unlatched window somewhere in this mammoth pile of stones— there had to be.

Aha! Above her room and to the right, a curtain fluttered through an open window. Without further ado, Anne tore a strip off her petticoat, then used it to tie her skirt up out of the way, the way Aunt Sidonia had instructed her when teaching her the various methods for escaping from a burning building.

Of course, Aunt Sidonia had never anticipated that she, Anne, would need to climb into a building, to escape from a man's burning kisses. In fact, now that Anne thought about it, Aunt Sidonia had been strangely reticent on the entire subject of kissing.

"Pssst! Drew!" Anthony slid out of bed and scurried across the floor to his brother's bed. "Wake up, Drew!"

"Wha . . . ?"

Anthony laid his hand over his brother's mouth. "Don't make any noise," he hissed. "Someone's climbing up the wall outside our room."

"You're dreaming." Andrew muttered, rolling over on his side and pulling the covers up over his head.

Anthony jerked the blankets back down again. "No, no, I'm not dreaming. Look!" He pointed at the floor, where a gigantic shadow appeared in the moonlight, a misshapen shadow that grew even larger while they watched.

The thing was so fearsome that Anthony, who was not normally a coward, quickly dived under the covers beside his brother.

His curiosity proved stronger than his anxiety, however, and when he heard footsteps beside the bed, he had to take the risk of peeking out.

"Anne?"

There was a muffled gasp, then a low laugh.

"Anne!" Andrew elbowed his brother in the face when he sat up. "What are you doing here, Anne? Tony said you were a monster."

Anne looked down at the two faces staring up at her. She should have known that the only ones in the house not afraid of the miasmas in the night air, the only ones daring enough to leave their windows open would be the twins.

She started to fob them off with a blithe answer about having locked herself out of the house, when something compelled her to take them into her confidence. Lord knows, she was going to need some help on the morrow if she was to avoid Dear Aunt Rosemary and Dear Cousin Rosabelle.

Seating herself on the bed beside the boys, she began her explanation. "Do you remember that I told you my real name is Lady Gloriana? And that when I was a little younger than you two, I went to live with some relatives who only cared about me because I had a title?"

"We remember," one shadowy figure beside her said.

"Well, they are here now. In this house."

"Oh."

"Yes, oh. And if they discover I am employed here as the governess, I am afraid certain people are going to be unhappy that I kept my identity a secret."

"You did not keep it a secret from us. And after all, you are our governess, not Uncle Bronson's."

"But he is my employer." For a moment Anne remembered what Lord Leatham had said about being a very lenient employer, but she suspected even that leniency might be strained to the limit, were he to discover she was not precisely who she claimed to be.

"As I see it," one of the boys said very seriously, "the only thing to do is keep you out of their sight for a few hours tomorrow."

"A few hours? I think you fail to understand. She is undoubtedly planning an extended visit. She brought along enough luggage for a trip to the moon."

Beside her a twin giggled, but the other one said quite calmly, "Oh, but Uncle Bronson never lets them stay long."

"They have come here before? Why did you not mention it earlier?"

"No, no, not these specific females. Others. You know, Anne—"

"The mamas with their silly daughters—"

"Pretending their carriages have broken down—"

"Even when everyone knows that the lane leading to Wylington Manor doesn't go anywhere but here."

"You know."

"Yes," she sighed, "I know well the stratagems used to trap a man into marriage."

"Yes, but Uncle Bronson is too clever."

"He has a special arrangement with Thomas Curry—"

"The wheelwright in Tavistock."

"And your cousins will be all fixed up and on the road again before noon."

"And we can hide you until noon."

"Easy."

"We once hid—"

"For a week. Yes, I know," Anne said. "But I have no intention of hiding in the house. Not when we have lessons to do. So I shall meet you in the lower gardens at seven, and we shall spend the day on the moors."

"And I shall have cook fix us a picnic lunch," one of the boys added.

"Although we could, of course, snare a rabbit and roast it over a fire we built ourselves," the other boy suggested.

"I do not doubt it," Anne said, smiling to herself. "But as we have already completed the lessons in foraging for food, it might be better to speak to the cook. And see if you can provide us with a substantial breakfast, also, because I do not think I will risk eating in the morning room. Dear Aunt Rosemary cannot be relied upon to sleep until noon."

"I wish you will stop fidgeting with my neckcloth, Wyke. It is vastly more important that we plan the next attempt on the twins' lives than that I present a good appearance here in the back of beyond." Creighton Trussell started to pour himself another brandy, but the bottle was already empty, so he tossed it aside.

"If I may be allowed to express my opinion, sir, I am not at all convinced of the wisdom of taking such a risk."

"Do my ears deceive me? You are questioning my instructions? May I remind you that it is not for you to decide policy; that is my prerogative. It is merely for you to help determine the best way to implement my plan."

"Surely there is no hurry. It would appear that Lord Leatham is settled in here for the summer."

"No hurry? Of course there is a need for haste. To begin with, the gossip about the shooting attempt has completely died down. For another, not only am I missing the end of the Season in London, but all of my friends are probably even now preparing to remove to Brighton. Did you expect that I should be content to spend the summer here on the moor, where no one would even care if I were to appear at dinner wearing the same waistcoat two nights in a row? Really, Wyke, sometimes you astound me.''

"I beg pardon, sir. I was not thinking clearly.''

"Well, you had better start pulling your wits together, because I intend to make the attempt tomorrow night.''

"So soon?'' Wyke had never regretted anything so much in his life as he now did his delay at writing to the lusty widow. Oh, if only she were here now, to take control of this—this monster—this little man with delusions of power—this imitation Napoleon, making his grandiose plans.

"Yes, so soon. I see no reason to delay, unless you have still failed to procure a map of the moor?''

"No, I have one right here.'' Wyke pulled it out of his pocket and handed it very reluctantly to his employer, who eagerly spread it out on his lap.

"I believe you have it upside down, sir.''

"Of course, of course.'' Trussell righted it. "Now then . . . hmmm . . . yes. . . .''

With one last prayer to the gods who had obviously forsaken him, Wyke moved around behind the chair, reached over Trussell's shoulder, and pointed to a little spot on the map. "We are here, sir, and here is the lane leading back to the main road.''

"Oh, yes, of course, quite right.''

"And here is—''

There was a loud knock at the door, and Trussell immediately started trying to refold the map. Before he succeeded, the door opened and Mrs. Pierce-Smythe entered the room without so much as a by-your-leave.

In total panic, Trussell shoved the map at Wyke, who calmly held it behind his back. Then, while the others were talking, he considered how best to dispose of the incriminating evidence.

"Wh-wh-wh-what are *you* doing here?'' The disordered state of Trussell's mind was evidenced by the fact that he did not even follow the rudiments of courtesy and rise to his feet, but remained instead cowering in his chair.

"Now, is that any way to greet your beloved after such a long absence?"

Mrs. Pierce-Smythe was smiling at Trussell, but if she was intending to calm him, thought Wyke, she was bound to fail. She had the look about her of a cat that has cornered a mouse and is toying with it.

Surreptitiously he moved backward, step by careful step, until he felt the dressing table behind him. Carefully he eased a drawer open and stuffed the map into it.

"But—but—but— you can't—" Trussell had still not completely regained his power of speech.

"Listen closely, my little man. Tomorrow you will arise at a goodly hour. By that I mean eight of the clock, not noon. You will seek me out in whatever room breakfast is normally served in, and you will invite me to stay on here at Wylington Manor for an extended visit, *is that clear*?"

Her voice was so forceful, even Wyke took another involuntary step backward, inadvertently pushing the drawer closed on his fingers. With an indrawn breath caused by the pain, he tugged at the draw until he finally managed to release his hand.

Trussell, meanwhile did not even attempt to speak, but just nodded his head up and down, up and down, as if once put into motion he could no longer control it.

The widow stared at him fixedly for a few moments, as if to reassure herself that he had indeed gotten her meaning, then she turned to Wyke, who barely stifled the urge to cringe before her.

"I shall hold you responsible for seeing that he is there on time, sober and presentable, and with his lines practiced."

"As you wish, madame." His mien carefully impassive, Wyke executed a correct bow, and moments later the woman was gone.

Although Wyke rather thought he had carried it off well—certainly better than Trussell had—still, his palms were clammy and his knees were shaking. What kind of fiend had he conjured up? To be sure, the lusty widow could easily control his master, but why had it never occurred to him to wonder who would control her?

Turning to speak to Trussell, Wyke discovered the lily-livered coward had fainted dead away in his chair.

Chapter Eleven

BRONSON WAS NOT in an especially good mood the next day when he descended to the morning room with the intention of breaking his fast. To begin with, he had not slept well the night before; his mind had been too filled with thoughts of Miss Hemsworth. Then, upon awakening, he had spoken to Daws, who had exhibited an unwavering reluctance—nay, an outright refusal—to undertake the supervision of the twins for even a few hours. To put the finishing touches on his ill humor, Bronson now had to endure the company of the two stranded females.

He had assumed that they would sleep late after their previous evening's adventures, but voices in the hallway half an hour earlier had forewarned him that he would not be able to drink his coffee in peace. Noon, he promised himself. He had only to hold onto his sanity until twelve, and then he would be rid of the intruders.

Gritting his teeth, he pushed open the door to the small room at the back of the house where breakfast was normally served. Chorley was there before him, efficiently serving the two females. Miss Hemsworth was noticeable only by her absence.

"Ah, good morning, my lord. I was just commenting to my daughter on what a pretty little room this is. So merry, with the sunbeams dancing in through the windows. I do like a breakfast room with a southern exposure, do you not also?" Mrs. Pierce-Smythe regarded him with an arch look.

The devil take the woman, it was going to be worse than he had thought. Apparently she was one of that appalling breed who not only yapped constantly, but who continually asked fatuous questions, demanding of her listeners that they make token responses. Well he was not going to give her the slightest encouragement. Unfortunately, the black look he gave her failed utterly to intimidate her.

"Try some of the coddled eggs, my lord, I am sure I have never eaten better anywhere, and I have a French chef, whom Lady Stansford is forever trying to steal away from me, but I am afraid she is doomed to disappointment, because Pierre will never allow himself to be lured away. The last time she made him an offer, I simply doubled his salary and bought him a new enclosed stove, and that was the end of that."

Without saying a word, Chorley set a mug of steaming coffee in front of Bronson, who grabbed it with the relief of a drowning man.

"Merciful heavens, are you having coffee so early in the day? Such a heathen custom. Are you sure you would not prefer a nice cup of tea? Or perhaps some hot chocolate? If you wish, I can ring for—"

"No!" He was more abrupt than he had intended, and she stared at him open-mouthed. "Thank you," he added more mildly, "but on my travels I grew accustomed to coffee in the morning." And peace and quiet with breakfast, he wanted to add.

"My dear husband, God rest his soul, preferred to take his breakfast on a tray in his room, but I have always enjoyed having a pleasant conversation with my meals." She continued to rattle on, while Bronson did his best to close his ears to her chatter.

Her husband, the late unlamented Mr. Pierce-Smythe, had had the right idea: At this moment, breakfast on a tray in his room held great appeal for Bronson.

About halfway through the meal, the door opened, and he looked up eagerly, expecting it to be Miss Hemsworth, who usually joined him before this. To his total astonishment, it was Trussell, who never set foot outside his room until the sun was high in the sky.

"Good morning, Leatham," Trussell said, then he did a double-take. "My word! Mrs. Pierce-Smythe, can it be you?"

"Why, 'tis Mr. Trussell. Look Rosabelle, it is our good friend Mr. Creighton Trussell. I had no idea you lived here in Devon. What a coincidence that we should have had our little accident right on your doorstep, so to speak." She languidly extended her hand, and Trussell hurried across the room to bow low over it.

"But my dear madame, whatever are you doing in Devon? I thought you were fixed in London for the Season."

"As did I, but I found myself absolutely burnt to the socket with all the partying, and decided we needed to take a short repairing lease. A friend of mine offered us her house in Plymouth, and I thought perhaps a bit of sea air . . ."

Her voice trailed off, and she looked at Trussell expectantly. To Bronson, everything suddenly became so clear that he had to raise his napkin to his face to smother his chuckles.

What a conceited fool he had been, thinking the widow was seeking to entrap him. She had her eye on other game. Now that he realized what the situation was, he could recognize the signs—the proprietary look the widow was giving Trussell, combined with the furtive sideways glances Trussell was giving him all added up to a different scenario than Bronson had originally thought.

"But my dear madame," Trussell said, sounding like a very bad actor on a provincial stage, "you and your daughter must stay here with us for a few days—er, weeks, that is. We would be delighted to have some company, would we not, Leatham?"

The invitation, coming as it did from someone who was himself technically a guest in the house, would have irritated Bronson no end, had not the humor of the situation tickled his fancy. Well, if Trussell were able to catch himself a rich widow, even if she were rather vulgar, then Bronson would not only be the first to wish him well, but he would do everything in his power to aid and abet him.

"To be sure, madame. Please feel free to extend your stay with us."

The look Trussell now gave him was surprisingly hostile, but the widow was all amiability when she finally begged to be excused so that she might see about unpacking.

No sooner was the door closed behind her and her daughter than Trussell exploded. "How could you invite that woman to stay here!"

"How could I? Pray remember, the invitation was yours. I merely seconded it. But do not worry, my dear Trussell. I am sure the widow's intentions are honorable. And may I be the first to wish you happy? Or has someone been before me?"

His breakfast companion looked as if he had been poleaxed. First his face turned puce, then stark white, and finally settled on an alarming shade of green. "She is not—that is to say, you have misinterpreted everything, Léatham. She is not interested in marrying me."

"Oh? Then does she intend merely to—uh—toy with your affections, I believe it is called?" It was a good thing Miss Hemsworth was not present at breakfast this morning, else she would call him to order with as much speed and firmness as she did the twins. But in her absence Bronson could not resist the temptation to tease Trussell, who rose so beautifully to the bait.

"Not at all, she—oh, dash it all, Leatham, if you must know, the woman is after me to gain her *entrée* into society. That is her purpose in coming here—er, I mean, that is why she was so happy to run into me so, ah, accidently, as it were."

Definitely, the woman had brought her own rock along with which to break the wheel. There was no longer the slightest doubt in Bronson's mind. "Gain her *entrée*? When she is positively burnt to the socket with partying?"

"That is all a hum, and do not try to persuade me that you believed a word she said. I am not that gullible. The woman barely hangs onto the fringes of society, as you have already deduced. Yet she is bound and determined to marry that chit of hers off to a peer of the realm. I tell you, Leatham, man to man, for the first time in my life I am grateful that my cousin stands before me to inherit my grandfather's title, else that blasted woman would in truth have her eye on me as a prospective son-in-law."

Bronson had not the slightest doubt that he had discovered the source of the money Trussell had been spending so wildly—but the price Trussell would be called on to pay was steeper than anything he would have been charged had he gone to a cent-per-cent.

Trussell looked at him now with a casual expression, behind which Bronson could see the naked calculation. "I have been thinking—if you have no objections, perhaps we could invite the Bainetons over for dinner this evening?" There was the merest whisper of desperation in the dandy's voice.

"I seriously doubt that Thorverton would be interested in the chit. She is not at all his type," Bronson replied calmly.

"No, no, I had no expectations along that line," Trussell was quick to correct. "I was thinking that perhaps Lady Thorverton might—"

"Might take over the responsibility of introducing Mrs. Pierce-Smythe into society? Now you are indeed clutching at straws. Lady Thorverton has vast experience in depressing the pretensions of the mushroom class."

"Oh, I say, Mrs. Pierce-Smythe is not precisely a mushroom. She is related to the Pierces of Lincolnshire—"

"You need go no further; I have already heard the lady's pedigree recited in exquisite detail. For what it is worth, you may invite whomever you wish. Just be sure that you consult with the cook before you make plans to entertain in too grandiose a manner."

To the litany of Trussell's heartfelt thanks being repeated over and over again, Bronson wandered off in search of the twins and Miss Hemsworth. He was in a much more cheerful frame of mind than before breakfast.

Really, the next few days held promise of being vastly entertaining. Although Trussell would undoubtedly put up a fierce struggle, Bronson was willing to give odds that the widow would eventually lure the unfortunate dandy into parson's mousetrap. That her interest in Trussell was limited solely to his connections in society Bronson did not believe for one moment.

In the meantime, Bronson could emulate the late Mr. Pierce-Smythe and take most of his meals on a tray in his room. Or better yet, he could join the twins in the schoolroom for meals. Coincidentally, that would mean he might be able to spend even more hours of the day in the company of the delightful Miss Hemsworth.

Anne paced back and forth in the schoolroom. "Oh, how I wish I could be a fly on the wall this evening and hear what they will all be saying at dinner."

Anthony looked at Andrew and Andrew looked right back. Something about their expressions made her instantly suspicious.

"All right, you two, what mischief are you plotting now?"

"We are not planning any actual mischief yet," Andrew said slowly. He looked at his brother, and Anthony nodded. "But if you truly want to eavesdrop—"

"Which you did say you disapprove of—"

"We know how you can do it."

Their eyes round, they looked at her, and she opened her mouth to say of course they must not any of them stoop so low as to eavesdrop—but she could not quite bring herself to utter the words.

"It might actually be a wise thing to do," Andrew commented to his brother. Both of them were now rather obviously avoiding looking at Anne.

"It would not, strictly speaking, be eavesdropping," Anthony added slowly.

"We should think of it as spying on the enemy," Andrew said thoughtfully.

"Because Mrs. and Miss Pierce-Smythe may be relatives—"

"But they are *not* friends."

"And we might actually *need* to know what they are planning to do."

"They might, themselves, be planning some kind of mischief—"

"Or plotting some misdeeds of their own."

"And forewarned is forearmed, as Aunt Sidonia would say."

Anne heard the echo of her words coming out of the boys' mouths. She knew she should say no . . . knew she should be firm . . . knew she should resist the temptation . . .

But the day spent on the moor avoiding Dear Aunt Rosemary had seemed an eternity, made longer by the fact that all she had thought about with every breath she took was seeing Lord Leatham again . . . talking to him again . . .

All right, she said to the little voice in her head that was mocking her, I admit it. I want to kiss him again. But I cannot allow myself to indulge in such things, no matter how lenient an employer he says he is. Kissing one's employer is, after all, conduct unbecoming a governess. And at the end of the summer, the boys will be packed off to Harrow, and Lord Leatham will vanish on another one of his journeys, and I . . . I . . .

She fought back the tears that were threatening to embarrass her.

Mrs. Wiggins will find me a suitable position as governess to some young lady who is all sweet compliance and no ingenuity at all, and I shall undoubtedly be driven to put a frog in her reticule.

Oh, I am not cut out to be a governess. Inside my prim and proper exterior, I am more a heathen than Skanadajiwah, who is really quite civilized. It is no wonder that Lord Leatham kisses me.

Turning her back on the twins, Anne walked to the window and stood looking out at the sunset. This was the evening she and the twins and Lord Leatham had planned to look at the stars again. If only her cousins' unexpected visit had not interfered!

"Just how do you propose we go about this spying?" she asked.

"Well, there is a secret passageway—"

"Which we discovered quite by accident."

"We found a diagram that explained how to open the secret doors."

"The chart was concealed in a hollowed-out book in the library."

Egads, Anne thought, next it will be ghosts. She stifled a laugh and turned to face the boys. "I cannot approve of eavesdropping, even if you do call it by the fancy name of spying. But sometimes all of us are weaker than we wish to think we are, so lead on. I should like to make use of this secret tunnel—"

"Passageway," Andrew corrected.

"And if you feel too guilty," Anthony assured her, "tomorrow you can forgo eating any clotted cream with strawberries."

"As punishment," his brother added. "And we shall translate an extra five pages of Cicero."

"That should be adequate," Anne replied, wishing life were really so simple.

* * *

An ill-assorted party was gathered in the rose salon before dinner. Trussell was seated between Mrs. Pierce-Smythe and Lady Thorverton, and from the frozen expression on the latter's face, the dandy was having a rocky time of it.

Looking like a veritable moonling, Collier was ensconced on the settee beside young Miss Pierce-Smythe, who was batting her long eyelashes at him, simpering, and frequently rapping him playfully with her fan.

"My brother seems determined to make a cake of himself," Thorverton remarked. "But then it is, I believe, his first case of calf-love. Were we ever that young?"

Bronson smiled. "When I was sixteen, I was totally smitten with Adler's sister, who was nineteen. Her charms, if I remember correctly, consisted of the boxes of chocolates she sent him once a month, and which he shared willingly with anyone bigger than he was. You, I believe, were always more interested in your fillies and mares than in two-legged beauties. But then you had Diana."

At the mention of his former betrothed, the other man looked uncommonly grim, and Bronson began to think his friend's affections had been more deeply engaged than he had realized. "Are you sorry that . . . ?"

Thorverton glanced at him in surprise. "Did I look as if I regretted it? Quite the contrary. Just for a moment there I had a horrific vision of what my life would be like right now if Hazelmore had not cut me out. The narrowness of my escape unmans me. Just thinking about it gives me the shakes."

Chorley opened the doors to the dining room and announced in a stentorian voice that dinner was served.

"What is this, Leatham? Do you not allow Anne to join us for dinner? I had not thought you such a snob."

"I could call you out for that, Thorverton, but my disappointment is as great as yours. No, Miss Hemsworth was invited, but she sent word that she has the headache and prefers to dine in her room. Which leaves you the odd man out, I am afraid. Unless you wish to compete with Trussell for the honor of escorting Mrs. Pierce-Smythe? You do outrank him, and if we are to stand on strict precedence—"

With alacrity Thorverton declined the privilege, leaving

Bronson to escort Lady Thorverton, Trussell to follow with Mrs. Pierce-Smythe, Collier Baineton with Miss Pierce-Smythe, and Thorverton to bring up the rear with no partner.

As the footmen began to serve the food and Mrs. Pierce-Smythe began again to recite her pedigree, this time apparently for Lady Thorverton's benefit, Bronson's thoughts turned to the empty place at the table where Miss Hemsworth should have been sitting. He did not believe for a moment her excuse that she had a sick headache.

No, after a day of trying to catch up with her, he had finally realized late in the afternoon that she was deliberately avoiding him. Unfortunately for his peace of mind, it was not hard to figure out why.

She was employed here as governess, and so far each of the two "gentlemen" in this household had gone beyond the bounds of what was allowable. To be sure, he himself had only kissed her . . . repeatedly . . . on two separate occasions . . . and held her in his arms . . . that was all.

Trussell, on the other hand, had attacked her in her bed chamber, but the difference between them was only a matter of degree. Where the dandy had been direct and had gone for the frontal assault, Bronson had been more subtle. He had lured Miss Hemsworth into the library, then had goaded her into his arms, then had—

Even now, the memory of the previous evening could not evoke in him the proper feelings of guilt and remorse. Just thinking about kissing her made him want to forget everything he had ever learned about the proper way for a gentleman to act—made him want to throw caution and restraint to the winds and go find Miss Hemsworth in her bedroom . . . and kiss her again and again . . . .

Granted, from his perspective, it had been an enjoyable moment, but if he considered it from her point of view? Was she at this very moment, in spite of his threat to force her to remain through the entire summer, making preparations for her departure? Could he in all fairness expect her to remain when staying meant being perpetually obliged to fight off unwelcome advances?

It was obvious to him that she would not at this very moment be hiding in her room if he had not taken liberties with her in the library. It was a sobering thought.

From her hiding place inside the wall, Anne could observe all the people gathered around the dining table, although regrettably, Lord Leatham had his back to her so she could not read the expression on his face.

It was a strange sensation to see and yet not be seen. Almost like watching a play on stage, but in essence vastly different. To begin with, in the theater actors and actresses know they are being observed, they have memorized their lines, and they are deliberately playing roles.

But the longer Anne watched and listened, the more she realized that here, too, lines were being recited by rote and the roles that were being acted out owed all to artifice and nothing to nature. Whoever the playwright had been, however, he was not on a par with Shakespeare. Lady Thorverton was but a caricature of the snobbish, society matron, Collier was ridiculous as the lovesick youth, Trussell was overdone as the foppish dandy, and her cousins . . .

Age had not been kind to Dear Aunt Rosemary. Too much of her character could now be read on her face—the selfishness, the pettiness, the narrow-mindedness, the greed, the conceit.

And Cousin Rosabelle, poor little thing, had been well trained not to have a thought in her head or a care in the world beyond what her mirror might show her. True, she was beautiful to look at, but she had no more personality and wit than a Brussels sprout.

Looking at her younger cousin, Anne felt no stirrings of affection, only a deep revulsion. Just so would she have been, had she not had the good fortune to come under the influence of Great-Aunt Sidonia. If nothing else was given to her in her life, Anne must still be grateful for having received such a blessing.

"And have I mentioned, my lord, that the Countess of Faussley, my dear cousin, lived with us many years after the demise of her dear husband?"

Bronson, who had not been paying any especial note to the empty prattle of the female seated beside him, now suddenly found himself all rapt attention. Mrs. Pierce-Smythe was related to the Countess of Faussley? But that would mean . . .

"Yes, we took her in, Mr. Pierce-Smythe and I, when she and her daughter had no place else to go, poor things."

Poor things? Bronson raised his napkin to his face and tried with indifferent success to turn his laugh into a cough. This ridiculous woman was categorizing Miss Hemsworth as a "poor thing"?

By Jove, the implication of what she was saying fully struck him. *This*, then, must be why Anne—that is to say, Miss Hemsworth—had been playing least-in-sight all day. It was not because of the kisses he had bestowed on her. "Tell me more, my dear Mrs. Pierce-Smythe, about your cousins."

"Dear Lady Gloriana," she began, "such a sweet child she was."

Unexpectedly, Bronson heard a slight scuffling sound behind him. He glanced over his shoulder to see who had made the noise, but there was no footman behind him, nor any other servant.

For a moment he toyed with the absurd idea that the twins might have sneaked into the room and secreted themselves, but that was clearly impossible. There were no draperies or pieces of furniture large enough to provide them the means of concealing themselves.

More than likely it was just rats in the wainscoting. He would speak to Chorley tomorrow about securing the services of a ferret or two.

"Dear Rosabelle and I were so attached to Lady Gloriana. It was positively wrenching when her great-aunt, Lady Sidonia, insisted upon dragging her away from us."

This time it was definitely a snicker behind him, and a very recognizable snicker, too, although whether it was Andrew or Anthony he could not have said. Belatedly, it occurred to him that the twins must have been more successful than he and his cousin had been. As boys, the two of them had spent many a rainy afternoon searching for the secret passages said to have been built in Wylington Manor during Cromwell's time.

The question that remained in his mind was, if the twins were now hiding in a concealed passageway, was Anne lying down in her room or was she also there a few feet behind him watching and listening? Could she have been so tempted to deviate from the strait and narrow path that she would deliberately eavesdrop?

Remembering the way she had thrown propriety to the wind and responded to his kisses, he rather suspected that there were three spies crowded into what must be a very narrow passageway indeed.

Lord Leatham did not appear to have heard them. Anne slowly let out the breath she had been holding, and beside her Anthony squeezed her hand in reassurance.

Really, this business of spying was trickier than she had thought. And so far they had learned nothing that was of the slightest benefit. It would be better by far if they abandoned their listening posts and retired to their own rooms, but if they so much as moved an inch, the sound of their footsteps would undoubtedly betray them.

To make her torment that much worse, she had only nibbled at her supper, and now the sight of Chorley carrying in platter after platter of succulent dishes made her positively weak. Surely the dinner must be ending soon?

Ah, at last one of the footmen was bringing in the sweets. Soon the ladies would be withdrawing to leave the gentlemen to their brandy. During the general commotion that would result, she and the twins would have an opportunity to make good their escape without fear of discovery.

But despite her cramped limbs and growling stomach, Anne could not completely control her insatiable curiosity, which had been her downfall on many a previous occasion. Long had she wondered what men talked about when there were no women present, and now, at last, she had the opportunity to find out.

"If you cannot bear to be separated from your newfound love, Collier, you are free to join the ladies," Thorverton said in a teasing voice.

Collier blushed, stammered something confused, and hurried from the room.

"Undoubtedly true love," Bronson commented wryly, reaching for the bottle of brandy. "But here I am neglecting my duties as host. My dear Trussell, do you care to join us in imbibing some of this divine potation from the vines of Bacchus, brought to these shores courtesy of the Gentlemen? Or do you also prefer to join the, uh, ladies?"

"The devil take you!" Red-faced, the dandy rose from the table, and with a glare at Bronson, stalked from the room.

"What the deuce has gotten into him?" Thorverton stared at the closed door in amazement, then turned to Bronson. "You were only being polite, yet he reacted as if you had insulted him."

Bronson poured himself and Thorverton each a measure of the rejected brandy. "You must excuse him. I fear Trussell is not himself today. Hag-ridden, I expect." Glass in hand, he rose to his feet and began methodically to inspect the wall behind him.

"You don't mean—you cannot mean Mrs. Pierce-Smythe?"

"Exactly. It would seem the merry widow has her claws sunk so far into him, he will ne'er escape." He heard a gasp emanating from the wall—a feminine gasp, and slightly to his left if he was not mistaken.

"A toast!" Behind him, Thorverton raised his glass. "To bachelorhood! Long may we both live in freedom from all feminine shackles!"

Bronson did not make a move to raise his own glass.

"But you are not drinking? Come, come, my friend, you have already expressed your views on the subject of women and matrimony. Did you not tell me—"

"Do not throw my former folly in my face," Bronson interrupted smoothly before his friend could totally offend the beautiful eavesdropper. The last thing he wanted at this moment was for her to get her back up. "Whatever my opinion of women may have been, it has changed radically since I met Miss Hemsworth."

Ah, there, slightly below normal eye level, a carved oak leaf was out of alignment, revealing a small peephole. There was not enough light to see who, if anyone, was making use of it, but even while he watched, the leaf slowly moved back into proper position.

"Since making the acquaintance of the redoubtable governess, I have been seriously contemplating matrimony," he said.

He was rewarded for his audacious statement by the sound of rapidly retreating footsteps, which made no attempt at stealth.

Chapter Twelve

"SURELY YOU ARE NOT seriously intending to carry out the kidnapping now? When there are so many extra people in the house?" Thoroughly aghast, Wyke stared at his employer in dismay.

"I must, I must, I have no choice," Trussell said, pacing back and forth in a veritable frenzy. "You do not understand. The widow has possession of my notes of hand, and she threatens to send me to debtor's prison if I do not secure her *entrée* into the highest level of the *ton*."

"Which would be less risky by far than what you intend."

Trussell grabbed the valet by his labels and spoke directly into his face. "It will not be less risky. It will be impossible. If you had been there this evening, if you had seen the way Lady Thorverton reacted, you would know that no power on earth is enough to pry open the portals of Almack's for that female and her daughter. I am sure of failure if I follow that route, but if we make this attempt now, at least there is a chance of success. You said we must wait until the moon was full. Well, 'tis full tonight, and tonight we shall do it. We must, I tell you, we must!"

His voice rose higher and higher in incipient hysteria, and the valet could only be grateful for the thick walls and doors in Wylington Manor, which with luck would keep anyone from hearing what Trussell seemed intent on proclaiming to all and sundry.

Wyke carefully removed Trussell's hands from his jacket, which was now sadly crumpled. Perhaps his employer was correct . . . and, on the other hand, assuming he was wrong, might there not be more money made out of the failure? If the widow learned of this misdeed, might she not pay handsomely?

"Very well," Wyke said in a placating tone of voice, "if you insist, but we must wait until quite, quite late, to be sure that everyone is asleep. And before we begin, are you absolutely sure you remember the plan?''

"Of course. It is simple enough. I will carry one of the twins and you will carry the other, and the ether will guarantee that neither of them puts up a struggle or cries out."

Wyke held the handkerchief he had stolen from Lord Leatham's room across the twin's face. The boy stirred fitfully for a moment, but then the ether with which the piece of fabric was soaked began to take effect, and the lad quieted down and lay motionless.

On the other side of the room there was an unexpected noise, which Wyke identified to his profound regret as the sound a bottle makes when it falls to the floor.

"Blast," his partner in crime muttered under his breath.

"Shhhh!" The valet left his designated victim and tiptoed across the room to help Trussell with the other twin.

Too late. Wyke could smell the fumes from the dropped bottle even before he reached Trussell, and he barely caught his woozy employer in time to prevent him from collapsing across the bed. With difficulty he assisted the idiot out of the room. Propping him up against the wall, Wyke left him in the corridor and returned to the job at hand.

Already, not ten minutes into the kidnapping, and everything was going wrong. One twin was properly out cold, but the other twin . . .

Wyke leaned over the bed and heard the slow, steady breathing of a sleeping boy. Good, they still had a chance to make a recovery. He took a step closer and his foot came into contact with the bottle, which skittered across the floor and under the bed.

Crawling underneath to retrieve it, Wyke got a dose of the ether himself, and he was forced to stick his head out the open window, lest he also succumb to the effect of the fumes.

Leaning over the windowsill, fighting off the nausea, he made his decision. As soon as was feasible, he was going to leave his jingle-brained employer and find someone more worthy of his talents. Or perhaps he would set himself up in business, where he could be his own boss.

By the time Wyke's head had cleared and he had hoisted the one twin over his shoulder, Trussell had also recovered his wits enough to follow them through the long, meandering hallways and down assorted stairs and out the small side door they had chosen for their exit.

"But we were supposed to take both boys," Trussell protested once they were out of earshot of the house. "You are changing my plan without permission."

"One will be adequate," Wyke replied tersely, only with great effort refraining from pointing out to his employer just who had fouled up the plan and who had salvaged at least the essential part of it.

"I suppose you are correct," Trussell said grudgingly. "Are you sure we are going in the proper direction? I thought we were supposed to head southeast."

"We are going southeast."

"No, no, I am sure you are mistaken. We are definitely going northeast."

It was too much. Wyke gritted his teeth and marched onward, leaving Trussell to follow or not. Ten minutes of walking and he came to the outcroppng of stone where he had secreted the lantern and rope, plus a pair of Leatham's boots, likewise removed from the baron's room when both he and Daws were absent.

"You see? Here is the equipment we need, right where we left it. Now if you will bring it along—"

"I? Why should I carry everything, pray? Surely your duties as valet include carrying things."

At these words Wyke totally lost control. "Do as I tell you," he hissed in a voice that brooked no nonsense. "Unless you prefer to carry the child, in which case I shall be more than happy to carry the other things."

"Oh, no, no, I have no objection to doing my share. It merely slipped my mind that you were already so burdened down."

It had slipped his mind that they were in the middle of a kidnapping? Wyke was appalled at his master's totty-headed inability to concentrate on what they were doing. And what else had Trussell forgotten? Had it also slipped his mind that if they were caught red-handed, they would likely be transported to

Australia, or even worse, to Van Diemen's Land? And what else might slip Trussell's mind? Or would it be a slip of his tongue that betrayed them?

Wyke, who had not once set foot inside a church since he was ten years old and had left his parents' house to go into service, now began to pray more earnestly than he had ever before done in his life.

Anthony was chilly and his head ached. "Drew, shut the window, 'tis too cold in here." There was no answer from the other side of the room, so he decided to shut the window himself.

He tried to roll over in bed, but he bumped into something hard—something that did not belong in his bed. Sleepily, he opened one eye, then in astonishment he opened the other.

He was not in his bed—not in his room—not in Wylington Manor—not in any building, in fact. He was lying on a blanket inside a circle of stones, with the starry heavens as the only roof over his head. In the west the full moon was setting, and in the east the sky was already starting to lighten.

It took him only a moment longer to discover his hands and feet were tied. Immediately enraged, he yelled at the top of his lungs.

No one replied. No one came. For a moment he just lay there, too angry to be scared. Then he managed to sit up and look around. He was out on the moor, and the only light within view was the moon, which was bright enough that he could see the ropes that bound his wrists and ankles.

Whoever had tied him up knew not the first thing about knots, that much was evident. To begin with, his hands had been tied in front of him, which made it ridiculously easy for him to use his teeth to untie his wrists.

Well, perhaps not ridiculously easy, but it did not take him more than ten minutes of effort, after which he disposed of the ropes on his ankles even more quickly.

Standing up, he had a better view of his surroundings, but he still could see no sign of habitation, nor did he recognize any of the rock formations around him. Knowing which way was east did not help him in the slightest, since he had no way of knowing if he was north or south or east or west of Wylington Manor.

More than likely he was south. That was the only part of the moor they were forbidden to explore on their own, because it had too many dangerous fens and mires.

He wanted very much to run home as fast as he could, but common sense and Anne's admonitions to stay in one place if lost kept him from setting out in the dark. He would not have very long to wait; the sky in the east was becoming rosier by the minute.

Picking up the blanket, he wrapped himself in it and sat down to wait.

Anne lay in her bed watching the slow arrival of the dawn. She had spent the night thinking about Lord Leatham and what he said to Lord Thorverton at dinner . . . or perhaps, he had said it to her, Anne, knowing from the beginning that she was hiding in the wall.

There was no doubt in her mind that he had known by the end of the evening that she was there. After the ladies had left, followed by Collier and Mr. Trussell, Lord Leatham had stood up and casually moved out of her range of view, although she could still hear him talking to Thorverton, and then suddenly Lord Leatham had been there, standing directly in front of her, blocking her view of the room and staring straight at her through the peephole.

Or so it had seemed. Knowing the darkness in the passageway would make it impossible, or at least highly difficult, for him to see her, she had not panicked—at least not right away. She had slowly and carefully eased the peephole shut, breathed a soundless sigh of relief, then heard him say those fateful words: "Since making the acquaintance of the redoubtable governess, I have begun seriously contemplating matrimony."

It was at that point that she had totally lost her composure and had fled from the scene. A bad mistake on her part, as the twins had not hesitated to point out to her. Had she remained motionless where she was they could have all escaped detection.

What the boys did not mention, but what had been driving

her crazy ever since, was the knowledge that by running away as she had, she had forever lost her chance to hear what else Lord Leatham might have said concerning marriage.

She rolled over in bed and pulled the covers over her head to shut out the sunrise. As long as the night had seemed, she was not yet ready to face what daylight would bring. The meeting with Dear Aunt Rosemary and Dear Cousin Rosabelle, which she had dreaded so much the day before, now seemed the least of her worries. More nerve-wracking was the thought of seeing Lord Leatham again. She had just spent many hours of darkness trying to figure out how to delay that inevitable confrontation.

To be sure, she had not been awake the entire night. Off and on she had slept briefly, but her dreams had been just as filled with Lord Leatham as her thoughts were when she was awake. The only difference had been that in her dreams he had each time looked her straight in the eye, had said, ''Marry me, Miss Hemsworth,'' and had then deliberately kissed her.

And each time, instead of being able to enjoy the kiss properly, she had invariably awakened, her heart pounding in her chest, her senses completely alert. All in all, it had been a most frustrating night.

Her dreams were not really the problem now, nor was her problem her inability to sleep. Her problem was first of all the question of whether Lord Leatham was seriously contemplating asking her to marry him. And if he was, there was the even more difficult question of whether she should accept him or reject him.

If she said yes to his proposal, assuming he made one, she would, in Aunt Sidonia's words, be burdening herself for life with that most useless of encumbrances, a husband, without whom women were free to do as they pleased, to live their own lives, and to think their own thoughts.

On the other hand, if she said, ''No thank you, my lord, I do not wish to marry you,'' then at the end of the summer she would of necessity have to leave Wylington Manor forever, in the process severing her relationship with the twins. Moreover, Lord Leatham would undoubtedly depart on another of his long journeys, and it was highly unlikely that their paths would ever cross again.

In essence, she would have to choose between freedom and entanglements, between remaining detached and becoming involved in the lives of others. Although she had held three previous positions as governess and had lived in intimate contact with three different families, she had never felt herself to be the least bit emotionally involved with them. She had always felt herself to be the impartial observer of the follies of others.

That those others had depended heavily on her was not to be denied. The point was, she could have walked away from them at any moment without looking back. In truth, when the time had come that her job was finished, she had indeed left without a backward glance or thought.

Could she leave the twins that easily? Or Lord Leatham, who she suspected was becoming just as emotionally attached to her as the twins were?

That they would miss her was a foregone conclusion, but that she would miss the three of them was a radically new idea. To be honest, every time she thought about leaving Devon, thought about how difficult it would be, she felt herself trapped.

Not trapped by their need for her services as a governess and a managing female, but trapped by her love for them.

It was exactly as Aunt Sidonia had warned her. Just so were women down through the centuries lured into permanent relationships with men.

What Aunt Sidonia had not mentioned was that it felt rather nice to be so involved. Compared to life here in Devon with her three lords, freedom seemed rather empty and forlorn and vastly overrated. Looking back, her years as a governess in more normal households seemed so boring, lacking as it did the mental stimulation of dealing with the twins' ingenuity . . . and the physical stimulation of Lord Leatham's kisses.

When she thought of his arms around her and his lips pressing against hers, her mind automatically returned to contemplating her first problem: Had Lord Leatham, knowing she was hiding in the wall, merely been toying with her in an attempt—success-ful, as it turned out—to teach her a lesson on the folly of eavesdropping? Or had he been serious when he mentioned marriage?

Bronson stood at the window of his room and glared out at the moor, which had a strange beauty all its own, bathed as it was in the rosy morning light. His thoughts, however, were not rosy, and his mood was becoming darker, rather than lighter.

He had not, of course, been serious when he had mentioned marriage the evening before. He had merely said the first out-rageous thing that had entered his mind, his goal being to provoke whoever was hiding in the secret passageway.

So why now, when it was the dawning of a new day, did his remark seem not the least bit preposterous? Why did it seem so completely natural? So totally rational and logical?

Bah, marriage was nothing but a trap. The whole idea of shackling himself to a woman for life was ridiculous—was madness—was the first step toward self-destruction. Demetrius was a case in point, saved only by a stroke of unexpected luck. With his friend's experience as a horrible example, how could he even for a moment contemplate following such a course?

What he needed was an early-morning ride—alone—to clear his brain of such foggy, illogical notions as marriage. Without bothering to wake Daws, he dressed quickly in his riding clothes, except for his newest pair of boots, which he was unable to find. Finally he settled for an older pair, which, although comfortable, had lost forever their perfect shine.

Holding them in his hands, he walked quietly in stockinged feet out of his room and along the corridor of the sleeping house. As soon as he judged himself far enough away from the occupied bedrooms, he balanced on one foot and pulled on his boot. He had just gotten the second one on when a small shadow came hurtling out of the darkness at the end of the corridor and crashed into him.

Together, they went down in a tangle of limbs large and small, and in the resulting confusion it took him a moment to realize that the boy, whichever twin it was, was crying. Not whimpering as one might do because of a bumped head or a banged knee, but sobbing as if wracked by desperate grief.

More than likely a nightmare, Bronson thought. ''There, there,'' he soothed, wishing Anne were at hand. She undoubtedly had more experience at chasing away the demons that lurked in the dark hours of the night. " 'Twill be all right.''

Instead of having a calming effect, his words only produced more hysteria. "No, no, you don't understand. Anne, Anne,'' the boy wailed, struggling to get out of Bronson's arms.

"Shhh, shhh, you will wake everyone,'' Bronson murmured, rising to his feet.

With a sudden desperate lunge, the boy broke free and darted down the corridor in the direction of Miss Hemsworth's room. Blast it all, thought Bronson. He stood where he was, still longing for his solitary ride, but feeling he should do something to help.

Which was ridiculous. Miss Hemsworth was perfectly capable of handling bad dreams. Besides, the boy had already rejected his attempt to help, obviously preferring his governess's attentions.

Bronson took a step in the direction of freedom, but he could not ignore his feelings of responsibility—not the responsibility he had accepted years previous, to see that the twins' estate was properly managed and their funds prudently invested, but a personal responsibility, which he was feeling for the first time in his life.

He discovered he could no more walk away from the desperately unhappy boy than he could have a few weeks earlier abandoned Demetrius in his hour of need.

Retracing his steps, he hurried back to Miss Hemsworth's room. The door was ajar, and he pushed it the rest of the way open, expecting to find that the governess had handled everything in her usual competent manner. In that he was wrong.

Looking up, she saw him standing in the doorway. "Andrew says that Anthony has disappeared out of his bed.''

She was so beautiful sitting on the edge of her bed. Wearing something white and gauzy, her hair in tumbled curls around her shoulders, she was cradling the boy in her arms. Bronson felt his stomach clench in unexpected jealousy at the sight.

Then the meaning of her words sank in. "More than likely he is just hiding again,'' he said calmly.

"No, no, he is not!'' Like a whirlwind Andrew flew at him and began beating him with his fists. "He is not hiding, he's not! He would never go off without me, never! He would not, he would not!''

Bronson caught the fists that were ineffectually striking him, and Andrew collapsed against him. ''Very well,'' Bronson said, lifting the sobbing boy into his arms and crossing the room to sit beside Miss Hemsworth. ''Then if Anthony is truly lost, we shall just have to find him. What do you think, Miss Hemsworth?''

For a moment she did not speak, then amazingly her head came down to rest wearily on his shoulder, and in a voice that quavered in a very un-Miss-Hemsworth fashion, she said softly, ''I am thinking of the shot that was fired, my lord.''

''Nonsense,'' Bronson said, although he knew very well it was not nonsense. ''More than likely we will find Anthony in the kitchen eating a slice of bread and jam. Or he might even be back in his own room by now, wondering what has happened to Andrew.''

His voice was carefully nonchalant, and it had a soothing effect on the boy in his arms, whose crying gradually died down into deep shuddering breaths.

But when Miss Hemsworth lifted her head from his shoulder, he turned and met her gaze, and his eyes silently acknowledged the truth of her fears. Like her, he suspected a second attempt had been made to injure or kill one of the twins. He could only pray to God it had not been successful.

''It is probably a prank, my lord, intended to keep all of us from our rightful duties.'' Chorley was not to be budged in his convictions, and the rest of the servants were equally unobliging, all of them having at one time or another been the victims of the twins' ingenuity.

Anne could not really blame them, but she decided then and there that as soon as she had both boys safely together again, she would sit them down and tell them the story of the little boy who cried wolf.

''I really have no interest in your opinion,'' Lord Leatham said in a soft voice that was surprisingly full of menace. ''You will do as you are instructed and organize a search of the house and grounds, and you will do it *at once*,'' his voice suddenly rang out, and the servants' attempted rebellion died before it had properly been born.

"I want to help search, too," Andrew tugged at the hand restraining him, but Lord Leatham refused to release him.

"We have one lost boy already," he said, "and I see absolutely no reason to have two lost boys. You will stay right by my side where I can see you."

And where no one can hurt you or kill you, too, Anne thought. Again her eyes met Lord Leatham's, and she could read the same thought in his.

Wishing someone would come and find him, Anthony stood up and surveyed the area around him. Nothing he saw changed his earlier estimate of where he was. The landscape was too desolate to lie anywhere except to the south of Wylington Manor. Perhaps a bit to the east, but in general south.

He was rather disgusted with his situation. Anne had taught them such useful things, such as how to start a fire with two sticks—except he had no sticks. He could, of course, unravel the rope and make snares out of the fibers, but he was not sure there were even any rabbits in the area, so sparse was the vegetation. Besides which, he would rather go home and eat a regular breakfast.

It was all very well for Anne to say he should stay in one place if he was lost, but she hadn't told him what he was supposed to do to avoid suffering from excruciating boredom. The next time he was lost, he decided, he would make sure Drew was with him.

But since he wasn't, there was no sense staying lost any longer, not when it was now light enough that he could be sure he would not inadvertently step in a bog.

He carefully coiled the rope and folded the blanket, then with one over his shoulder and the other tucked under his arm, he looked to the north. Selecting a particular outcropping of rock, he headed toward it. Not only was he careful to glance down frequently to check his footing, but he also paused now and again and turned around to look back the way he had come, in case he found it necessary to retrace his footsteps.

About halfway to the rocks, he saw something that encouraged him in his belief that he was headed in the right direction. At the edge of a boggy place were some footprints in the damp ground. He walked over to look at them more closely.

They were large. No one he knew wore boots quite that large except Uncle Bronson. How ridiculous, Anthony thought. As if anyone would believe Uncle Bronson had had a hand in this affair.

Checking his direction again with the rocks he had picked out, Anthony continued along the route he had chosen. To begin with, if Uncle Bronson had tied him up, he would have done it properly. But then, Uncle Bronson would never have gone off and left him in the middle of the moor, and especially not the moor south of the house.

Anthony could still remember the day when he and Drew had decided to explore the moor south of the house. Although they had only been five or six years old, they had known perfectly well that they were forbidden to go in that direction.

Uncle Bronson had found them after about half an hour and he had not scolded them, he had simply paddled their bottoms all the way back to the house. Hard enough to hurt. Hard enough that the next time they were bored they did not even consider going off in the forbidden direction, even though Uncle Bronson was away on one of his journeys again and could have done nothing to stop them.

But Uncle Bronson was here in Devon now, and Anthony amused himself while he walked by considering with blood-thirsty relish how his guardian would punish whoever had done such a stupid, stupid thing.

It was better by far to think about that than to think about how alone he was for the first time in his life. He was not so much worried about himself, of course, as he was worried about his brother. Drew might be safe back at Wylington Manor . . . but then again, someone might have abducted him, too.

Anne wiped the dust from her hands and gazed around the low-ceilinged attic. There appeared to be no nook or cranny she had not checked. For the moment, she was alone. Lord Leatham had joined the men who were searching the grounds outside, taking Andrew along only when the boy swore an oath "on the egg" that he would not leave his uncle's side.

The female servants were all helping her conduct a very thorough and methodical search inside the house, and the grooms, gardeners, and farm workers had divided up to search in ever widening circles around the house.

"Beg pardon, ma'am." Sally came up the narrow stairs into the attic, followed by another of the maids and a footman. "We haven't found hide nor hair of the boy, but we found some things we thought you ought to know about."

She handed Anne a man's handkerchief. " 'Tis Lord Leatham's. It has his monogram embroidered there in one corner. I found it by Lord Andrew's pillow."

The other maid then handed Anne a small bottle of cobalt blue glass. "And I found this under Lord Wylington's bed. I ain't never seen it in this house before. It's got something writ on it."

Ether, Anne read with a sinking heart. Any last hopes she might have had, no matter how faint, now died. This was not a childish prank. Whoever had taken the boy had carefully planned the abduction.

"And I found these tucked behind a bush by the little side door that is usually kept locked." The footman held up a pair of muddy boots. "His lordship's new pair. It appears they've been worn in a bog. And there's no bogs here about, except if you go south, and no one in this house has any business going in that direction."

From the size of them, Anne could not doubt that they did in truth belong to Lord Leatham. Nor could she doubt the condemnation that was written on the servants' faces as plainly as the word *ether* was written on the label.

With a feeling of revulsion, she set the blue bottle down on the windowsill, where it sparkled prettily in the sunlight, its evilness disguised as completely as the evilness of whoever had thought up this plot.

Chapter Thirteen

ANNE WAS FEELING VERY DISCOURAGED. She and the servants had searched the entire house from cellars to attics, and the only result of the search was that she now had cobwebs in her hair, smudges on her face, grubby hands, and an extemely long mental list of housekeeping jobs that should be undertaken.

But of Anthony, the object of their search, there was no sign nor had they found any other clues to his disappearance other than the monogrammed handkerchief, the ether bottle, and the muddy boots.

Unfortunately, checking the house was a minor task compared to checking the endless moor around them. She decided to wash the dirt from her face and hands, then join the men searching the moor.

The unwelcome presence of Mrs. Pierce-Smythe in Anne's room was an unexpected inconvenience, but a very minor one. With only a glance at her cousin, Anne poured some water from the pitcher into the basin and began to wash her hands.

"So, my dear Lady Gloriana, it is indeed you. When my servants reported there was a giantess living here, I thought it could be no one but you, and see, I was correct in my assumption, for here you are in truth. How very propitious to find you here."

Mrs. Pierce-Smythe's feline smile indicated she thought it was more than propitious, that it was a veritable stroke of good fortune, and the cold and calculating look in her eyes made it a sure thing that she would do her best to take full advantage of said luck.

With her mind full of anxiety for the missing child, Anne was unwilling to devote proper attention to Dear Aunt Rosemary's social ambitions. "Propitious? In what way?" Actually, Anne had not the slightest doubt what Mrs. Pierce-Smythe had in mind, but she wondered to herself just how blatant her cousin's attempt at manipulation would be.

"I am afraid I do not know a delicate way to put it, but have you perhaps kept your identity a deep, dark secret here? The servants refer to you simply as Miss Hemsworth, rather than as Lady Gloriana."

Anne was suddenly tired of all the assumed coyness, and she decided that even if Dear Aunt Rosemary were determined to hint around, she herself was equally determined to come right to the point. "If you intend to blackmail me by threatening to reveal my 'deep, dark secret,' feel free. I care not one way or another who knows that my father was the Earl of Faussley."

Momentarily taken aback, the widow made a game recovery. "But surely it will cost you your job if Lord Leatham discovers you have deceived him. Surely you do not wish that, when I ask so little of you. Merely to use your influence on my behalf . . ." Again Mrs. Pierce-Smythe let her voice trail off, rather than coming right out and saying what she had in mind.

A wicked impulse tempted Anne, and such was her mood that she made no attempt to suppress it. "Oh, my dear cousin, I had no idea you wished for my help. Why of course, I shall be delighted to speak on your behalf. Blood is thicker than water, after all, and you did take me in when I was a penniless orphan."

"Why, my dear child, that is truly generous of you." Mrs. Pierce-Smythe was at once all smiles. "I should have known you would not forget your dear cousins."

"I would have come forward sooner, but I had no idea you were fallen upon such hard times. But you need worry no longer. I am sure Mrs. Wiggins can find you a suitable position, perhaps as companion to some elderly lady? I am afraid you do not have the proper credentials to be a governess, but with me to vouch for you, I am sure Mrs. Wiggins can find you gainful employment."

"Mrs. Wiggins? Employment?" Mrs. Pierce-Smythe's look of shock was rapidly replaced by hostility, which she no longer made any effort to disguise.

"Why, yes. Did you not say you wished me to use my influence on your behalf?" Anne feigned confusion.

Mrs. Pierce-Smythe was truly stunned speechless, but

unfortunately for Anne, the condition was only temporary.

"I have *not* fallen upon hard times, and I do *not* wish to have anything to do with your Mrs. Wiggins."

Anne finished washing up, and her towel was very convenient for hiding her smile. When she was fully recovered and no trace of amusement lingered on her face, she turned again toward her cousin.

"But what else could you mean? Oh, surely you did not think I have any influence in society?" She allowed her jaw to drop open in pretended astonishment. "But my Dear Aunt Rosemary, you cannot have thought things through carefully. I have no 'place' in society other than as a mere governess—although 'mere' is perhaps not the best description for an overly large governess, do you not agree?" And then Anne gave in to laughter she could no longer suppress.

It was indeed fortunate Dear Aunt Rosemary had never been one to pay much note to other people's feelings, except in so far as they related to herself and to her own ambitions, else she might have realized the laughter was caused more by Anne's overset nerves than by the humor of the request, and indeed, it was only with great difficulty that Anne was able to keep the laughter from becoming tears.

As soon as Mrs. Pierce-Smythe had left the room in a huff, however, Anne collapsed on the bed and allowed her tears for Anthony's safety to surface. But a few minutes later, her practical nature and common sense reasserted themselves, and she rose, dried her eyes, and went to join the others.

Anthony arrived at the rocks he was heading for, then scrambled up on the tallest one and surveyed his surroundings from that vantage point. Far off in the distance and slightly to the left a bit he saw some other rocks that looked vaguely familiar. There was a tall one at the west end, and three shorter ones to the east, and the last short one jutted out at an angle, rather than standing erect.

From the window of the schoolroom he could, on a clear day, see a similar arrangement of rocks. If they were indeed the back side of the same formation, he was not all that far from home. And breakfast, his stomach reminded him.

He was only halfway to the rocks when he became aware of several other figures on the moor, moving back and forth in sweeping patterns. One smaller figure suddenly began running toward him, and he realized it was Drew. All his anxieties vanished, now that they were together again.

His brother stopped a few feet away and regarded him with a critical eye. "You were gone," Andrew said in an accusing voice. "Without me."

"Somebody carried me out onto the moor and left me tied up." Anthony held up the rope. "But they didn't know anything about real knots, so I didn't have much trouble getting untied."

"Whoever it was, they should have taken both of us."

"That's what I thought. You want to carry the rope?" Anthony offered magnanimously.

"Course," his brother replied.

The two of them walked shoulder to shoulder back to meet their guardian, who stood about a hundred yards away waiting for them, an impassive expression on his face.

Anne was taking tea on the upper terrace with the twins and Lord Leatham. It was the day after the great adventure, as the boys had taken to calling it. Anne could only be grateful the experience had made them indignant rather than fearful.

Much to her relief, Mrs. Pierce-Smythe had earlier in the day coerced Trussell into accompanying her and her daughter into Tavistock to go shopping. Anne was relishing not only the resulting peace and quiet, but also the chance to be private with the twins and Lord Leatham.

To be sure, she could not keep from wishing Trussell and the two ladies would keep right on driving through Tavistock and on to London, but she would be grateful for what she had received.

"Have you noticed the gardener is spending more time watching us than tending to the roses?" Lord Leatham interrupted her thoughts to comment in a low voice.

"That is hardly surprising, considering how worried all the servants have been since they realized it was not another of the twins' pranks," she replied. "I think it is rather touching that they are all conspiring now to keep a careful watch over the boys, so that the perpetrator will not have a chance to strike again.''

"Touching? I had not thought you a fool, Miss Hemsworth."

"I see nothing foolish in taking special precautions, Lord Leatham. Surely you cannot doubt that someone has on two occasions acted with deliberate malice aforethought?''

"You delude yourself. You see only what you wish to see."

"Meaning?"

"Meaning the servants are not making an effort to watch over the boys. It is me they are determined not to let out of their sights, since they have cast me in the role of archvillain.''

"You? But—''

"But what? But they could not possibly suspect me? But they could not believe that I am trying to murder my wards so that I can inherit the title and the estate? But what, Miss Hemsworth?''

Anne was silent. Now that he had called it to her attention, she did realize that the only time during the day when there had been no servant in sight was the hour Lord Leatham had closeted himself in the study with the bailiff.

"Do you wish to have me enumerate the evidence against me?'' he continued when she did not respond. ''To begin with, there was the shot fired from my dueling pistol. Then my handkerchief was used when the other was administered, and it was my boots that apparently decided to go for a walk in that bog. And as for motive, it is the oldest in the world—title, land, and money, it all comes to me if the boys die with no heirs.''

There was nothing Anne could say to refute the bald facts he had just recited. But the conclusions the servants had drawn were all wrong, of that she was certain.

"I think it is pointless to dwell on what is past, my lord. More to the point, we should be figuring out how to prevent a third incident.''

The boys had stopped their own conversation and were now listening intently to the adults.

"And how do you purpose to do that, Miss Hemsworth? Look around you,'' Lord Leatham waved his hand at the moor and then at Wylington Manor. ''It would take an army of servants watching, and still the villain will be able to find an opportunity. And the next time, if he is only patient and chooses his time wisely, he will doubtless be more successful.''

"So are you still of the opinion that it is a servant wanting revenge for a childish prank?'' she asked.

"Who else? There have been no strangers around, or we would have seen them. I would, of course, prefer to cast Mrs. Pierce-Smythe in the role of villainess, but unfortunately she was still racketing around London when the pistol shot was fired.''

"It could be Uncle Creighton,'' Anthony piped up.

"He is not really very fond of us,'' Andrew pointed out. "Although he pretends to be.''

"And we are not fond of him, so we wouldn't mind at all if he got sent to jail,'' Anthony pointed out.

"But your uncle lacks a motive,'' Anne explained.

"Yes,'' Lord Leatham added, "and furthermore, he knows very well that if I inherit Wylington Manor, he will be out on his ear in an instant, with no place he can retire to when the tipstaffs are after him in London.''

"But he is stupid enough to have done it,'' Andrew explained.

"Unfortunately, stupidity is not considered reason to send people to jail,'' Anne said.

"Else the jails would be full,'' Lord Leatham added under his breath.

"We had better all go on a trip around the world,'' Anthony suggested.

Anne started to explain why that was impossible, but then it occurred to her that although an extended trip might be out of the question, a shorter one might actually be very practical. Turning to Lord Leatham, she asked, "Do you not think it might indeed be wise for the boys to leave Wylington Manor for a while? Since we do not know which of the servants to be wary of?''

"Not just Tony and me; all four of us must go,'' Andrew said.

"Drew and me and you and Uncle Bronson,'' Anthony added.

"I am afraid it would not be proper for me to go with you,'' Anne started to explain. "You would be staying at inns and—''

"No," Lord Leatham said flatly. "No inns. They are by far too public to be safe. I think it would be better if we simply removed to Sidmouth."

"Sidmouth? Why Sidmouth?" she asked, puzzled by his seemingly random choice of destination.

"Because it is on the seacoast," Anthony said.

"And because we can go bathing in the ocean," Andrew explained.

"And because we have been wanting Uncle Bronson to take us there for ages."

"I own a house in Sidmouth," Lord Leatham explained. "So it will be an ideal place for what we need. And we shall take none of the servants with us—no nanny, no grooms, no maids, no footmen."

"And no Mrs. Pierce-Smythe," Anne remarked under her breath.

Lord Leatham's eyes met hers, and his held such an intensity of emotion, she began to suspect he had not been joking when he had made that remark about marriage. Then he smiled, and she decided it was a good thing she was sitting down because the look in his eyes was making her knees feel all trembly, the same as if he were actually kissing her.

For a brief moment she wished the twins had accompanied the others to Tavistock, so that she and Lord Leatham could have a private tête-à-tête.

"I have a housekeeper there, and a cook, so we will manage very nicely," Lord Leatham's eyes conveyed the silent message that she had only to be patient, and soon they would have all the privacy she had just discovered she wanted.

Their announcement of the impromptu journey had created quite a furor. Jouncing along on the way to Sidmouth, Anne thought back over the protests, searching for a clue in some servant's remark or someone else's tone of voice, but there was nothing.

The number of people demanding to go with them had rather surprised her. Sally had not been the only one to act insulted that the slightest possible suspicion should fall upon her.

Virtually every servant had appeared to argue his or her case before Anne. Why they all thought she was the one to approach instead of Lord Leatham, she could not have said.

Even Trussell had been in a state of total panic when he had learned of their impending departure. He had been truly piteous when he begged not to be left alone with Mrs. Pierce-Smythe, but Lord Leatham had been adamant: No one was allowed to accompany the four of them.

The boys had wanted to ride cross-country to the coast, but as the four of them had a sizeable amount of luggage, they were traveling in style in an ancient landau that had belonged to the boys' grandmother.

Old-fashioned though it was, the coach was surprisingly well sprung, and the only complaint Anne had was that since Lord Leatham was acting as coachman, she was denied his company and conversation on the trip, except for the short periods of time when they had stopped to change horses.

Having left behind the person engaged in malicious mischief directed against the twins, and having given the boys a piece of string and shown them the intricacies of cat's cradle, Anne was finally free to turn her attention once more to the subject of marriage, more specifically marriage with Lord Leatham.

After his infamous remark the evening of the dinner party, she had expected to feel some degree of self-consciousness in his presence, but the search for Anthony had put them on a very informal basis with one another. Once Lord Leatham had even called her Anne, although he had apparently not realized it.

Well, at least she was now sure in her own mind what her answer would be. If he was indeed serious about marriage, and from the looks he had been giving her, that seemed not a totally impossible assumption, and if he did ask her formally for her hand, then she would definitely say yes.

One thing the kidnapping had shown her clearly was her own heart. She could not love the twins more if she were their own mother, and as for Bronson . . . well, she was not sure if what she felt for him was love, but she quite definitely liked him.

More important, after living in the same household with him and after watching the way he handled the twins, she was sure he was an exception to Aunt Sidonia's rule. He would not be an encumbrance like most husbands, but rather a friend, a partner, and a—

Lover was the other word that darted through her mind, and she felt her face flush. Luckily the coach was beginning its descent to Sidmouth, so the boys were more interested in the sights outside the coach than inside. By the time Lord Leatham pulled the horses to a stop in front of his residence, she had her emotions under control again.

It was a tall, narrow town house of gray stone, and she liked it from the moment she saw it, even though she had to admit to herself that it was probably the fact that Lord Leatham owned it that made it stand out from its neighbors with such distinction.

The boys darted up the steps without waiting for Anne, and were already pounding on the front door by the time Lord Leatham helped her descend from the traveling coach.

There was a considerable wait, however, before the big front door was eased open a crack. "Oh, Lord Leatham, we were not expecting you," a woman's voice said. Then the door was flung open the rest of the way. "Come in, come in, I shall tell Mrs. Uglow you are here so she can prepare some rooms."

Anne stood frozen to the spot as if she had been turned to stone. Welcoming them into Lord Leatham's house was his mistress, the mother of his child, the woman he had shaken so roughly on the street in Tavistock.

How could she have forgotten that incident, which had revealed to her Lord Leatham's true nature? How could she have forgotten the woman and especially the boy, who looked so much like the twins?

Inside herself Anne felt something die, something delicate and soft that had just begun to take root and that had not had a proper chance to grow and flower.

Choking back a sob of despair, she realized her aunt was right: Men would always betray the women who loved them. And she did love Lord Leatham. She had to, else this discovery would not hurt so much.

Her own life as a governess now stretched before her, inevitably bleak, lonely, and loveless. She could have forgiven Lord Leatham a mistress. What she could not forgive was the neglect of an innocent child. She could never marry a man who fathered a child and then refused to acknowledge his own offspring.

Bronson wandered through one familiar room after another, wondering why he felt no sense of homecoming. This was, after all, his home, where he had lived continuously until he was sent off to Harrow, and intermittently for years after that, coming back here for vacations until he attained his majority, after which he had studiously avoided Sidmouth.

Home. The word implied something more than wood and stone and plastered walls, more than Aubusson carpets and damask-covered chairs and Sèvres vases.

Home implied family, but his parents had lived together only long enough to produce the required heir, then they had gone their separate ways, leaving him behind . . . alone.

Not that he had ever minded being alone. Indeed, at school and later at university he had made it a point to avoid close friendships. He had a large circle of acquaintances, to be sure, but he had never allowed any of them to have an important place in his life.

Why do you travel so much? people had asked him repeatedly, and he had told them what he had believed to be true, namely that it was in his blood. His father had spent his life traveling, and he was also destined by nature to be a wanderer.

But now for the first time Bronson had to ask himself whether that was true . . . or whether he had actually been wandering in search of a home? The home he had never realized he missed—at least he had not realized he missed having one until this summer, when he had seen how devoted the twins were to one another. For the first time in his life, he had truly wished he'd had a brother when he was growing up.

And more significantly, for the first time in years he had remained in one place for more than a week or two without feeling a compelling need to set forth on another journey.

Now, back in the house where his life had begun, he climbed up the stairs to the floor that held the schoolroom. Even before he reached it, he could hear voices—the twins' high and excited, Miss Hemsworth's lower and calmer.

Approaching the open door quietly, he was able for a few moments to observe the three of them before they noticed him. Andrew had discovered the lead soldiers and was lining them up in formation. Anthony was galloping wildly on a rocking horse, which was barely big enough to hold him. And Miss Hemsworth was industriously unpacking some of the boys' own toys, which they had not wanted to leave behind.

Becoming aware that he was standing there, she turned toward him. As their eyes met, the realization sprang into his mind, full blown, leaving no room for doubt: Home was where Anne was.

He could no more leave her and resume his aimless traveling than he could cut off his own right hand. Not that he had any desire to be separated from her, even for a short period of time. What he wanted was to stay by her side forever—night and day—to be married, to step into parson's mousetrap, to be leg-shackled for life. In whatever disparaging terms it was described, it was still what he wanted more than anything else.

The only question that remained was whether or not he could persuade the enchanting Miss Hemsworth to accept such a ramshackle old bachelor as himself.

Why, why? Anne asked herself. Why did Lord Leatham still look so appealing, even with what she knew about him? Why did her heart still race when he smiled at her? Eyes downcast, she continued to unpack the twins' toys, afraid to look again at the despicable baron lest she fall further under his spell.

"Miss Hemsworth," he said, but still she declined to look at him.

"Miss Hemsworth, if I might have a word with you in private?"

"No, indeed, my lord. I am much too busy now for idle chatter," she replied, her heart pounding in her chest. Oh, how could she stop him from broaching the subject of marriage? She did not want to reject him out of hand; it would be far more agreeable for all concerned if they simply avoided the topic altogether. The twins had become very quiet, and she knew they were undoubtedly listening to every word with fascination.

"I did not intend discussing the weather, Miss Hemsworth."

"Perhaps another day," she demurred. "Next week, perhaps? I may have some time free then."

She risked peeking up at him. He was lounging against the doorjamb, a look of unholy amusement on his face.

"I find I am a very impatient man, Miss Hemsworth. May I call you Anne?"

"No!" she blurted out. "That is, I feel we should not have such a degree of informality between us, since I am in your employ. People might gain a false opinion of our relationship. . . ." Her voice trailed off.

"That is what I wished to discuss with you, my dear Miss Hemsworth—our relationship."

"Oh," she said, "well, perhaps we should not have this discussion now, in front of the boys." She felt her face become hot, and she knew she was blushing.

"Oh, but—" one of the twins started to say, but then stopped.

She looked up at him, Anthony it was, and saw he was grinning at Lord Leatham. Really, this was an impossible situation. They should definitely not be discussing such matters in front of the boys—or indeed anywhere.

She would have to be firm—blunt, even. "I feel I should make it perfectly clear to you, my lord, that I intend to remain a governess all my life. I feel I have a calling to educate young minds—"

"You can be our governess, forever and ever," Andrew piped up. "We don't particularly want to go to Harrow anyway."

"Yes, you can stay with us at Wylington Manor, forever and ever," Anthony reaffirmed.

"Capital idea, really splendid," Lord Leatham interposed. "And I shall cease wandering around the world and we shall all live together in Devon and be as merry as grigs."

"Say you'll stay, Anne, do say you'll stay," Andrew said.

"You don't want to leave us, do you, Anne?" Anthony asked with a slight tremor in his voice.

The black look that Anne gave Lord Leatham should have made it clear to him that she was not at all pleased with the way he had manipulated her, but he showed no sign of remorse.

And what of your other son? she wanted to ask. Will he be

living with us in Wylington Manor? And what of his mother? Where will she be? And do you still plan to visit her occasionally?

Methodically, Anne began again to unpack the toys, until at the bottom of the portmanteau she found something wrapped in silver paper. When she opened it, two little figures fell out into her lap. "What on earth?"

"Oh, these are sugar mice," Andrew explained, picking one up.

"Haven't you ever eaten one?" Anthony asked.

"Quite a favorite of mine when I was a boy," Lord Leatham contributed.

"If you want, you may have one of these," Anthony offered.

"Yes," Andrew agreed, "Tony and I can divide one, and you can have the other."

She probably would have declined, except she was in the mood to bite someone's head off, and a sugar mouse was better than nothing. Feeling quite like a kitchen cat, she bit the head off the sugary little animal and chewed, while the others watched her intently, waiting to see if she liked it.

"Very strange flavor," she commented. "What is the filling made of?"

"Filling?" Lord Leatham repeated, his expression very strange.

"Yes, the filling." She held up the uneaten half of the sugar mouse for him to see. "What is the green filling inside the fondant?"

He turned a rather sickly shade of green himself, then knocked the remaining piece of confection out of her hand. "Spit it out," he ordered in a frantic voice. "Spit it all out!"

"I swallowed it," she said faintly, already starting to feel queasy.

Chapter Fourteen

WRAPPED IN A BLANKET, Anne sat on Lord Leatham's lap in the kitchen of his house in Sidmouth. Gathered in a circle around her were the twins, Mrs. Uglow, and Martha Miller and her son, Adrian.

It had been a rather eventful hour. Lord Leatham had first stuck his finger down her throat, which, unpleasant though it was, had brought up most of the poisoned candy. Then he had carried her in his arms down to the servants' quarters, where Martha had mixed up a repulsive concoction, which Lord Leatham had then forced her to drink. It had tasted much nastier than the poisoned sugar mouse, but it had apparently been efficacious. Her stomach was already feeling much better, and the chills and cramping had eased.

"Can anyone tell me how those two sugar mice got into the portmanteau?" Leatham asked, his hand still soothing her hair. "Andrew? Anthony?"

Both boys denied any knowledge of the confections.

Anne was feeling amazingly comfortable ensconced on the baron's lap, and she did not want to think about such things as assassins, kidnappers, and poisoners. She just wanted to rest and let Lord Leatham handle everything.

Did Aunt Sidonia have any idea how comforting it could be to let a man take charge in an emergency? But then, Aunt Sidonia's husband had not been of much use in emergencies, so perhaps she had just cause for her low opinion of men.

Creighton Trussell, for example, would no doubt have been useless in such an emergency, too worried about the condition of his clothing to get near anyone who was being violently ill.

As if reading her thoughts, Martha spoke up now. "Mr. Trussell once, while he was still courting me, gave me some sugar mice that he had filled with Epson salts. As a joke, he said, and he laughed when I bit into one, although I did not find it at all funny. Quite put me off, although he sulked until I forgave him.''

''Trussell?'' Lord Leatham asked in an ominously quiet voice.

Anne lost all interest in the poisoned sugar mice. Instead, all her attention was focused on what Martha had said about being courted. Trussell had been courting Martha? Then perhaps . . . perhaps Lord Leatham was not Adrian's father? Perhaps Trussell . . . ?

Sitting up straight, Anne looked at Adrian, and she could see clearly that although he resembled the twins, he in no way resembled Lord Leatham. Indeed, he had the exact same coloring, the same blond hair and green eyes, as the twins—and as Creighton Trussell had, also.

Why had she never noticed before? The twins had apparently gotten their features from their father's side of the family and their coloring from their mother's side. It would explain so much.

''I am afraid,'' Martha said, ''that he can be rather cruel . . . in a rather off-hand sort of way. I fear it is simply that he does not truly care about anyone but himself, or so it seemed to me by the time he left me.''

''Hah! I suspected Uncle Creighton was behind all this. Didn't I say it might be him?'' Andrew said with great glee.

''Actually, I said it first,'' Anthony pointed out.

''But we both agreed he is stupid enough,'' Andrew said, and his brother nodded.

''But if Trussell is behind this, what does he hope to achieve by killing the boys?'' Lord Leatham asked. ''He does not stand to inherit a penny if they die.''

''Well,'' Anne said thoughtfully, ''he has not actually killed anyone. Or even hurt anyone, although it might easily have turned out more seriously than it did. All Trussell has done, really, is cast suspicion on you.'' She sat up on Lord Leatham's lap and looked directly in his face. The worry and concern she saw there made her wonder how she could ever have doubted his basic honest and integrity.

''I heard from some of the servants at Wylington Manor, my lord, that when the twins' parents died, and Trussell learned that you had been appointed guardian, that he had his nose bent out of shape good and proper," Mrs. Uglow said, adding her two cents' worth. "It would not surprise me to learn that he has been trying to have you thrown into jail so that he might be appointed guardian in your stead."

Martha nodded her head. "Yes, that sounds quite like him. Devious and deceitful and the slyest thing imaginable, but a total coward when it comes to physical violence."

Anne struggled free from Lord Leatham's embrace and stood up. Hands on her hips, she declared, "Well, he has plenty to be afraid of now, for I intend to return to Wylington Manor at once and force the truth out of him."

Lord Leatham attempted to catch hold of her again. "It can wait until tomorrow," he insisted. "Until you are feeling more the thing."

"I am feeling perfectly all right," she replied, stalking angrily around the kitchen. "And I am going to Wylington Manor today if I have to walk all the way."

The twins were equally enthusiastic about returning to confront their uncle, and within the hour fresh horses had been procured and hitched to the coach, the luggage had been dumped unceremoniously back into the boot, and they had set off on their return journey.

In spite of her eagerness to ride on the driver's seat next to Lord Leatham, Anne was again overruled. Because of the poison she had swallowed, both he and the boys insisted she ride inside the coach, where as if to prove they were correct in their concern, she quickly fell into a light doze.

Her thoughts were happy, however, because before they left Sidmouth, she had managed to have a private conversation with Martha, and that good woman had confirmed that Trussell was indeed the father of her son, and that Lord Leatham had always acted the complete gentleman toward her.

Now all Anne had to do, besides shaking the truth out of Trussell, was manage to have a private conversation with Lord Leatham who, she could only hope, still wished to speak privately with her on matters concerning her future . . . and his.

"You did what! This is unbelievable! Have your wits gone entirely begging?" Wyke stared at his master in astonishment.

"You needn't get so excited. All I did was put poisoned sugar mice in the twins' luggage. When they eat them, Lord Leatham is sure to be arrested," Trussell said quite cheerily.

The questions flew thick and fast through Wyke's mind, the main one being just why Trussell assumed suspicion would be cast on Lord Leatham and not on himself. There did not, however, appear to be any point in trying to make the dandy recognize his mistake. No, the time had come, Wyke decided, to cut his losses and make a rapid exit from the scene, before everything fell apart.

And the first person Wyke planned to speak to was Zizette, Mrs. Pierce-Smythe's phony French maid. Not only was she pleasing to look at and a proper armful for a man, but she also appeared to have her eye on the main chance. She had hinted at a willingness to throw her lot in with Wyke, and in all ways, she seemed a more worthy partner than this posturing dandy, who was bound to come to a sorry end sooner or later.

With the fear that it might be sooner rather than later, and with the feeling that time was running out more swiftly than he might wish, Wyke invented a barely plausible errand, and left his master to seek out the maid.

Zizette, when he found her, was as quick to catch on to the dangers in Wyke's situation as Trussell was slow. "Lord preserve us, but I think your master is not dealing from a full deck."

"That has long been my opinion," Wyke confirmed. "And I fear if I stay here he will attempt to cast all blame on my shoulders."

"Well," she said judiciously, "you are not entirely blameless. On the other 'and—" she winked at him, "—you do 'ave a certain style about you that is quite appealing."

"And I have not been idle the last few months," he added, putting his arms around her waist. "I have taken full advantage of your mistress's generosity, and have quite a tidy nest egg saved up."

She curled her arms around his neck. "And I," she murmured, "have likewise not been a slow top. I think you will find my nest quite well feathered."

"Then," he said, lowering his face to meet hers, "what say we combine our resources and set up in business together?"

"As partners?" she asked, pulling back slightly.

"As marriage partners," he replied, "and as business partners."

"Agreed," she said, and they promptly sealed their bargain with a kiss.

"But we have not much time. We must be away from here before Lord Leatham returns. The farther the better."

"But before we go . . ." She smiled coyly at him.

"Of course, my sweet," he replied. "We must dip our fingers once more into the pie and see what a magnificent plum we may pull out this time."

With a delightful giggle, Zizette—or Susie Porter, as she confessed to Wyke her real name was—led the way to find Mrs. Pierce-Smythe and sell her the information Wyke possessed.

Soon, soon, this will all be mine, Trussell thought. In a day or two, when the magistrate has bound the baron over for trial, I will be in complete control here. Then we shall see how compliant that stuck-up governess is, how she will bend to my every whim, how she will dance to my tune, how she will yield to my every demand. . . .

His feet not quite touching the floor, he sat in the oversized chair behind Leatham's desk in the library. Sparing not a thought for his unwelcome house guests, Mrs. Pierce-Smythe and daughter, he poured himself another glass of brandy and held it up to the light. Beautiful, truly beautiful. Perhaps he should have a waistcoat made of just such a color. . . .

His tranquility was shattered when the door to the library was thrown open and an army marched into the room, an army that resolved itself into his two nephews, their guardian, and their governess.

Somehow, he had forgotten just how big Leatham was—but even more formidable was Miss Hemsworth, who appeared a veritable Juno or Athena or whoever the goddess of war was. The governess loomed over him, her eyes flashing fire, and involuntarily he shrank back in the chair.

Before he could protect himself, although he could not even think how he might do that, she had grabbed him by the ends of his cravat and hoisted him up out of the chair.

He attempted to speak, but all that came out was a squawk, after which regaining the ability to breathe seemed more important than demanding explanations.

"Is she going to strangle him?" one of his bloodthirsty nephews asked.

"More than likely," the other replied calmly, while Trussell clutched desperately at his cravat, which was relentlessly cutting off his breath.

"Might I suggest, my dear Miss Hemsworth, that it will be less of an inconvenience for us if we let the law handle him?" Lord Leatham commented. "It is only a suggestion, to be sure. If you feel it is necessary, by all means, feel free to strangle him."

Trussell tried to indicate his approval of Leatham's first suggestion, but was unable to manage so much as a croak.

Fortunately, the giantess threw him back down in the chair, where he collapsed in a heap, each desperate breath hurting his poor, mangled throat.

"You fired a gun at the twins," the giantess said accusingly.

When he did not immediately answer—and indeed, he had not recovered enough breath to speak—she reached for him again, but he eluded her grasp, his head bobbing up and down of its own accord.

"So, you admit it at least."

To his relief, she lowered her hands.

"And you were the one who drugged Anthony and left him out on the moor."

She stated it as a known fact, rather than a question, but Trussell thought it prudent to admit his misdeeds openly. "Yes, yes, I did it," he managed to croak out.

"And put the poisoned sugar mice in the portmanteau," she continued relentlessly.

"I'm sorry, I'm sorry," he said. Indeed, he felt so desperately sorry for himself that he began to cry.

At last, to his relief, the baron took the governess's arm and moved her gently aside. Perhaps Leatham might be more reasonable? Surely, as a man, he could understand better the untenable position he, Trussell, had found himself in with the widow—be able to sympathize.

"I would turn you over to the magistrate, and if you fail to cooperate, I still might do so," Leatham said mildly. "I am not inclined, however, to allow such a scandal as that would entail. So you are free to go. Bear in mind, however, that you may never return to Wylington Manor. Indeed, if you ever so much as set foot in Devon, I shall doubtless feel compelled to overcome my scruples regarding scandal and lay charges against you. Likewise, if I hear one word of this bruited about in London, I shall see that you are sent to the hulks."

"I promise, I promise," Trussell stammered out, still keeping a wary eye on the governess, who watched him as unblinkingly as a poisonous snake. "Not a word of this shall ever pass my lips." To his relief, this seemed to satisfy his accusers.

"Then I shall order the coachman to drive you to Tavistock within the hour," Lord Leatham said. "See that you are ready in good time, or you shall depart without your luggage."

"But, but, I have no funds," Trussell cried in despair. "How can I catch the stage in Tavistock?"

Lord Leatham cast some coins on the desk. Trussell grabbed for them, but some rolled onto the floor and out of his reach. While he was scrambling on his knees after them, he heard the footsteps of the others leaving the room, then the welcome sound of the door shutting behind them.

With them safely gone, he cursed them with a fury he had never felt before, but which made him feel only marginally better. Surely there must still be some way to come about—

"You missed a half-crown over here," a female voice said.

Recognizing Mrs. Pierce-Smythe's cultured tones, Trussell's heart skipped a beat. Unwilling to believe the evidence of his ears, he crawled on hands and knees around the chair, which was arranged so that its back faced the room.

There she sat, the widow, smiling down at him like the predator she was. She was only slightly less fearsome than that wretched governess.

"This will make a very delightful story in London," she said in dulcet tones.

"No, no," he begged, clutching at the hem of her dress. "Please, please, I will do anything you ask, only do not reveal what has happened here. You heard what Leatham said; he will have me sent to the hulks if I breath so much as a word of this to anyone."

"Why, since you ask so prettily, I must tell you, I should never dream of serving my dear husband such a back-handed turn."

She smiled so sweetly, for a moment he did not comprehend her meaning, thinking she was referring to her deceased first husband. Then when he realized she meant to force him to marry her, he fainted dead away.

"Are you sure you don't need our help?" Anthony asked.

"We are really very ingenious," Andrew added.

Bronson regarded his cravat in the mirror of his dressing table. Sheer perfection.

"Indeed, I do not need any help. There are some things a gentleman must be able to do for himself. One is to tie his own cravat." He allowed Daws to help him into his new, gold-embroidered waistcoat. "And the other thing he must be able to do is to propose marriage to the lady of his choice without assistance."

The twins looked solemnly at one another, then Andrew explained, "It is not that we think she will reject you—"

"Because then she would have to leave Wylington Manor—"

"And she rather likes it here."

"She has all sorts of ideas, in fact—"

"For setting everything to rights."

"It's just that—"

"If you say the wrong thing—"

"You're liable to get her back up."

"And sometimes when she's in a temper—"

"She does have a temper, you know," Anthony explained.

"Yes, I have noticed that," Bronson said with a smile, remembering the delightful kiss that had resulted the last time he had gotten her into a temper.

"Well, sometimes when grown-ups are in a temper—"

"They say things they don't really mean."

"And if they say no, they don't like to admit they are wrong and say yes later."

There was a significant pause, and Bronson turned to see both twins regarding him expectantly. It dawned on him that *he* was the one who was now supposed to admit he was wrong, and agree to let them accompany him to speak with Miss Hemsworth.

"Keep in mind," Andrew said, "what might very well happen around here if she decides to leave rather than marrying you."

Bronson's smile vanished, and he said very sternly, "And the two of you keep in mind that this is no game. A gentleman does not coerce a lady into accepting his hand in marriage, no matter how much he desires it. So we will have no pranks or even threats of pranks, is that clear?" He turned so that Daws could help him on with his new russet jacket.

The twins nodded, but then Anthony inquired in a too casual voice, "If she does say no, may we ask her to stay on as our governess anyway? Or will you insist that we go to Harrow as planned?"

Bronson could feel his temper rising at their lack of confidence in him. But with effort he managed to keep his voice even when he replied. "In the unlikely event that she turns down my proposal, you have my permission to offer her continued employment."

On the other hand, was it really so unlikely? He turned to regard himself in the mirror and was not very satisfied with what he saw there. In spite of the new clothes, direct from London and of the latest mode, no amount of tailoring could disguise the fact that he was far too large and muscular to look a proper gentleman. And his skin, which was naturally swarthy, had darkened even more on his latest journey through the tropics.

In addition, he rather needed a haircut, his hands were calloused from the rough life he had been leading . . . and he had thirty-five years in his basket to her twenty-seven. Would she want such a travel-worn specimen as himself?

The only thing in his favor was that he was a few inches taller than she was, but would that really signify to someone of her

superior intellect? After all, in what way could the length of
a thighbone indicate a man's worth?

"Actually," Andrew interrupted his thoughts, "I think she'll
accept you."

"Yes," his brother agreed. "She always smiles more when
you're around."

With those words of encouragement, Bronson set out to find
and woo his fair lady.

Anne had been standing at the window of her room for a full
hour, staring out at the moor. Ever since Dear Aunt Rosemary
had driven away in triumph with her prize—although why
anyone would think Trussell was a prize was beyond Anne's
comprehension—ever since then, Anne had been arguing with
herself in her mind.

The twins were no longer in danger, she was no longer
laboring under the misapprehension that Lord Leatham was the
father of Martha Miller's son, and she no longer had the slightest
reluctance to give up her single state for married life, so there
should have been no obstacle preventing the baron from asking
for and receiving Anne's hand in marriage. Except . . .

Lord Leatham himself, she had realized while changing into
her prettiest dress, harbored some misconceptions about her,
and it would be not only dishonest but also dishonorable to allow
him, so long as he remained in ignorance of her true nature,
to make her an offer in form.

There was, of course, a chance—a very slight chance—that
if he learned the truth about her, he would still wish to marry
her, but it was vital that she tell him before he made any commit-
ment, else he might, as a gentleman, persist in his offer rather
than drawing back, even though he felt nothing but disgust for
her.

Bronson found the door to Anne's room ajar and the room
empty. The library was also empty, and for a moment he was
afraid that she was again hiding from him. It was almost
discouraging enough to make him retreat to his own room, but
Chorley, when questioned, informed him that Miss Hemsworth
was taking tea on the lower terrace.

Bronson paused on the upper level and looked down at her. She was wearing a blue dress and her hair was done in a softer style, and she looked ridiculously young and vulnerable sitting there. For a moment he felt despair, but adjuring himself not to be a total coward, he went down the few steps to join her.

Coming up behind her, he unintentionally startled her, and she spilled a few drops of tea in her saucer. But she regained her composure with unnerving speed.

"Won't you sit down, my lord? Would you care for some tea, my lord? It is a pleasant day, is it not, my lord?"

She was evidently determined to hold him at arm's length, and he became equally determined not to let her. Sitting down beside her, he took the cup of tea she held out to him, promptly set it down on the table, and took her right hand in both of his instead. The slight tremble he could feel in her fingers reassured him that she was not as calm as she was trying to appear.

"Miss Hemsworth," he said, knowing no way to do the thing other than simply to get on with it, "will you do me the honor—"

"Stop!" she said, laying her left hand against his mouth.

He kissed her finger, and she jerked her hand back as if it were burnt, but he managed to retain his hold on her right hand.

"Before you say another word, my lord, there are some things about me you should know." She again tried tentatively to retrieve her right hand, but to no avail. Taking a deep breath, she continued. "To begin with, I am not Anne Hemsworth. That is to say, I am she, but not completely. That is— Oh, dear, this is a muddle. Here I have lectured the boys on how telling part of the truth can be just as deceitful as telling an outright lie, while all the time I myself—"

"You are Lady Gloriana Hemsworth, the daughter of the Earl of Faussley," Bronson aided her, since she did not seem able to explain very well. Her confusion was absolutely delightful, but he wished very much to determine if she meant to have him in the end.

"How did you know that?" She regarded him with suspicion. "I told no one but the twins, and I cannot believe that they—"

"No, I am afraid I must take the blame."

"Blame?"

"I hired a Bow Street runner to investigate Trussell, who I feared was dipping into the twins' funds, and in the course of his investigation, he found out Trussell had hired you, and that you were not exactly who you claimed to be. It is perfectly understandable of you not to mention your father. I also have relatives I would as lief not acknowledge."

"You hired a runner?" she said, her tone mild, but the merest spark of temper in her eyes.

"As I said, I admit I am to blame." He waited, but she made no effort to berate him for such a despicable action, which rather made him suspect she had given up on him.

"There is more," she said tentatively. "I know I have impeccable references, and everyone thinks my behavior is above reproach, but actually I have done some very disgraceful things."

It belatedly occurred to Bronson that she would not be going to all this effort to convince him that she was not worthy of marrying him if she intended to reject him out of hand, and his anxiety was replaced by undiluted happiness. He was, in fact, hard pressed to keep from laughing aloud out of pure joy.

"For example," she continued, "I told the twins that eavesdropping was wrong, and that I did not approve of it, and yet, when the opportunity arose, I set a very bad example for them."

"And hid in the secret passageway."

She nodded. "Not only that, but I have lectured them on the necessity of being honest with oneself and warned them against making excuses for what is really inexcusable behavior. Yet when the time came, I immediately thought up several ways to justify my eavesdropping. So you see, my lord, I am afraid that I am a thorough hypocrite."

"Bronson."

"Excuse me?"

"You said, 'my lord,' and I feel that we have reached the stage of intimacy where we should be allowed to use given names with one another."

She blushed a very becoming shade of pink. "I am not sure—"

"It is not so difficult. Just say, 'I am a hypocrite, Bronson, and a thoroughly bad example for impressionable minds—' ''

"I would not go *that* far," she said indignantly.

"Bronson," he said smoothly. "You seem to have trouble saying that name. My middle name is Alden, if you find it easier to pronounce."

"I am trying to have a serious discussion, *Bronson,* but if you persist in mocking me—"

"There, you see, my dear Anne, we are perfectly suited for one another—you are a hypocrite and I am an irreverent scoffer."

The corner of her mouth twitched slightly, as if she were having trouble repressing a smile. "If you will not interrupt, my lord—I mean, Bronson—I shall continue with what I have to tell you."

He nodded agreeably. "As you wish, my dear Anne."

"Although I prefer to think of myself as a calm, rational human being who uses intellectual reasoning instead of brute force, I have discovered I not only have a temper, but I also, when under the influence of that temper, still have a deplorable tendency to resort to physical violence." She looked at him expectantly.

"If you are waiting for me to condemn you for manhandling Trussell, you will have a long wait. I can only applaud your style, my dear Anne. And as for your temper, I admit I have derived a great deal of enjoyment from each of the times you have lost it." He smiled, and she blushed again.

"You are no gentleman," she said, but her effort to censure his conduct failed miserably, because this time she could not completely control her expression, and despite her most determined effort, a shy smile crept out. "And I am no lady," she continued, her smile fading away. She turned her head away and looked at the far horizon.

"I know people think I am quite proper, but—" she hesitated, but he did nothing to prompt her, "—the truth of the matter is, I sometimes behave quite improperly. When you k-kissed me," she said, stuttering a bit over the word, "and when I sat on your lap in Sidmouth, I am afraid my thoughts were quite shocking and highly improper."

He could not help smiling, and he tugged on her hand, urging her closer, but she still resisted. "My sweet, sweet, Anne. Wherever did you get the ludicrous notion that men prefer women who think of propriety when they kiss?"

"Well, you see," she answered seriously, "kissing was not a subject that was covered adequately in my education."

"I would never have guessed," he replied. "If that is indeed the truth, then I must say you show a remarkable aptitude for it. If you would wish me to speak truthfully and openly, I have never in all my travels and all my vast experience, enjoyed anyone's kisses as much as yours."

She started to smile again, but then almost immediately looked stricken. "The worst is yet to come, I am afraid. Before we go any farther, you must know that for a while I suspected you."

"*What!*" Bronson dropped her hand and stood up, glaring down at her. "You suspected I was trying to harm the twins?"

Instantly the picture of outrage, she likewise leaped to her feet. "Of course not, you dolt! I never for a moment suspected you of that. I suspected that you, *in your vast experience,* had seduced Martha Miller and were the father of her child."

Her lower lip was thrust out pugnaciously, and Bronson could only be thankful she was not as prone to resorting to physical violence as she thought she was.

"I apologize, my dear Anne."

"And I have not given you leave to use my given name." She continued to scowl at him.

He stepped closer to her, and her gaze faltered. Another step and he was within kissing distance. "Are you done enumerating your failings and shortcomings?" he murmured softly. "Because if you are, I have something to ask you."

"There may be something I have forgotten," she said in an equally soft voice, all trace of temper gone from her expression.

"It doesn't really matter," he said, stroking her face lightly with his fingertips. "I like you fine the way you are."

She caught his hand and pressed it against her cheek.

He bent his head slightly and brushed his lips against hers. He was taking unfair advantage of her emotions, but he didn't particularly care. Whatever it took to convince her to marry him . . .

"Marry me," he said, pulling her the rest of the way into

his arms. "Marry me," he repeated when she did not immediately reply.

"Kiss me," she said, wrapping her arms around his neck.

After a long while he lifted his head and said calmly, "Now you shall have to marry me."

She leaned her head back so that she could see his face. "And why is that, my lord?"

"Bronson," he said, correcting her once more. "Because you have thoroughly compromised me."

Still standing in the circle of his arms, she glanced over her shoulder. Not six feet away were the twins, grinning from ear to ear, and behind them were gathered virtually every servant on the estate. Embarrassed, she buried her face in Bronson's chest.

"You may congratulate me," he said loudly. "The redoubtable Miss Hemsworth has agreed to marry me and stay here in Devon forever."

A cheer went up from the assembled servants, and under the cover of their huzzahs Anne whispered indignantly, "But I have not yet said I will marry you."

"Ah, but I have three weeks while the banns are being called, during which time I am confident that I can persuade you."

She looked up into his eyes and experienced again that feeling of unspoken communication. Happiness welled up inside of her. "I am quite looking forward to your persuasion, Bronson. You are so eloquent—"

"I had not planned to use intellectual reasoning, my dearest darling," he murmured for her ears only.

She trembled in his arms. "In that case, I must be sure to demur as long as possible."

"But in the end?" he asked, suddenly unsure of himself.

She smiled up at him. "In the end? Well, if all else fails, there is always clotted cream with strawberries."

Epilogue

OVER A CUP OF HOT CHOCOLATE, Lady Letitia Morrough perused the morning paper. She smiled with satisfaction when she noticed a small announcement: "Married, in Tavistock, Devon, Lady Gloriana Hemsworth and Bronson Roebuck, Lord Leatham."

Succinct, but sufficiently informative for those who cared about them. She must remember, Lady Letitia thought, to invite Dorothy Wiggins over for lunch one day soon to celebrate their success. And perhaps at the same time she would invite the widowed banker her husband had brought home to dinner Saturday a week ago. Mr. Cartwell might just be the one for dear Dorothy, who had been without a husband long enough.

Lady Letitia laid the paper aside and was pouring herself another cup of hot chocolate when Amelia Carlisle was announced.

"My dear Amelia, how fine you are looking. Is that a new bonnet?"

"Oh, Letty, do you think it will do?" Amelia hurried over to check her appearance in the mirror hanging above the sideboard.

"Do? Do for what?" Lady Letitia asked.

Amelia blushed. "Well, I have met the most wonderful man."

"How interesting, my dear. Sit down and have a cup of hot chocolate with me, or tea if you prefer, and tell me all about him."

Amelia sat down, but waved away the proffered refreshment. "No, no, I am too excited to drink a drop. I met him quite by chance, and he has the most fascinating hobby. He has been studying the art of spying—"

"Spying? He is a military man then?"

"Military?"

220

"You said spying. I presumed you meant spying on the French."

"The French? Oh, no, no, nothing like that. He is practicing to be a Bow Street runner. Or rather, he is practicing their techniques, but of course he would never actually become a runner."

"Of course," Lady Letitia murmured, taking another sip of hot chocolate.

"Mostly he has been following people, and you will never believe what he has discovered. Did you know, for example, that Lady Brownell is definitely having an affair with a captain in the Horse Guards? And Lord Ahrendale is not only sleeping with Toveson's new bride, but also with the Gravenstoke's widow?"

"But really, Amelia, a runner?"

"Oh, he is not a real runner, of course. He is Felix Sommerton. You know, Sommervale's younger brother."

"Younger? My dear Amelia, have you taken to robbing the cradle?"

"Oh, pooh, he is not that much younger than we are. And he says I am quite well preserved for my age. Besides, I have not mentioned one word about marriage."

"But you have stars in your eyes, and a certain tone in your voice when you say his name. . . ."

"It shows?" Amelia gave a girlish giggle. "You have found me out. I am indeed in love, and I am sure my feelings are reciprocated. You do not think I am too old to consider marriage, do you? To be sure, I am already a grandmother, but I was a very *young* bride—"

"Oh, absolutely."

"And besides, dear Felix says that one is only as old as one feels, and I feel positively fifty again."

"And you do not look a day over forty in that bonnet."

"Do you think so?" Amelia jumped up again to check her appearance in the mirror.

While she was occupied, Lady Letitia glanced down at the paper once more and her eye was caught by another nuptial announcement, this one so unexpected she dropped her cup, spilling chocolate all over the table.

''Letty, good heavens, what are you about?'' Amelia hurried to mop up the hot liquid, since Letty was laughing too hard even to attempt it.

''Read, read,'' Lady Letitia finally managed to say, pointing with her finger at the small announcement.

Picking up the paper by one corner and holding it so that the chocolate would not drip on her clothes, Amelia managed to decipher through the brown stain: ''Married, in St. George's London, Mrs. Rosemary Pierce-Smythe née Pierce and Mr. Creighton Trussell.'' For a moment she looked puzzled, then with drawning comprehension, she exclaimed, ''The mushroom's widow! But however did she catch Trussell? Is he not the grandson of the Earl of Bardeswythe, or am I thinking of a different Trussell?''

''No, you have the correct man. But it is quite a long story, and unfortunately you are pressed for time.'' Lady Letitia could not resist a smile.

''Nonsense, Letty,'' Amelia replied, seating herself again on the settee and removing her bonnet. ''I always have time for a comfortable coze with you. Ring for a pot of fresh tea and tell me every detail!''